C000102772

HEEL OF ACHILLES

A MAX FORTIS THRILLER

MATTHEW J. EVANS

ISBN: 978-1-7394834-1-8

DISCLAIMER

Heel of Achilles is a work of fiction. Names, characters, businesses, schools, police operations, and criminal cases are a product of the author's imagination or used in a fictitious manner. Any resemblance to actual persons alive or dead, or actual events is purely coincidental.

For Ozzy.

PROLOGUE

Kamlai has stopped breathing. Her bed is drenched with blood and sweat, her eyes wide open and still. Janie's eyes are locked onto her sister's, and she rocks gently over her, humming their mother's favourite song. She wonders if she could travel with Kamlai once more. But this journey is for Kamlai alone.

'Be strong, sister.' Those were her last words to Janie.

'Be strong, sweet Kamlai.'

Janie's tears have stopped, and now the rain takes over, pattering on the corrugated roof. The sour stench of death is growing in the air. The others are silent. They lie in their beds, turning away from her. Janie carries her burden alone.

A shaft of light punctures the darkness as the door unlocks and opens. Dennis is here, and a woman Janie has never seen before comes in behind him. She's carrying a long black bag, which she places open on the cold concrete floor. Dennis and the woman lift Kamlai from her bed and put her inside the bag, along with her bedding. The bag is closed, and Kamlai's tiny body is lifted over Dennis's shoulder. She's gone. The door closes and locks. Darkness, rain, and bitter loneliness fill Janie's world.

CHAPTER 1

Two men in charcoal suits join me at the table, effusing a heady mix of musk and testosterone. My back's against the wall, the bar is busy, and music beats a pulse from a speaker above my head. They sit facing me, leaving an empty chair between them. One is my height and build—tall, broad, and bald. His mother would be proud. The other is shorter, with sandy hair. He's doing his best to look tough, but he doesn't have the jaw for it. He's the bald man's subordinate. Both are wearing earpieces—wireless and subtle, but I see them. Their expressions are vacant, listening to instructions.

'Just to let you know, gentlemen,' I say, 'I don't kiss on the first date.'

No response—straight faces. The suits are looking towards the entrance and won't engage with me.

As we wait, the pub gets busier. Outside, the door staff set up the queue barriers, and nervous teens show them their IDs. It's early evening on the last Friday of the month, and most people are still sober, but they're getting there.

I pick up my pint and take a sip, sensing my new friends'

heightened nerves—the licking of lips, the fidgeting fingers. Their twitchiness is bugging me. Both men have weapons concealed under their jackets. My reputation must precede me.

The bald man stands as a woman enters. His boss. She's a white, frowning forty-something in a brown trouser suit, straight brown hair, and brown-framed glasses. She hurries over, not looking up, and sits in the empty chair, a suspicious brown filling in a stooge sandwich.

'A rose between two thorns,' I say.

Not even a smile.

'Mr Fortis.' She gets straight to it. 'I'm Commander Janice Lacey. You spoke to my PA on the phone.'

'And the Chuckle Brothers here?'

'They're here to keep me safe.'

'Who from? Where's the trouble?'

She takes off her glasses and produces a tissue to clean them. 'Only from you, Mr Fortis. You're an unknown quantity to me. Why didn't you return my calls?'

'Why should I?'

'We need to discuss why you left.'

'You may do, but I don't. Six months on, and you people are still banging on that old drum.'

'But things were about to get interesting.'

'I'd had enough, and someone else needed me more.'

'Was that *our* fault?' I smell garlic on her breath.

'Ah, the blame game again. Is that what this is all about? New management seeking to distance themselves from the past. Dump the responsibility on someone else. I gave my reasons for leaving to your predecessor. I have nothing more to add, Janice.'

'It's *Commander* Lacey.'

'I don't give a fig what your rank is. It has nothing to do with me anymore.'

She replaces her glasses and blinks at me. The lenses make her eyes look too large for her face. 'Are you going to be a threat to us now that you're a free agent? There are things you know that could undermine national security. So…'

'I'm still one of the good guys. That's all you need to know.'

Lacey leans back in between the burly shoulders on either side of her. Her boys have relaxed a little. That's not good practice—they don't know me. I could turn at any moment. What are they teaching them these days?

'A little birdy told me you've set up a private detective business.'

'Your little birdy is correct,' I say.

'How sweet. Where?'

'None of your business unless you have a marital dispute you need help with.'

'I'm not married, but thanks for the offer.'

'Really? I am surprised.' There's a brief twist of a smile on the bald man's lips.

'I don't get it,' says Lacey, shaking her head. 'You're one of the best there is. The threat to this country hasn't been so great since the Cold War. Chinese spies in Westminster—did you hear about that? Researchers, for God's sake. Then you decide to throw it all in and become some do-good private eye.'

'Someone I cared about got hurt, so I took a safer option, for all our sakes.'

Lacey examines her nails. 'It wasn't you, though, was it. You weren't hurt. Strange that, considering what happened. It was a miracle you survived.' She takes a sharp intake of breath. 'Did you have a tip-off? A bit of inside information, perhaps. Who got to you?'

'You're new to this, so try reading my file. No one got to me. It was my choice to leave.'

'But you can see how it looks, surely. You didn't even go back to your police team.'

'There wasn't a position available.'

I can sense her growing frustration with me. Her little head twitches on her skinny neck, and she keeps flashing her teeth.

'What happened to your loved ones was very unfortunate. There's going to be an internal inquiry.'

'Why? An inquiry won't fix anything or anyone. It was all in the line of duty. A risk we all took.'

'Of course.' She sighs, and her attention turns to a gathering of girls dressed as nuns, meeting for a hen night. 'Who are your clients? Assuming you have *actual* clients. Not Russians or Chinese, I hope.'

I think that was an attempt at sarcasm.

'Just the good people of Sussex and Hampshire. Normal people. People who don't see an undercover agent everywhere they look.'

Lacey scoffs, and I finish up my drink. She leans forward again and lowers her voice in a friendly, *I'm going to kill you* kind of way. 'I want to make something very clear, Mr Fortis. If I consider you a national security threat, then I will deal with you robustly. I'm not afraid of you, whatever your skills are. This isn't the police. These are different rules. I can shut down your bank accounts and lock you up as a terrorist.'

'Was that really necessary?' I say. 'I've had enough of this.'

I stand to leave, and both men rise from their chairs, their hands slipping inside their jackets.

'Sit down!' barks the shorter one. 'We haven't finished yet.'

'But I have. And don't threaten me, shorty.'

Baldy slaps his hand on my shoulder, trying to push me down. I think he's jealous of my hair. His fingers grip me, searching for the pressure point under my collarbone. Then, three things happen fast. My thumb digs deep into the top of his hand, and his grip fails. I wrench his forearm away, and his head follows, dipping towards the tabletop. Then I smack his head down hard enough to stun him.

'You alright over there, Max?' It's the landlord calling from the bar.

I raise my hand and smile at him. 'All good. He's had a few too many shandies. Lightweight.'

Lacey hisses at me like she's some kind of feral cat. She pulls the bald man up off the table.

'What is it with you?' I say. 'Don't you have something more important to do? You could have been nice. That's all it needed. I'm a friendly guy, Janice. Really friendly. You need to rewrite your e-learning package about me. I'm more adaptable than you think. And your boys here are lucky I'm in a good mood today. Anyone who pulls out a nine on me usually ends up six feet under. Look at me—I'm living proof. Reasonable force in the circumstances—measure for measure. Now leave me alone.'

Lacey swears at the other man as he thinks about drawing his weapon. 'I'll be watching you, Mr Fortis. Put one foot out of line…'

I shake my head and wave, giving her the finger.

As I back away, the bald man stands upright again. If he's going to do anything, he'll do it now. But he holds back, fuming, still under Lacey's control. So I turn and walk out of the Locomotive Inn into the cool evening.

———

I walk north for about thirty yards and reach the front door of my office. I'm aware of someone standing in the shadows on the corner of Southgate, which is another twenty yards from me. It's a woman, and she appears to be waiting for someone.

I have a flat above the office, and as I'm finding my keys, I'm thinking about Commander Lacey. If she had turned up at my door with a packet of custard creams and a smile, I would have given her a better reception. Still, she's brand new in her role and finding her feet. Her little birdy didn't tell her how close my office was. Her threats are empty. There's nothing she can do to satisfy her paranoid curiosity. She's pissed she didn't get her way. But I was prepared for that and The Firm's reaction to my leaving. The mutual mistrust has never gone away.

After locking the door to the street behind me, I climb a set of dark, narrow stairs to the flat's front door. I didn't realise how weary I was. The door swings open as I turn the key.

I rent the flat. It's clean, modern, and basic. It's my crash pad for when I work late. It has an adequate shower, and I keep a change of clothes here. There's a TV if ever I feel like it, and it's in range of the Wi-Fi signal in my office below. I like my solitude, so best of all, there are no neighbours.

A fresh coffee is in my hand, and a pizza delivery is on its way. Standing at my window, I'm watching Chichester's finest out on the razzle tonight. Girls in short skirts and impossible heels walk along Southgate with packs of drunk lads following them—all freshers from the university. A police car crawls past them, windows open. *When in town, windows down*, we used to say when looking for the drunk and disorderly to tuck us up with paperwork for the night. It made the hours go by faster and was better than sitting with suicidal, sick people in the hospital for the entire shift.

I sip my coffee. It's the only vice I have. I'm not a heavy drinker or a smoker. That professional stereotype has never fit me. I keep myself healthy and strong, more for my state of mind than anything else. My body feeds on training, and I'll sink into a hole if I miss it. I've never used drugs—not once. I was in The Job, the police, for sixteen years, and I've seen where addiction leads too many times—and that was the police officers. The Job has made me more cynical, darker, and less trusting of people, and I don't always tell the truth anymore. But at least I know I'm not a good person.

I hear the buzzer on the door. If that's my pizza already, they can't be busy tonight. When I get downstairs, I open the door to a woman. She's the one I saw standing on the corner, and she's not delivering pizza. She's silhouetted by the street-lights and has a mobile phone in front of her face, giving off an eery glow. I can't make out her features, but she has long, dark hair and is wearing a short black leather jacket and a tight skirt. She has a handbag over her shoulder.

'Hi,' I say. She steps back into the light, and there's a look of horror on her face.

'I can't do this,' she says.

She backs away, turns around, and crosses the one-way system, leaving me standing there.

'Okay, bye then.' I shrug.

She must have got the wrong address or something. Now she's standing alone and still, her hands in her jacket pockets. She could be waiting for a taxi. She pulls out a mobile from her bag and checks it. She reminds me of someone, and I feel something going on with my stomach. I must be hungry, so I return to my flat and wait.

When my pizza arrives, I go down again and take it from the boy on the bike. The woman is still there, but now she's sobbing, sitting on the wall outside the magistrates' court, clutching her handbag as if it's her only friend in the world. It's not any of my business, and I turn to take my pizza into the flat. But a nagging doubt stops me right there. Of course, it does. If that were some guy over there, I wouldn't think twice about going back inside. Instead, I tuck the pepperoni pizza box under my arm and put the door on the latch. I cross the one-way system and stand in front of the woman until she notices me.

'You buzzed my door. Do you need help?' I say.

From this distance, I can see her clearly. She's an attractive forty-something with good cheekbones and a great figure, wearing killer heels with red soles. She dabs her eyes with a tissue and glares at me. That feeling of familiarity hits me again.

'Leave me alone!' she says. 'I can't talk to you.'

'Fair enough.' It doesn't bother me, so I go to walk away.

'Hey!' she says. 'I'm sorry, but thank you.'

'Don't worry,' I say and shrug again. 'I get that a lot.' I step back to cross the road and get halfway.

'I *really am* sorry,' she calls out. I recognise something in her voice, but I can't place her. It's jangling my nerves, and my brain has gone into some deep-rooted subroutine to find her in my memory.

I return to her against my better judgement—she could be drunk or drugged.

'Can I call a taxi for you?'

'No.' I think she's expecting something from me. Then she turns her head away, swearing under her breath. 'Memory is a strange thing, don't you think? And you don't, do you.'

'I don't understand. Have we met before?' I say.

She shakes her head. 'No. This was a bad idea. I've made a mistake. The people we love come first. I've got a taxi coming —I have to be somewhere.'

She has an attractive smile, but something is going on behind those dark eyes I don't want to get involved with. It could be drink *and* drugs. Whoever she is, she doesn't want to talk to me—so nothing I can do.

I hear the rattle of a diesel engine, and a taxi pulls up—a silver saloon—it could be a city cab. The driver calls out. 'Taxi for Garcia?'

'That's me,' she says.

Garcia—it's a name I know from somewhere, but the face doesn't match. She slides into the back seat of the car and says something to the taxi driver. She closes her door and watches me through her window. It's a look I've seen before. Someone from years ago. Something has scared her, and now there's no way out. Our eyes lock, and there's regret. She should have told me something. I step towards her, but the taxi pulls away. It drives south over the railway line, and soon, it's a pair of taillights heading out of the city.

I can't shake the doubt that's come over me. Why was she talking about memories? Maybe it was the drink, but there was more to it than that. The look, the regret, the fear. And as the neural connections find their match, it hits me like a sledge-hammer to my gut. I know who she is, and my head is firing question after question. How did she ever find me after all these years? What did she want from me? Now she's gone, and I'll never know.

CHAPTER 2

On Saturday morning, a police car eases down the hill on the narrow road through Houghton village, passing the George and Dragon pub, then flint walls and charming cottages. The views here stretch east over the South Downs, with a rich farmland valley and an unfurling ridge of hills scarred by a chalk cliff face.

As the car continues down, the River Arun comes into view. Its winding waters are green and churning with muddy-brown swirls after the recent heavy rainfall. The car slows as it crosses a stone bridge over the river and stops beside a woman wearing a long black cardigan and dress. The bridge has no footpath, so she's standing in one of the recesses to avoid the passing traffic. The rear reds flash on the police car's light bar, and the officer leans forward to see what the woman is pointing at.

He nods. 'Stay there a mo. I'll park up.'

He drives a little further over the bridge and into a pub car park—The Travellers Rest. Returning to the woman guarding her find, he dons his reflective jacket and a cap.

'It took you long enough,' she says to him. The woman pulls her cardigan around her. 'I've been standing here for forty-five minutes. Rain'll be here soon.'

'Sorry,' says the police officer. 'It's only me available. Everyone else is busy with a suicidal missing person. The world and his wife are looking for her—helicopters, search teams. A famous author—I can't tell you who, though. Show me what you've found.'

The woman steps aside. 'I'm the landlady of the Travellers. I was walking my dog this morning and saw them here.'

'What time was that?'

'It was shortly after eight.'

'Mrs Whitcliff, isn't it? I'll come by your pub in a moment to grab your details. It'll be safer for you if you wait there.'

She nods and walks back to the pub. Tucked into the recess where she had been standing is a pair of black high heels placed together. Next to them is a black handbag with a gold-coloured chain strap. The officer crouches, puts on protective gloves, and turns on his body-worn video camera. Without picking up the bag, he unclips the clasp and lifts the flap with a fingertip. Inside is a purse—no cash—door keys, lipstick, scrunched-up tissues, and a small photograph of a young woman. There's a zip pocket inside. He opens it and finds a mobile phone—an iPhone showing forty-nine missed calls.

The officer stands and peers as far over the edge of the bridge as he can. The river flows fast beneath him, the current making the surface swirl with miniature whirlpools. He squints into the chill morning light, and his eyes follow the river's path as it bends to the right and the left. Trees and shrubs are on the left bank at the first bend. At first, he thinks it's an animal in the water, a long, dark shape bobbing against the muddy bank, caught in the reeds. Then his heart sinks, and he presses the talk button on his radio.

'Control from Alpha-Zero-Three. I have an urgent update.'

A voice replies over the radio. 'Alpha-Zero-Three. Go ahead.'

'I can confirm what the informant reported regarding the shoes and the handbag. But now I'm standing on the bridge looking south, and there appears to be a body in the water.'

The tide is retreating along Southsea Beach, exposing a line of fine shingle and rotting sargassum. New sea defences of grey Norwegian granite encrust the shoreline along with thousands of tons of imported sand.

Tourists walk the esplanade, enjoying the end of summer's entertainment. There are queues for the aquarium, and the castle on the waterfront is putting on a show of military reen-actments, with guns and cannons booming. But the weather is turning, and soon the crowds will seek cover. The wind has carried dark clouds inland, and the bright August sunshine fades.

'Keep up, Juliet!' says Clarice. She sweeps her black hair out of her eyes as the sudden south-westerly breeze catches it.

The little girl walks faster, and Phil holds out his hand to her. Juliet giggles as he moves out of reach, teasing her to increase her pace. Clarice watches them together. He's so good with her, she thinks.

'Keep hold of my hand, sweetheart,' he says, 'then Grandma won't nag you.'

'I'm not nagging,' says Clarice. 'It's going to pour down any minute. I don't want us to get soaked.'

Phil sweeps the little girl up into his arms and raises her high in the air. A gust of wind catches his tie, which lands over his shoulder. Juliet laughs at all the excitement, holding out her arms like a bird. Then, as he lowers her, she runs her fingers across his beard stubble.

'Your chin feels funny,' says Juliet.

Phil straightens his glasses after Juliet dislodges them. He smiles at her. 'Well, your grandma says I look quite fetching with a beard. So it's staying.'

Large droplets fall from above, and now the colour of the sky over the Solent has turned a muddy grey.

Phil holds Juliet under one arm, takes Clarice's hand, and they run together past the D-Day Museum and towards Clarice's BMW X5 parked nose-in on the side of the road. The heavens unleash their load as they get into the car. The rain washes down on the windscreen, drumming on the roof.

'Made it,' says Clarice, laughing. She's sitting in the driver's seat.

'I think I'll wait here for a bit,' says Phil, wiping his glasses with his tie.

Clarice hasn't felt this happy for a long time. She takes his hand and squeezes it. 'It's been a wonderful morning, Phil. Thank you. Do you have to work this afternoon? It is Saturday, after all.'

'I'm afraid so. Those accounts won't do themselves, but at least we've spent some time together.' They kiss, and Phil sweeps a stray hair away from her cheek.

Clarice strokes his face. 'You look like someone's taken a weight from your shoulders.'

Phil smiles. 'More like a millstone. My wife is now officially an ex-wife. I'm free at last.'

'You're no longer married?'

'I was going to surprise you with it, but I can't keep it in any longer. That chapter's finally closed. It caused me nothing but grief. Now, all I care about is you... and Juliet. Your happiness is the most important thing to me now.'

'Can we get chips now?' says Juliet from the back seat.

'Are you still hungry?' He makes a grunting noise like a pig, and Juliet laughs.

As fast as it began, the rain stops, and the clouds break apart. Umbrellas go down, and people emerge from under the cover of the trees.

'Are you sure I can't drop you anywhere?' says Clarice, starting the engine.

'Thank you, but my car's only in Duchess Street, and I'm meeting my client there.' Phil looks out of the window. 'Anyway, the rain has stopped. It's going to be fine now.'

'Are you still working in that awful club?'

'They're still a business that needs their accounts put in order, and the client is a stickler for punctuality. I'd better go.'

'You promise me you'll keep your eyes on your work.'

He opens the door and kisses Clarice once again. 'Don't worry, Clarice. I work in the office upstairs, and I only have eyes for you. I promise. Loyalty is everything.' He glances at his watch. 'I'd better go. Bye, Juliet. See you again soon. Look after your grandma for me, okay?'

Juliet nods with a smile.

Clarice watches him in the rearview mirror as he walks away over the green. He's on his phone straight away. His gait changes, and his shoulders roll back. He's like a different man when he's working, but Clarice believes Phil is kind. It's a kindness people take advantage of. She's listened to Phil's horror stories about his ex-wife. He told her how she was unfaithful to him and even tried to kill him, forcing him into hiding.

Phil was Clarice's accountant for a while. That's how they met. He was nervous of her, never self-assured. But that changed when she got to know him. He helped her fledgling business and found a better way for her to invest her money in an offshore account. After a burglary of her home, Phil turned up at her front door one night with a curry and a bottle of wine. She felt safe with him, and he made everything okay again.

Seeing him stride away now, more confident than before, she knows this man is here to stay. He is loyal to her, and she is to him. She has nothing to fear.

CHAPTER 3

As soon as he shakes his head, she covers her eyes. This isn't what she wanted to hear today.

'We still have nothing for you, Ella,' he says, sitting back in his creaking office chair.

Ella's known *Jack the Hack* for years. He's looking tired and old now, and he's put on a few pounds since she first met him when she was a bubbly, bright young reporter, full of hope and unwavering enthusiasm. That tie he's wearing has seen better days, too.

She slumps and sighs, groaning into her hands. She comes in most Monday mornings now, always hopeful he will say yes. She tugs at her red hair in frustration. Jack has always been straight with her, and even though he's a busy man, he still makes time for her. She gazes through his office windows with envy as she sees how busy they are preparing this week's magazine edition. She could do their jobs, no problem.

'But there was a position here for a features writer two weeks ago. I'm more than capable of doing that.'

'That position's taken. You were too late to apply.'

'My mother was in hospital!'

'I'm sorry to hear that. Is she okay?'

'Yes, she's fine. A UTI. But the job was for a features writer, Jack!'

'It wasn't even here in Chichester. It would have meant you travelling to Hastings.'

'Hastings!'

'Yep.' He sits forward, and his eyes show some sympathy for her. 'I've seen your work, and believe me, you're good. We're happy to receive freelance submissions from you. I think that's some of your best work. But we don't have anything permanent. Times are hard, Ella. Online news is king now. Local rags like this one are struggling to adapt.'

'But I'm desperate.'

'I can tell, believe me—it's bloody obvious. I dream about you coming in here, asking me for work. My wife's wondering if I'm having an affair.' He smiles, and she isn't sure if he's joking. 'I'm sorry.' He tilts his head and frowns. 'Wasn't there something you were working on? Some secret philanthropist project? That sounds exciting. That would interest a lot of editors.'

'Yes, but it's slow, and I need money now. I've had to move in with my mother.'

'Not ideal.'

'No.'

'I promise you, if I hear of anything or if something comes up here, I'll call. In the meantime, continue with your free-lance work.'

She nods. 'Thanks, Jack. It's the same story everywhere I go.'

'Write a book. Everyone's doing that.' He glances at his watch and smiles.

'I may do one day,' says Ella. 'Okay. Thanks for your time.'

She leaves the office and heads back out into the city. It's raining again, so she puts up her umbrella and walks back along the East Street precinct towards the cathedral. She twists her heel on a loose brick and stops to check she hasn't broken it. She sees she's stopped outside Simon's favourite Italian restaurant and has a flashback of their last meal there. That was when he told her his news. She swallows hard and turns, moving onward.

'No, Ella,' she says to herself. 'Don't go there.'

When she reaches the clock tower, The Cross, she sits on the stone seat. The air is filled with the aroma of roasting coffee and the ambient sound of morning shoppers. She could do with a coffee. She thinks about that project she started, and *Jack the Hack* is right. The story would sell well. She must keep going with it since she has already come so far. What is she afraid of? Perhaps there's some more background work she can do first. Find out where he lives and who his friends and family are. Talk to his clients, then get up the courage to ask for an interview.

It's turned into a grey, wet Monday morning—the kind of morning you wish you could skip straight over or even take a flight to somewhere that isn't here. Summer never arrived this year.

I'm weary of this gloomy beige office. Why am I doing this? I could have stayed home or taken the boat out into the harbour. There are plenty of things I could be doing today. But no, I'm here. Sitting alone in the semi-darkness. Thinking about a woman I used to know and wondering what the hell happened to her.

I'm about to make another coffee when someone presses the buzzer on the front door. Detective Constable Gary Bates is in the street, hunched against the rain, trying to get my attention. I open the door latch, and he blunders in, overweight, too scruffy for the job, and wishing he was me. Gary and I go back several years. We were PCs on the same team in Chichester but chose different career paths. He's okay, but can be dense sometimes and socially awkward. His raincoat is dripping, making puddles on my floor.

'Hey, Max,' he says. 'God, awful weather! I got your message. Do you realise you can come to me sometimes? The nick's only five minutes away.'

I'd forgotten I'd sent him a text on Sunday morning. I pass over my iPad to show him the news report on the screen. It's a photo of an attractive, dark-haired woman—a publicity shot. The police had pulled Mariana Garcia's body out of the River Arun on Saturday morning—an apparent suicide.

He reads the report and nods. 'You're sure it was Mariana Garcia you saw?'

'The taxi driver called out her name,' I say, 'and I recognise her in this photo. I didn't realise she was a celebrity. Probably why she was cautious of me.'

'I'd never heard of her either—a rich author. Made all her money in the last five years.' He drops into a chair and looks around my office. 'And with all *your* money, why don't you get a bigger place? Something more upmarket.'

'People will think they can't afford me.'

He laughs. 'You don't even need to work, lucky sod. And you still drive that old rust bucket. Why do you do it?'

'That's my business, and it's not a rust bucket.' I turn the focus away from me. 'So, what's the verdict on Garcia?'

'We're certain it was suicide—well, my sergeant is. She'd sent her agent a message telling her she was going to end it all. There's going to be an inquest.'

'Did you find her phone?'

'In her handbag,' says Gary.

'Was the phone locked?'

'What is this, Max?' He frowns at me. 'Do you know something? Did you two meet up for anything on Friday night?'

'No,' I say. 'She was sitting over there, crying to herself.' I point out the window to the law courts. There's a woman over there now, standing under a red umbrella. Gary glances at her. 'Garcia was where that woman is. I went over to check if she was okay.'

'And was she?' he says.

I can't tell him how I once knew Mariana Garcia. That's personal to me.

'She was upset about something,' I say, 'but she didn't want to talk to me. Then she went off in a taxi.'

Gary studies me. He has this sly look that doesn't do him any favours. 'She was a good-looking woman. You're sure you didn't invite her in for a drink?'

I glare at him, and he turns his head away. 'She was in a bad way, Gary. I don't take advantage of vulnerable women.'

He coughs. The fool glances around him to see if no one's listening. 'I shouldn't be telling you this, but the phone wasn't locked.'

I nod. 'No, you shouldn't. Where did she go in the water?'

'Off Houghton Bridge into the Arun. Her daughter had called the police in the early hours of Saturday morning. Mariana's agent had contacted her, worried after she'd received the suicide message.'

'Her daughter reported her as a missing person?'

'Yep. The duty inspector assessed her as a high-risk, vulnerable misper. The landlady of a local pub found Garcia's handbag and heels on the bridge around eight on Saturday morning. A police officer found her body around nine o'clock. The river didn't take her far. She'd got caught up in the reeds on the first bend.'

'Her shoes and handbag on the bridge?' I say. 'How long was she in the water?'

'Between eight and ten hours, according to the pathologist.'

'Leave a note?'

'Nope. Only the WhatsApp message to her agent.'

'Are they certain she went into the river from the bridge?'

He nods. 'As sure as they can be.'

'What was in the handbag?'

'Shit, Max, you don't ask for much.' He looks up at the ceiling tiles to remember. 'Keys, purse, bank cards, and a mobile phone. Sundry bits and pieces like lipstick and a photo of a woman.'

'Did Forensics find anything?'

Gary raises his eyebrows. 'That's all you're getting. Why are you so interested? Do you know something I don't?'

'Of course not. She didn't look like she was going to kill herself.'

He scoffs. 'Come on, you can't tell by looking at someone. Can you give me anything new? Or is this one-way traffic? I assume you didn't want me to come here just to get me soaked.'

I shrug.

He gets up and heads to the door, looking again at the office. 'This place.' He tuts. 'Think about it, Max. Take early retirement. It makes sense.'

He's gone back out into the rain—not happy. There are things I can't tell anyone, not even Gary. It was the nature of the job. Garcia and I spoke for less than a minute on Friday, and everything was in that last look she gave me. Understanding memory isn't straightforward. It relies on context, and there wasn't context at first on Friday night. There is now.

The only case I'm working on is some stupid dispute over a will. That can wait. I head out of the office through the back door, get into my blue Volvo V70 estate, and head off to Amberley and Houghton Bridge.

CHAPTER 4

The car park at The Travellers Rest pub is a convenient place to park the Volvo and is next to Houghton Bridge. By the time I arrive, the clouds have parted, and the rain has stopped. The air is thick, humid, and earthy-sweet.

It's late August, and the light is changing as summer fades. I notice it in the shadows of the leaves as I pass beneath a tree. They're less defined along the edges.

The bridge spans the River Arun, about a hundred and fifty yards long, and is wide enough for traffic to pass both ways with no footpath. Although it appears medieval, I remember from somewhere that it's less than two centuries old.

I walk past a token police sign by the pub asking for witnesses. I doubt there will be any. It's clear where they focused the crime scene. There are small turret-like recesses in the bridge, and one has yellow marks and arrows sprayed on it. Crossing the bridge whilst dodging the traffic isn't easy, and I've had to dip in and out of the recesses until I reach the one I want.

They couldn't have got fingerprints off the stonework, but

I expect they've swabbed for fibres, blood, and DNA. I watch the flow of the river, and with the sun in my eyes, I squint towards the first bend, perhaps forty feet or so away. An unconscious body would take about twenty seconds to get there in this current. People can die a few seconds after inhaling water, so she could have been dead by then.

Why choose to end your life here? Why at some time after midnight? I gauge the height of the wall on the bridge. It wouldn't be easy to lift yourself up and over, and you'd need two people to raise a deadweight and throw it in the river. The dead are heavy. And how did she get here, anyway? She didn't have a car that night. There's a railway station three hundred yards away, but she took a taxi. Someone must have driven her here, so the taxi's the next obvious line of enquiry.

Too many questions. I take a deep breath to focus my mind. When things get complicated, experience tells me I'm going in the wrong direction. My stomach rumbles as I've only had coffee for breakfast, and my shoulders ache after the extra hours in the dojo yesterday. I must get something to eat soon.

I make some mental notes to recap. Mariana, a ghost from the past, appeared at my door on Friday night. She wanted to tell me something but changed her mind. They found her dead on Saturday morning, and she left her shoes and handbag behind on a bridge in the middle of nowhere. There's an unlocked phone and a suicide message to her agent. Someone drove her here. This is a busy road during the day. But there'd be plenty of time to dispose of a body at night. This all stinks. She didn't kill herself. She was murdered.

'You one of those bloggers?' A man in chef whites and a headscarf is standing beside me. He takes me by surprise.

'What do you mean?' I say.

'We've had all sorts here after they found her body.' He

leans against the wall and lights a cigarette. 'My wife's read all her books. Mariana Garcia. Romance crime thrillers, she called them.'

'Do you work at the Travellers Rest?'

He looks down at his clothes and laughs. 'Amateur sleuth, eh? And that's your old Volvo in our car park, I imagine.'

'I'm just going.'

'No need. We're not exactly busy. It was full of police vans at the weekend and girls in white bunny suits. Pretty things, they were. CSI, they call them. The whole bloody road was closed for the day. We lost all our usual customers. Ended up feeding the coppers instead.'

'Do you live in the pub?'

'Yep. Me and my missus. That doesn't mean we heard anything on Friday night.' He coughs into a tissue and turns away. 'Foxes sound like screaming women. We get plenty of foxes around here. The males make that noise, warning the competition.'

'Would you have heard someone scream, do you think? I mean, you're less than fifty yards away.'

'Guess I would,' he says. 'I'm a light sleeper. I didn't hear the foxes either.'

'Who found the handbag and shoes?'

'My missus.'

I nod and smile. 'Do you serve an all-day English breakfast?'

I follow the man back to the pub, placing an order for a full English, minus the black pudding. Striking up a conversation with the chef's wife, the pub's landlady, she tells me about finding the shoes placed together on the bridge. *Louboutin*, she says—red soles and black patent leather—not her size. And the bag was Chanel. No jacket, she says. That's a strange thing to tell me. I never asked her about a jacket, but that gets me thinking. Was Garcia wearing it when she went in? The jacket was a pretty tight fit when I saw her wearing it. I give the landlady my card and tell her to call me if she remembers anything else.

I take one last look at the bridge and think about the direction Mariana could have come from. To the west is the A29, from Bognor Regis to London. That leads onto the A27 and Chichester. The other way is east towards Storrington, Worthing, and London. She would have come from the west. Driven by who?

On my way back to the office, I get a call from DC Gary Bates, and I take it on the hands-free.

'What do you remember about the taxi that took Garcia?' he asks me. I hear the stress in his voice.

'I was just thinking about that. It was one of the city cabs,' I say. 'I can't remember which one. He said he was a taxi for Garcia.'

'None of the taxi companies picked her up.'

'One of them did.'

'No, they didn't. We checked.'

'What are you saying?' I say.

'Maybe you got it wrong.'

I'm on the A27, and the cathedral spire comes into view as I approach the Portfield roundabout.

'Have you checked CCTV in Southgate?' I ask.

'They took it down. Chichester City Council cut-backs.'

'Why are you checking taxi companies if you think it was suicide?'

He hesitates. 'I can't say.'

'She had to have been driven to Houghton.'

'There's a railway station a few hundred yards from the bridge.'

'Do you honestly believe she got out of the taxi and took a train?'

'No,' he says.

'My thoughts exactly. The taxi took her to the bridge, or someone else drove her. What are *you* saying happened?'

'I can't tell you,' he says, but he wants to tell me something.

'You've got the toxicology results back. What do they say?'

'Max, it's part of a police investigation.'

'I can give you something in return,' I say.

'What?'

'Was she wearing her jacket when they pulled out of the river?'

'A jacket?' Gary thinks. 'What kind of jacket?'

'So, she wasn't.'

'I never said that.'

'Yes, you did,' I say. 'But she was wearing one when I saw her. Black leather with zips.'

'Perhaps it came off in the water,' says Gary.

'No, it didn't. It was too tight. Do you want to know where it is?'

'You have it?'

'No, not me!' I'm pulling into my parking space behind the office. 'If I tell you, then you tell me about the toxicology results.'

His end of the line goes quiet for a few seconds, and he sighs into the phone. 'There was a trace of GHB in her blood.'

'The date rape drug? Was she sexually assaulted?'

'Not according to the pathologist. We don't know if she

was recovering from it when you saw her or if someone gave it to her afterwards. We're still going with suicide, but my sergeant wants to know more about your involvement.'

'My involvement? I had nothing more to do with her.'

'That taxi you said you saw—we can't find it. It's a major line of investigation, and you're a key witness. You're the last person to see her alive.'

'How about the driver? He was the last person to see her alive.'

'Aren't you listening, Max? As far as my sergeant is concerned, there was no taxi.'

'Not my problem,' I say.

'He thinks it is.'

'He can think what he likes. Stop fretting. I'll come in and give a statement.'

'Okay,' says Gary, letting it go. 'Now, what about the jacket?'

'The landlady of the Travellers Rest took it.'

'How do you know? Did you go to Amberley?'

'Of course I did. She has an eye for fashion,' I say. 'The shoes weren't her size, and the handbag was too personal for her. Something about it spooked her from taking it. Probably that photo or something else that was personal to Mariana.'

'The photo,' he says.

'I reckon someone drugged Mariana Garcia and dropped her into the river. Was there definitely water in her lungs?'

'Yes. She was alive when she went in.' I hear him move the phone to a different ear. 'Are you going to come in, Max?' There's tension in his voice.

'Yes, I'll give my statement. Nothing more.'

'Thanks, mate. It's not you. This has put me in a difficult position.'

'How?'

'Because you're my mate, and my sergeant knows it!'

After I end the call with Gary, I go back inside my office. Gary is right. This place is dull. I thought being in the city, I'd see a lot more business than I'm getting. But it's slow, and I'm bored. I don't need the money. This job is important to me for other reasons.

A few weeks ago, I looked for an office somewhere else. An estate agent called Gemma told me she had problems with a stalker. She needed my help, so I persuaded the stalker to move away. In return, Gemma helped me find another place that suited my needs. I hope to be out of here sometime soon.

I make a coffee, rub my shoulders, and stand by the window. I'm thinking I may need some help around the office. Someone to answer the phone and do some research for me. As long as they don't question my business model, I don't care. My work is *pro bono publico*, or they pay what they can afford. I get to choose my rates, not them. Most people won't understand it, but I don't care.

The rain is heavy again. We had the wettest July on record this year, and the woman walking close by my office must have made good use of her umbrella this summer. She's only a few inches from the glass. She glances at me and smiles. Nice —red hair and green eyes. She's waiting a few yards from my door. Her hair is reflected in my window. I could ask her if she wants a job—that might be a little creepy. And she's definitely my type, but that would mess with everything. She's taken a photo of something. The rain? Perhaps it was a selfie for a friend. And now she's gone.

I can't put off my existing work any longer. Mariana Garcia isn't my case until someone makes it mine. Can I shelve it after everything I know about her? I have other work

I'm obliged to finish, but I don't think Mariana is going to leave me alone anytime soon.

I check the time on my mobile. The police want me to give a statement about the taxi. I'd better get it over with before they start hammering on my door.

CHAPTER 5

Chichester Police Station is a little different from when I worked here. New carpets, new colours, and posters on the walls. The same smells and the same pained expression on the officers' faces as they go by. There's a customer-friendly feel now, with more ways to complain about the service you receive than ever before and more ways to shaft hard-working officers trying to get the job done.

I started my police career in Chichester before moving to the Met. After two years, I went into firearms and intelligence, somehow ending up in CID and Major Crimes for a while. But it all started right here as a student constable.

I still have dreams about this place where I'm walking through the corridors at night, killing zombie officers. The dreams where you're running through treacle, and your mother turns up to take you home. Perhaps it's only me who has those dreams.

I've been waiting for thirty minutes, and I'm now counting tiles on the ceiling. The door opens and a young, smart-looking detective has found me daydreaming in reception. He gives me a perfunctory greeting and leads me to the custody block for a *quick word*. I must have looked as young as him once. I glance at his face while we're waiting to be let into Custody. He has a thin trace of perspiration above his top lip, and he keeps swallowing.

'I'm DS Chambers.' He's remembered to tell me his name. 'Thanks for coming in for the interview. We're rushed off our feet here.'

He's a detective sergeant! Gary's manager—I am honoured. He must be older than he looks. And this is an interview? I thought I was giving a statement about the taxi. Gary didn't tell me that part.

'I didn't realise this was an interview,' I say.

'Really? Is that a problem?'

'Not a problem. Happy to help.' I wanted to make the point.

The door clicks, and we enter. The DS finds us a cosy interview room. I'm unsure what he knows about me, but I'm willing to play the game. He removes his jacket and sits opposite me. He's sweating under his arms. He takes a moment to review his notes, shuffling papers in question order. He's done his planning and preparation, but he's not asked me if I want a solicitor yet. It would piss him off if I said yes, and he'd have to arrange another time.

He hits the record button.

'I have a few questions for you,' he says. 'First, I need to tell you that you're not under arrest, and you're free to go whenever you want. While you're here, you are entitled to free and independent legal advice. Do you want a solicitor?'

'You're okay,' I say. 'I don't want one.'

'I'm Detective Sergeant Chambers, and this interview is being held in an interview room at Chichester Custody. This is regarding the death of Mariana Garcia on or around Friday, the 25th of August this year.'

'What do you want to know?'

'DC Bates tells me you used to be a police officer.'

'I used to be a DS like you,' I say.

'Where did you work?'

'Caution me, and I'll tell you.'

He rolls his eyes. Perhaps he didn't mean to, but it's a signal to me that something odd is going on. He cautions me, slow and deliberate. Once he's finished, I tell him I understand it, and I'm ready.

'I used to work for the Met in Protection Command,' I say. 'Royalty, Specialist, and Diplomatic Protection. Then later for MI5 in counter-espionage and domestic terrorism.'

He laughs. Does he think I'm joking? Most of that's gone above his head. I think he only heard blah-blah. He's got something else on his mind.

He reads his first question. 'What can you tell me about last Friday evening regarding Mariana Garcia?'

I tell him everything I saw and heard in my brief interaction with her, including when the taxi took her away. The DS makes notes during my statement, ready to challenge me.

'Describe the taxi to me,' he says.

'Silver or grey, a saloon type of car. Something like a Skoda Octavia. That sort of shape. It was difficult to be certain of the colour under the streetlights.'

'The driver?'

'I don't remember anything about him. I was watching Garcia'

'Did Ms Garcia go of her own free will?'

'I have no reason to believe otherwise.'

'Did you see a taxi meter in the car?'

'I didn't notice. She told me a taxi was coming, and I heard the man say taxi for Garcia. He had a European accent, I seem to remember.'

'Did you see a taxi licence plate at the back of the car?'

'I don't remember.'

'And it drove south, over the railway line?'

'Yes.'

'How well did you know Mariana?'

'I didn't know her. I only spoke to her for a minute.'

That's a lie, but there's nothing more I can say.

He sits back in his chair, tapping his pen on the table. I remember interviewing a terrorist once, and he grabbed my colleague's pen and plunged it into his own throat. Funny the things you remember. The interview room had to be redecorated after that.

'None of the Chichester taxi companies have a record of picking up Mariana Garcia. How do you account for that?'

'Why do I need to account for that?' I say, sitting forward.

'It seems strange that none of them know anything about it.'

'I agree.'

'You do?' he says.

'How would you account for that?' I ask.

'I don't need to, Mr Fortis.'

'And neither do I, DS Chambers.'

'Was there really a taxi, Mr Fortis? Or are you lying to me?'

That was sudden. 'There was a taxi.'

'Did you take Mariana Garcia back to your flat?'

'No.'

'Did you have a drink or a meal with Ms Garcia on Friday evening?'

'No.'

'Did you go anywhere with her in your car?'

'No.'

'What did you do Friday evening?'

'I stayed in my flat, eating pizza and researching office furniture. I live such a dirty rock and roll lifestyle. I'd be more interested to know what Mariana's movements were that evening *before* she met me. What was she doing in Chichester City Centre?'

'That's what we are trying to establish,' he says.

'Why was she all dressed up? It looked like she'd been out somewhere. Have you tried the local bars and restaurants?'

'Mr Fortis, I'm asking the questions.'

'Pointless ones.'

He glares at me, and I smile back.

'Why did you go to Houghton Bridge today?'

'I was trained to build a rapport with the people I interviewed, DS Chambers, even if I didn't like them. You're not getting the best out of me today.'

'I asked you why did you go to Houghton Bridge today?'

'Gary told you that, did he? Because I wanted to see where she died.'

'Why? You only spoke to her for a minute. What did you care?'

I smile at him. 'I have a morbid curiosity.'

'Are you an investigator, Mr Fortis, or are you a fantasist?'

I point at him. 'You got me there, DS Chambers.' I glance at my watch and stand up. 'I must go. See you around.'

'I haven't finished!'

'Remember, DS Chambers, I'm free to go whenever I want.'

'I can arrest you.'

'Necessity for arrest? You've already interviewed me. Seems to me you're clutching at straws. I'll see you at the inquest. See how that goes for you.'

Chambers flushes red. 'Interview terminated.'

Frank Pinto and Mikita help Councillor Fenz onto the boat moored at the quayside. The evening light seeps over Portsmouth, painting the grand Spinnaker Tower in a tangerine wash. Pinto loves Old Portsmouth—he has a history here. But the way events are playing out, he thinks his time here may soon be over.

He's in his dark suit and tie this evening, and his sizable form squashes into the boat's open cabin, where he takes the controls.

'This meeting with Mr Marlowe has been a long time coming,' says Fenz as he steps on board. His voice is unusually high-pitched and matches his weasel-like face. 'But I don't understand why it's so rushed. I haven't even been home from work. Why doesn't he want me to talk to anyone?'

'I'm sure you understand, Mr Fenz,' says Pinto, 'the nature of this meeting requires discretion on both sides.'

'True. But I'm glad Mr Marlowe has finally seen sense. And, of course, I always appreciate a meal out on the island.' He's uncomfortable as Mikita squeezes into the seat next to him.

Fenz is the head of the city's licensing committee. It's a job that has often put him at odds with Marlowe. Pinto knows his agenda. As a former nightclub owner, Fenz must understand the challenges of running a niche club in Southsea. Marlowe's venture, however, has got under Fenz's skin, and he's beginning to make unwelcome noises at the committee meetings. The rumours are that Fenz is about to call time on the Obsidian Rooms nightclub. The years of work Marlowe has put into building this business mean nothing to Fenz. As soon as he heard about the nature of the club's entertainment, he wanted to close the place down.

'It's the girls,' Fenz says. 'Surely your boss understands that. The entertainment is getting out of hand.'

Mikita has cast off. Pinto pushes the accelerator control, and the boat lurches forward. He navigates them out of the quay and takes the boat into Portsmouth Harbour, past the Round Tower, and into open water. He pushes the control forward again, and the boat speeds towards the Isle of Wight.

'It's got a lot of punch, this boat,' says Fenz. 'I'd like one like this.'

Pinto's wearing his shades now, and his bald head is lit red by the setting sun. He turns around, smiles, and nods.

'You not paid enough to converse with me, Pinto?' Fenz laughs to himself. 'You should ask for a rise.'

He looks across the bow, and the Isle of Wight drifts starboard. Mikita offers him a cigarette. He takes one, and Mikita lights it for him.

'You said Mr Marlowe is in Ryde? That's over there.' Fenz points.

'Don't worry, Councillor,' says Pinto. 'There's been a change of plan. My boss wants to meet you in Bembridge. There's a new fish restaurant he wants you to try.'

'Goodness!' says Fenz. 'I'm not dressed for any fancy restaurant, guys. Look at me.'

'You'll be fine,' says Mikita in his Belarusian accent.

They pass one of the Napoleonic forts, and Pinto nods at Mikita.

'I doubt the crabs will care what you're wearing,' says Pinto, and he laughs.

'You guys know Marlowe well, right?' He takes a long draw on the cigarette.

Pinto nods.

'What sort of offer is he going to make me? I assume he wants to keep the club running. We've had complaints about the girls you have on display. The neighbours aren't happy to see women in underwear appearing at the windows. I wouldn't mind, of course. But I have to be seen to be upholding standards.'

'But for a price, you'll turn a blind eye to your standards. Yes?'

'I wouldn't put it that way to Mr Marlowe. But if we're being brutally honest, then yes.' He drags on his cigarette and exhales a plume of smoke, giving a wheezy chuckle.

Pinto pulls back the accelerator, locking it into neutral. The boat slows to a stop.

'Hey, why have we stopped?'

'There's a red light at Bembridge,' says Pinto. 'Look. Can't go through a red light.'

Fenz stands and moves to the front of the boat. He's peering into the distance, and Bembridge comes into view around the island's northeast corner. He sees a yacht sailing into the harbour.

'What red light? Boats don't stop at red lights.'

Fenz doesn't know what's coming. Mikita slaps the side of his face with a large pair of pliers, gashing his cheek and knocking the man off his feet.

'Hey!' He's dazed. 'What the—'

Pinto hauls the stupefied Fenz off the floor, and Mikita

binds his wrists together with cable ties. Fenz panics as he struggles to breathe.

'The thing is, Councillor,' says Pinto, 'my boss won't agree to any deal with you. You have been a pain in his arse for far too long. Of all the people we thought would understand our business, it was you. But you've let us down.'

Mikita ties a rope around Fenz's ankle and nods at Pinto.

'So, Mr Fenz. It's time you were no longer here. It's time to feed the crabs. And say hello to the fishes.'

With a swipe of his foot, Pinto slides the iron weight tied to Fenz's ankles overboard. Fenz gasps. He tries to lean forward, struggling against the weight, and Pinto laughs. Then, with one last shove, Fenz hits the water with a splash, and he's gone. It's as if he was never there.

CHAPTER 6

It's a Monday in late September, a month after the police pulled Mariana Garcia from the river. Ten minutes ago, the coroner's inquest into her death closed in Chichester. They read out the statement I gave to the police, but I wasn't called to testify. DS Chambers tried to cast doubt on my account about the taxi, but he couldn't state for certain there wasn't one. In the coroner's summing up, he said Garcia's suicide message to her agent and the agent's testimony about her recent depression would suggest she took her life. But then the GHB traces in her blood, the location, the missing taxi, and the fact her phone was unlocked—anyone could have typed that WhatsApp message—persuaded him towards foul play. There was insufficient evidence either way, so the coroner recorded an open verdict. The problem was the police investigation had hit a dead end. DS Chambers wasn't able to pin anything on me.

Leaving Edes House, I head onto West Street in the direction of my office. The street isn't busy here, so hearing someone walking behind me wasn't difficult. Stopping, I turn to speak to a young woman in her early twenties with long dark hair, brown eyes, and a blue dress. She has a Spanish look about her, and I can see she has her mother's eyes.

'Mr Fortis,' she says. 'I'm Grace.'

'Mariana's daughter,' I say. She was at the inquest, sitting a few rows behind me.

I've been doing my homework on Mariana's family and her recent life. I already knew she was a widow, and she had only started writing about five years ago. Her books became international best-sellers overnight. Grace is her only child, and Mariana kept the details of her life with her late husband private.

'How can I help you?' I ask.

The man strolling up behind Grace is Spencer Ryan, her boyfriend. It's important for me to know who people are. It's the reason I do the homework. I'm always prepared—like a boy scout. He's good-looking. Blue eyes and perfect teeth. I get the feeling he's already worked out which side of his bread is buttered. Grace has money coming her way now.

The boyfriend is wearing black boots, polished and bulled to a mirror finish. He's giving off a suspicious vibe, like he's wondering if I'm some kind of competition for him. There's a red swelling under his left eye. Someone has punched him. He puts his hand on Grace's shoulder, more out of ownership than comfort.

'From what I gather,' says Grace, 'you're one of the last people to see my mother alive.'

I'm not sure what I should say. 'I doubt that, Miss Garcia.'

'You said in your statement my mother appeared to be distressed about something.'

'That's right,' I say.

'What do you think that was about?'

'I spoke to your mother for less than a minute. That was all the contact I had with her.'

There are tears in Grace Garcia's eyes. 'You're a private detective, aren't you?'

'Yes.'

'Can I meet with you to discuss something?'

'Of course.' I'm sure she suspects someone murdered her mother, too.

The boyfriend shifts his stance and whispers something in her ear. She shakes him off.

'When did you have in mind?' I say.

'Now?'

'I'd be delighted to. On your own, I take it?' The boyfriend is glaring at me. I know his type straight away.

'Yes.' She raises her chin as she says it.

'I'm in Southgate, near the Locomotive pub. There's a sign on the door. I'll meet you there in half an hour.'

'Thank you.'

As I walk away, I hear angry, hushed words exchanged between them.

Someone is running to catch up with me. He's heavy-footed, trying not to sound breathless.

'Gary,' I say without turning around.

'How did you know it was me?' he says, now even more out of breath.

'I could smell you coming.'

'That's not very friendly.'

'An open verdict, eh?' I say. 'How about that?'

'Well, it's a bit dodgy.'

'I've told you my thoughts.'

We pass the cathedral and turn right onto South Street.

'There's no evidence for anything else, Max.'

I slow my pace to help him catch his breath. 'What was inside Mariana Garcia's jacket?'

He's puzzled for a moment and then embarrassed. 'The landlady at the Travellers Rest denied seeing a jacket.'

'Gary, she has it. Too late now. She'll have thrown anything in the pockets.'

'Don't you have other work to keep you busy?' he says. He's a little irritated with me.

'I'm always busy.' I wonder why he's interested. 'Have you had anyone ask questions about me? Your bosses? People in suits?'

He laughs and blushes. 'Why do you think anyone would be interested in you?'

'No reason. Forget I asked.'

So he has. Lacey still wants to keep tabs on me, and she's asked Gary to help her. She's not the only one. There's the woman with red hair and the red umbrella I keep seeing. She could be working for Lacey, but she's pretty crap at surveillance if she is. She's been watching me on and off for the last six weeks. I've even seen her talking to a couple of my clients. Odd behaviour. Maybe she's in competition with me—another investigator. Do I need to keep an eye out for her?

'The trail's gone cold with this Garcia case,' says Gary. 'Was that Grace Garcia I saw you talking to?'

'It was,' I say.

'What did she want?'

I shrug. 'I'll find out soon.'

'If anything comes up, don't forget you have a duty to tell me.'

'Yes, Gary.' I salute him. 'It was murder. GHB isn't easy to come by. Who was Mariana Garcia with that evening?'

He shrugs.

'That is why your trail has gone cold. You've fallen at the first hurdle.'

Gary grunts something abusive at me and leaves me outside my office. He's more stressed these days—not good for his heart.

I open the door to Grace Garcia, and her overprotective boyfriend is following right behind her.

'Miss Garcia,' I say, 'so you're not alone.'

'No,' she says, embarrassed. 'Spencer wants to support me.'

Spencer is now without a tie. He has a thin-lipped smile, as if he's just beat me at tiddlywinks.

I move some chairs, and they take a seat in front of my desk. She surveys my office, and I don't think she's impressed.

'I'm not staying here,' I say. 'A bit too beige and brown for my liking.'

She smiles politely and nods while her boyfriend—the strong, silent, and controlling type—leans back and scowls.

I sit forward with my elbows on the desk. 'How can I help you, Miss Garcia?'

'Please, call me Grace.'

I nod, and Spencer rolls his eyes and folds his arms. I notice his Rolex watch. Not only is his bread buttered, it's spread thick with jam.

'I'm not convinced my mother took her own life.'

'Neither was the coroner,' I say.

'About a month before her death, she was happy and full of hope. She was researching a new book and loved hunting for story ideas. Then something happened. I'd gone away for the weekend. Spencer asked her for my hand in marriage. But she had suddenly changed.'

'Didn't she agree?' I ask Spencer.

'No,' he says.

'Why?'

'None of your business,' he says.

Grace rolls her eyes.

'Are you sure you don't want to talk to me privately, Grace?' I say.

Spencer sits forward. 'Yes, she's sure.'

'Nice watch,' I say to him. 'Birthday present?'

'It's okay, Mr Fortis,' says Grace. 'Spencer gets a bit…'

'Controlling?'

'I was going to say protective… of me.'

The stupid grin has slipped off his face now. I laugh.

'You were saying you went away,' I say to Grace, 'and when you returned, your mother was different somehow?'

'Yes. She was worried about something. Constantly looking at her phone.'

'And she wouldn't tell you when you asked her?'

'She'd smile at me and tell me it would be okay.'

Is this something to do with Spencer? He asked Mariana if he could marry his daughter, and then she changed. Or was there something else?

'What would you like me to do?' I say.

'I want you to find out what happened and why she's dead.'

'That's a pretty tall order. I'd need to do a lot of digging around people's private affairs.'

'Here we go, Grace,' says Spencer. 'He's about to rip you off. I told you this was a bad idea.'

I can hear a residue of an American accent in his voice.

'Shut up, Spencer!' Grace snaps.

'What I'm saying is,' I say, 'you're going to have to accept what I find. Good or bad. These things are seldom black and white. Bad guys, good guys. Sometimes, I uncover details that are difficult to hear.'

'Anything, Mr Fortis. All I want is the truth. What are your terms?'

'All my expenses, plus five hundred a day to the charity of my choice.' I know she can afford it now.

Spencer laughs. 'A charity?'

'Something funny?' I say. 'I can double it if you prefer?'

'Thank you, Mr Fortis,' says Grace, frowning at Spencer. 'It wasn't what I was expecting. I want to sign you up.'

'I'm happy to oblige, but I'd still like to know why your mother didn't want your boyfriend to marry you.'

Spencer shakes his head.

'She said no,' says Grace. 'That's all there was to it. It didn't matter. It was something Spencer did out of courtesy, anyway.'

'Funny,' I say to Spencer. 'I wouldn't have taken you for someone who asks permission for anything.'

'You're treading on thin ice, Fortis,' says Spencer, his nostrils flaring at me.

I laugh. 'Am I, now?'

'You don't know the first thing about me.'

'You're Spencer Ryan. Aged thirty-one years old, born in Chicago, Illinois, dual nationality. You spent a year in the British Army until you couldn't handle it anymore. You manage a second-hand car dealership, and I reckon Grace's mother bought you that shiny Rolex for a birthday present two months ago. Oh yes, you're also some wannabe cage fighter. A really tough man.'

The rage in his eyes was worth all the research on the family.

Grace laughs. 'You're definitely hired. But don't you want the money for yourself?'

'I don't need it. But there are plenty of people who do. Those are my terms. You'll need to sign them before I start.'

Clarice leaves work at lunchtime and stands in front of her car in the business centre's car park. She's too busy to see what's on her windscreen. She's lost in thought, looking for her keys with one hand while the other is scrolling on her mobile phone for any messages from Phil. He still hasn't called her this morning, and she's worried. He'd texted her to say he had a problem at work and couldn't talk.

She opens the car door, and there's a shadow on the windscreen. Something green and red. She gets out and finds a bouquet of red roses pinned by the stalks under the wipers. She can't help but smile. There's a note with them, which she rips open to read. *Lunch?* She puzzles for a moment.

'Well?' says a voice behind her.

The smile turns into a grin. 'If you're going to buy me flowers, how can I refuse?' She kisses Phil, and they hold each other. 'Where are you taking me?'

'To the park. We both only have half an hour, so…'

'Perfect!' she says.

'And I've got our lunch.' Phil opens a bag with sandwiches and fruit.

They cross over the busy road and walk into Milton Park, through the black iron gates, past the brick theatre building, where they find a bench.

'This is lovely, Phil,' says Clarice as she opens her sandwich. 'I'm so glad to see you. How is work this morning?'

'Not great. Trying to balance the books.'

'Must be hard being an accountant. You're a clever man. How is my investment going?'

'Your investment?' Phil looks blank and then smiles. 'Oh, yes! Your money's being put to good use—planting trees in the Amazon. An incredible project. Great returns.'

'Wow!'

'Did I tell you I didn't always want to be an accountant?'

'No?'

'I wanted to be a vet at first and then a police officer or a tree surgeon. It used to change every week.'

Clarice laughs. 'I can imagine you as a policeman. I bet you'd be a good one.'

'I don't think I've got the stomach for it now. I hate the sight of blood.'

Clarice glimpses Phil's hand. His knuckles are red-raw, and he has long scratches down his wrists.

'Oh my goodness, Phil! How did you do that?'

Phil inspects his knuckles and pauses. He doesn't answer straight away. 'I didn't realise it was as bad as that.'

'Have you been in a fight? Does it hurt?'

'It does look like that.' He laughs. 'A shelf fell on me at work. I heard it go. I had to put my hand up to stop it crashing on my head.'

'It must have caught you.'

'Yes. It must have.'

Clarice examines his hands with care. 'You have blood on your arm, too. You must wash them when you get back. You don't want an infection.'

'Thank you. I will.'

'It's good you don't mind the sight of your own blood.'

'Now there's a thing,' says Phil. 'When I was a boy, I used to throw up at the sight of a cut knee or a gash on the head. I seem to be cured.'

'A shelf?' says Clarice.

'That's right.'

Clarice turns away. She's ignoring the three strands of long black hair caught tight around the button on his shirt sleeve. She doesn't want to think about it. She has complete trust in him. Why would he lie?

CHAPTER 7

Grace Garcia hired me five hours ago. I've already been phoning around taxi companies and visiting their local offices. A friendly face is often better than a phone call, and I can turn on the charm if needed. I've travelled to the nearest major towns to the west, Emsworth and Havant, and bothered taxi offices there. None of them wanted to provide details of drivers on their books driving silver or grey saloons. The days of waving money in front of their eyes for information have long gone. Data protection includes audit trails nowadays. I reached a dead end pretty fast as far as that taxi goes. It could have come from further away, but that's unlikely.

Then I researched more on Grace's background and her mother's recent history, trying to fill in the blanks. That wasn't so difficult for me, as I already had some inside information on Mariana, even if it was over five years out of date. Grace inherits Mariana's fortune. All thirty-eight million of it, plus a house near Arundel and an apartment in London. She's still so young, and her whole life has turned upside down. She will never need to work again. An obvious motive, of course—

murder your mother for the inheritance. But I don't think she has it in her to kill anyone.

Taking a life changes you—she doesn't have that look about her. She could have asked Spencer to do it, but I doubt it. He'd kill his own mother for a packet of toffees. He'd get his share of the money once they're married. But Spencer Ryan is an ugly leech. I can tell. He's attached himself to Grace to suck her blood. He's done a job on his girlfriend, and he's my number one suspect before I start. It's funny how we can take an instant dislike to someone. The manipulative, controlling types are the ones I hate the most. Subtle body language—that hand on Grace's shoulder.

The last thing I've done today is arrange to speak to Mariana's literary agent in Soho, London. She might be able to give me some inside information. Talking is done better when it's face-to-face. That meeting's booked for tomorrow at their offices.

I'm thinking of returning to the house tonight, and then I can take a train from Bosham in the morning. Leon can take me to the station if he's not busy with something else.

Ima and Leon. They live with me and take care of the house. They're both retired, so they live there rent-free in return, plus a little extra. The house is in safe hands with them, and they are safe there, too. They were close friends of my uncle, and they cared for him in those last few days when he wanted to die at home.

My Uncle Arthur was my father's brother. They looked alike but were a different species from each other. Although my father killed people for a living, he was kind and easy-going—as weird as that sounds. My uncle showed all the outward signs of kindness, but he was shrewd and ruthless underneath. I get my stature from my father. He was tall and dark-haired, too. My mother fell for him at first sight, and he did the same for her. My father died in battle, and it broke my mother for many years.

I lock up my office and return to the Volvo parked at the back. As I'm about to get in, I glimpse that red-haired woman again. She's hard to miss. She's on her phone, walking into the multistorey car park behind the offices. If Lacey wanted someone to follow me, she wouldn't have chosen her. She sticks out too much. The red hair and the green eyes are far too memorable. It's time to bust her cover and find out who she is.

She's heading into the car park, going up the spiral steps in one of the round towers to the first level. The fluorescent lights spread a dreary glow under the cover of the concrete ceiling. I follow her from a distance—any closer, then I'll creep her out. She stops, and a light flickers. I slip behind a pillar as she senses someone following her. Perhaps she is surveillance-aware, after all.

She heads to the first row of cars and finds a silver Audi as the lights flash. After a brief struggle with her bag and phone, she gets in. While she's checking something on her mobile, I walk up to the driver's door and tap on the window. She's startled but then smiles and lets her window down six inches.

'Hi,' I say.

'Hi?' She's smiling—not the reaction I expected.

'You're working for Lacey.'

'Am I?' she says, now a little puzzled. 'Who's Lacey? Does she work at the head office?'

I'm pretty good at reading people, and I'm not backing down. 'You stick out too much to do close surveillance work. The hair and the good looks don't work for you.'

She's still smiling. 'Well, that's a line I've never heard before. Okay, I'll bear it in mind. It's a good job I'm a store manager then. Now, if it's okay with you, I must get home to my mother.'

She closes her window, locks the doors, and starts the engine. I back away in case she decides to run over my feet. How could I have got that so wrong? She smiles, waves her left hand at me, and drives down the tight curve of the down-ramp, the Audi's tyres squealing around the corners, echoing off the concrete walls. I'm left standing there like a fool.

I head back to my Volvo, thinking about the woman, kicking myself for blundering in there. She's smart and feisty. She could be a great actress, but I somehow doubt it. I'm trying to picture what store she works in. Her ring finger was bare, but there was a pale line.

With my embarrassment buried as a lesson learned, I take the road home, past Fishbourne, and on to Bosham, where the house that is now mine sits on the waterside on The Hoe. I pull onto the driveway and put the Volvo into one of the two double garages alongside the Range Rover and the *red car*. This was my uncle's place, and he left it to me. He also left me with more money than I would ever need in many lifetimes. He made his money in technology companies set up in the 1990s at the start of the Internet boom. He was handsome, married with no kids, and his wife left him when he was a simple millionaire. She had discovered one of his many affairs with younger women. If she'd waited a few more years, his bank account would have had some extra zeroes.

He bought a house built in the mid-1900s and applied many modern upgrades, including rendering the brickwork an off-white. It's now a mix of stylish curves and traditional design, set on three acres of land. It has two floors, six reception rooms, and a sizeable gymnasium. During the day, the rooms are lit by a wall of intelligent, bullet-proof glass patented by my uncle. I don't have a clue how it works, but it just does. The bright kitchen is the size of my old house, and it adjoins a huge conservatory with a high apex roof. The house has more bedrooms and ensuite bathrooms than I'd ever need. They look out over stunning gardens cared for by Ima and Leon. They are happy living here, but I'm still uncomfortable with the house. I'm glad they have a home now, as they are all the family I have.

One thing that isn't so obvious when you see the house from the outside is how secure it is. My uncle redesigned it to be a fortress. The surrounding walls are high and dangerous to climb. The place can lock down in an emergency, and thick, thorny bushes protect access from the waterside. There's even a no-fly zone over the house and gardens to deter inquisitive drones. There was a good reason for his security paranoia. And these days, it serves Ima and Leon well, too.

Ima greets me in the hallway with a smile and a cold beer, her long grey hair loose around her shoulders. I drop onto the sofa beside Leon, waking him up from a nap.

'Max!' he says. 'Excuse me, I was just having forty winks.'

'How are you, Leon?'

'I spent the day mowing, and now I'm exhausted.'

There are over two acres to mow, and I'm not sure how he keeps on top of it all. I may need to get him some help soon.

'You need to take it easy, Leon.'

'I'll take it easy when I'm dead. Not before.' He stands, stretches, and strokes back his thinning grey hair.

I laugh. 'I need to get to Bosham station tomorrow morning for eight-fifteen. Can you give me a lift?'

'Of course! Where are you off to?'

'London. I'm talking to a literary agent.'

'Oh. Are you writing a book?' Leon winks at me.

'Not this week,' I say. 'It's to do with this case I've taken on today.'

Leon nods. 'Are you hungry? I can knock us up a curry for dinner.'

'That sounds great. I'll be in the gym for an hour if that's okay?'

'Don't overdo your exercise, Max,' says Ima. 'Rest is important, too.'

'I'm not,' I say. 'It's reflex training.'

'I meant to say something to you yesterday,' says Leon. 'There's been a car turning around at the end of the drive every day this week. Different times of the day. I'm wondering if someone's taking photographs. So, I'll start closing the gates again. You never know who these people are.'

'What sort of car?' I say.

'I can't be certain. I was watching the driver.'

'A silver Audi,' says Ima, 'with a 2022 plate. I've written down the registration somewhere.'

'Was it a woman with red hair?' I ask Leon.

'It was,' he says.

'Oh, he noticed *her*,' laughs Ima. 'Long hair. Fiery auburn.'

'Do you know her?' says Leon.

'I will do soon.'

CHAPTER 8

The train arrives at London-Victoria after ten-fifteen, avoiding the morning rush hour. I grab a coffee and a doughnut, watch a man play blues on the piano, and find the taxi ranks. I don't like travelling by tube, so I take a cab to Soho to meet Maddy Abbott, Mariana Garcia's agent, in her offices down a side street. It's a building from the early 1960s. Square, uniform, and quite different from the surrounding architecture—no doubt replacing bombed-out buildings from the Blitz.

The inside is unexpected—modern, stylish, and professional. Soft lighting on the walls, blow-ups of book covers, and photos of famous-name authors looking severe and literary. They just make stuff up for a living, so the extra photogenic gravitas doesn't fool me.

While I'm waiting, I enjoy the cosy vibe. They go for orchids in a big way here. They've lined the windows and shelves with them, all in bloom. I like the orchid flowers, but not as much as they do. The roots look like dead rats' tails. I hate rats—vicious buggers when cornered—taste like rabbit.

An attentive receptionist finds me and leads the way to my

appointment. He's tall, has black curly hair, probably paid peanuts, and straight out of university. He introduces me to Maddy, a petite and friendly woman in her forties with drawn-on eyebrows. Why do some women pluck their perfectly adequate eyebrows and then draw them on again? The ones she's drawn today give her the expression of being permanently surprised.

'Mr Fortis,' she says. 'Good to meet you. Grace told me about you.' I tower over her as we shake hands. She offers me the chair in front of her desk while the receptionist gets us a coffee.

'Thanks, Ms Abbott, for meeting me.' The pleasantries are complete—now to business.

'We're still trying to get our heads around losing Mariana,' she says. 'Such a frightful shock.' She adds a touch of doleful drama when she speaks. 'I'm in despair. And when Grace called to say you're investigating her *murder*—I couldn't sleep!'

'Sorry to hear that, Ms Abbott. It's a disturbing business. You understand I'm not the police?'

'Yes.'

'I'm a private detective. Grace hired me after she heard the evidence at the coroner's inquest.'

'Please call me Maddy, Mr Fortis. I can't believe anyone would want to hurt dear Mariana. She'd been through so much in her life. Did you hear her husband used to abuse her?'

'I did.'

'She even went into hiding from him. Can you imagine such a thing? He died tragically five or six years ago.' She takes a moment to gaze pensively. 'I'd heard she'd jumped from a bridge. I would never have believed it from Mariana.

She would never have ended her life that way. Jumping from a bridge, of all things?' She slurps her cappuccino.

'Probably not jumped,' I say, 'but she entered the river somehow. I met her briefly a few hours before she died. She was distressed about something. In your statement to the coroner's inquest, you said she had sent you a message telling you she wanted to kill herself.'

'Ah, yes! Look.' Maddy Abbott picked up her mobile phone and brought up the WhatsApp message to show me. 'She sent it to me at 12:33 in the morning,' she says. 'It woke me up. I called her daughter straight away.'

'Do you mind if I grab a photo of this?'

'Please do.'

I take a photograph of her screen with my mobile, including their previous conversation. 'Is there anything about the language she used that seemed unfamiliar?'

I hand back her phone, and she reads out the message. '*ITS ALL TOO MUCH. SORRY I HAVE TO END IT ALL THIS WAY.*' She shakes her head. 'Mariana was a pedant. First, it's all in capitals—how abhorrent! Second, she would never have missed an apostrophe, even in a text. I know that sounds silly, but it was ingrained in her.' I knew that about her already. 'And then there's the repeat of *all*. It's so vague and impersonal!' Her eyes tear up. 'I was her friend as well as her agent.'

'Do you think she wrote it?' I ask.

'It didn't sound like her, I must admit. What are you saying?'

'I'm only trying to build a picture of what happened.' I wait for her to dry her eyes with a tissue and reassure her that her mascara hasn't run. 'What are your thoughts as her agent about her death?'

'Bloody terrible timing! She was about to sign a lucrative

TV deal. Lucrative for both of us, if I'm honest. I'm devastated.'

Maddy then went through the details of how they first met at a conference after Mariana's husband died. 'She started writing seriously as a form of therapy. It was authentic and passionate, and she knew how to touch the reader's heart. The genre combined crime and romantic fiction. Both are very popular.'

'It's all foreign to me,' I say, 'especially romantic fiction. You told the inquest you thought Mariana was depressed. What made you think that?'

'The last few weeks, she was difficult to get hold of. She wouldn't return my calls, and when I did manage to speak to her, she wasn't her usual self. She seemed withdrawn and worried.'

'Was she working on anything that affected her mood? Trouble with deadlines? Anything that made her feel like it was too much?'

'I don't believe so. Her latest novel was about a detective going undercover in a fishing village. Something or other about a criminal gang. She was always a stickler for research. It was her favourite part, but I don't remember her visiting any fishing villages.'

'Researching gangs? Did she reach out to anyone for her research?'

'Gosh, I hope not!'

'Have you got the manuscript she was writing?'

She hesitates. 'I have a short proposal document from her. She wrote it off the cuff. We met for lunch, and she talked about it. I'm not sure I should show you.'

'I can understand that, but I'm not planning on becoming a

crime writer overnight. You're quite safe. I'm trying to ascertain if there is a link or any clues.'

Maddy gets out of her chair and opens a filing cabinet next to the door. She spends some time searching for something, muttering under her breath. Her hair is flopping over her face, and I can't see her expression.

'I'm sure I put it in here,' she says. She goes to the door and calls out. 'Hector!'

The receptionist comes in. 'Mariana Garcia's last proposal document. Did you archive it?'

'No,' he says. 'She asked for it back that weekend you met with her. I thought she'd told you.'

'No, she didn't, Hector. What reason did she give?'

'She said she'd changed her mind about the whole thing. Said it wasn't going to work.'

'Bugger!' says Maddy. 'Thanks, Hector. She never spoke to me about it. So strange.'

The receptionist leaves a little flushed, pushing the door closed behind him.

'Never mind,' I say, breaking the silence. 'Where did Mariana do her writing?'

'In her house near Arundel. God, I hope someone's gone in and looked after her cats!'

'I'm sure they have,' I say. 'I'm interested in this research she was doing.'

'She kept much of it to herself. She may have told her daughter.'

'Okay, I'll ask her. Moving on, are you aware if she was in a recent relationship with anyone?'

'No, she kept that sort of thing private. I suspect there was an old flame she was trying to find, but I can't be certain. It was a few things she told me. As I said, she was a widow with many sad memories. That often makes a successful writer.'

I think that last part is bullshit. I make a few notes on my phone. There must be something in this. Maddy fidgets with her watch, telling me she wants this meeting to end. But I haven't finished yet.

'Any trouble with fans?' I ask.

'The occasional over-friendly admirer—nothing too scary. And nothing that the threat of a court injunction couldn't deal with.'

'This is important, Maddy. Did someone threaten her?'

'It was nothing. There was someone on social media, *The Real Bard*, he called himself. He creeped her out.'

'How long ago was that?'

'About nine months ago. Our solicitor threatened to trace him if he didn't stop.'

'And did it?'

'Yes, straight away.'

The Real Bard. Another lead, perhaps.

'And I assume the computer she used to write with is in her house?' I say.

'Probably, Mr Fortis. Look, I think that's all I can help you with today. I have a meeting with a client now.'

I thank her and shake her hand. I'm sensing there wasn't great affection for Mariana here. It was a business relationship, and I get that. What's the point in dressing it up as friendship? Maddy nurtured Mariana for profit, and she will now have to find someone else in her slush pile to grow from scratch.

CHAPTER 9

I leave the agency grateful for Maddy's help, but with more questions than answers. I need a walk to get things straight in my head. What caused Mariana's sudden mood change, and what was she researching for her book?

I glance to the side, and the hairs on the back of my neck stand up. Something in all of us spikes our brains when danger is near. Call it a sixth sense, or call it millions of years of evolution designed to keep us alive. Some people are more aware of it than others. I've trained myself to be one of those who are acutely aware. Like I am right now.

I take a route south down Frith Street, passing Ronnie Scott's club on the right, dodging men wheeling equipment in flight cases through the doors. Restaurants and takeaways are everywhere, and the spicy aromas are making me hungry. If I needed a massage, I'd be spoilt for choice down here, but I don't—not that kind of massage.

I continue south for a few minutes, heading towards China-town. My hunger has beaten me, so I drop into a Turkish take-away to order a doner kebab and some spicy lamb-filled manti in yoghurt. There's a bench outside, so I sit to eat and observe the two men who have been following me since I left Maddy Abbott's agency. They weren't hard to spot. As I begin my succulent kebab, they change their plan and slip into a side street. I can't help but find it amusing. I can lose these clowns, but I don't want to. I need to find out who they are, even though it's likely to end in a fight, and they are undoubtedly armed. But I will not miss out on my kebab for them, so they will have to wait.

First wiping down my greasy fingers on the paper serviette, I switch off my mobile and stand, dropping the wrappers into a bin. Glancing up, I can see they are watching me again, so I head south through Chinatown, and I've found Gerrard Street. Chains of red lanterns are strung overhead, and there's a whole new set of sweet, spicy aromas here.

I stop to do up my shoelace. My new friends turn to view the menu of a restaurant. They're both shorter than me, about five-ten, and similar in appearance—white-skinned with pink faces. One is wearing a baseball cap, and the other is bald with sticking-out ears. They're muscular under their grey jackets, and both are in jogging bottoms. It's hard to hide those knives down there.

I walk on, turning left and soon coming to Chinatown Gate. I'm now heading towards Leicester Square. My friends want to take me as I pass an alley, so I'm trying to oblige them. I find one, a passage into the rear entrance of a Chinese restaurant. It's gloomy down here, and it smells of cooking oil and urine. Walking halfway down, I pretend I've taken a wrong turn and change direction to return the way I came. The two men are blocking my way.

'I've gone the wrong way,' I say. 'Will you excuse me, please?'

They could be related. They even sneer at me the same way.

'Don't,' I say again. 'Neither of you will stand a chance. I'm a black belt in origami.' No answer. Not even a smile. 'Where are you boys from, and why are you following me?'

The one in the baseball cap takes a few steps towards me. He pulls out an eight-inch blade from a sheath under his track-suit bottoms. That couldn't have been comfortable.

'Why is it that no one ever listens to me?' I say to them. 'Don't do this. It's going to hurt you more than me.'

The man with the knife is holding it in his right hand. I'm a leftie. There is tension in his eyes as he walks forward, facing me. He's an amateur. He's going to swing that knife into me, hoping we get to hug after I block it. Then he'll stick it into my back as many times as he can. Most people make the mistake of trying to grab the knife hand. That's not going to work. I'm going to block his first strike and see what happens. This could be fun.

'This isn't going to end well for you,' I tell him. 'Don't say I didn't warn you.' But he carries on sneering like they taught him at sneer school.

Then it comes, and I'm right, but it's even worse for him. He sweeps the knife down towards my throat. I block it with my left, thrusting my right into the gap between his knife arm and neck. It's like I'm diving into a pool. He will want to thrust again behind my back, but I've trapped his forearm under my left arm, and my right hand strikes the side of his neck. Holding the pressure, I step back, still trapping his arm, bringing him with me, and he drops to the ground, gripping the knife.

'Let go of the knife!' I shout at him. He refuses, so I snap his arm and gouge his eye. That hurts. Then I kick the side of his head—not too hard, jarring his neck. His cap flies off. He's away with the fairies now with a dislocated jaw.

I leave the knife. I don't want my fingerprints all over it. Man number two, with the sticking-out ears, can't work out what to do. He's pulled out his knife, but his hands are shaking. I step over my new unconscious friend, and my hands are in front of me. Man number two glances behind to see if he can run, but he's still pointing his knife at me. He turns, but I rush forward, and my foot strikes the outside of his leg—his femoral nerve. He hits the ground, dropping the knife. I'm on top of him. I have one hand against his neck, pressing on his carotid artery, and a thumb digging behind his ear. Easy to do with his ears.

'Who sent you?' I say.

He hisses between his clenched teeth, and then he squeaks at me. 'Don't kill me!'

'I can't promise that. Tell me why you're trying to kill *me*, and I'll think about it.'

His face and neck are going beetroot. 'Jethro Matisse. I'll be a dead man if he finds out I told you.'

I release the pressure on his neck to keep him alive. 'Tell me more, or this will end badly for you. You can't win either way.'

I dig my thumb deeper, and he's in a lot of pain now.

'He knows you're on Garcia's case.'

'Who is Jethro Matisse? Where is he?'

'He's everywhere. He'll find you.'

I don't have time for this. Someone will find us soon. With a jerk, his wrist snaps, and he passes out. I drag him over the top of his unconscious friend and drop him. Putting the knife back into the hand with the broken wrist, I stick the blade into his leg, hitting the femur. I pick up the cap, put it on, and pull down the peak.

When I get out into the main street, I head towards Leicester Square, losing the cap in a bin. My phone is back on, and I book an Uber to take me to Victoria Station.

CCTV in London can trace everyone's journey twenty-four hours a day. What will it make of my journey? But I'll be long gone by the time anyone searches for me.

Phil Marlowe's office has views over the Solent and the Isle of Wight, looming grey in the distance. He grew up on the south coast and has always lived less than ten minutes from the sea. His father was a boatbuilder, working with glass fibre and resin, and his mother was a schoolteacher. Phil remembers the day trips to Portsmouth with his parents. He has a vague memory of a tour aboard a Royal Navy destroyer.

'Navy Days, they were called,' says a voice in his head. 'They don't do them now.'

'It's a shame,' says Phil.

Now he lives in Portsmouth, both his parents are dead, and his life is full of trouble. He'd love to relive those days again after his father's death, with only his mother for company.

Yet, he has Clarice, who lights up his days, balancing darkness with light. If it weren't for that urchin who stays with her while its mother works, everything would be perfect.

'Why not take little Juliet to the old docks, Phil?' says the voice.

Phil laughs at a thought that's come to him.

'Yes. You could get Mikita to take her for a ride on your boat. Tie her to a rock, give her a little shove, and no one would know. She'd be out of your life, and Clarice would be all yours.'

'That's not nice,' says Phil. 'Not nice at all.'

His eyes focus on the small photo frame on his desk. It contains that picture of him with Clarice after they'd first met. He only wanted her. Not her family. He can't tell her that, of course—she wouldn't understand. Sex with her is great, and she trusts him with her money. It's that little imp her daughter palms off on her three days a week—it's too much, and he's tired of sharing her.

Phil puts down his pen and goes over to the open window. He takes a deep breath of the salty air and stretches. Something in his trouser pocket is digging into him, and he pulls out a small, yellow plastic duck. Juliet gave it to him in the morning when he left Clarice's house. She'd stayed for a sleepover with her grandma *again*. He rubs his finger and thumb over the large orange beak and tosses it into the bin.

His mobile phone rings. It's Mikita, the Belarusian, who runs errands for him.

'We haven't heard from the contractors,' says Mikita. Phil struggles to understand his accent sometimes.

'Have you called them?'

'No, boss,' he says. 'They were due to provide an update, but they've vanished.'

'But we've paid them?'

'Yes, boss.'

'Okay. Any chance they've done a runner with the money?'

'Unlikely. They've done good work for us in the past. Fast, tidy, and accurate. Contractors with those skills are hard to find.'

'I doubt it, Mikita. I doubt that very much. Find them. If

they've taken the money without doing the job, then you'll pay for it. Understand?'

'Yes, boss.'

'I've got plans, Mikita. Big plans to grow our business. Now that Fenz has gone, we can expand the club and offer more shows. We can bring in more girls. Don't tell anyone this, but I've seen a place in Southampton. A possible second Obsidian Rooms. I don't want anything to scupper those plans before they even get started.'

'Yes, boss.'

'You're a good man, Mikita. Keep me updated. I hope they haven't failed to deliver.'

Phil ends the call and exhales. He's troubled by the incompetence of those around him. He's wondering if he should call Frank. Frank is always good in these situations.

The music starts up again from the rooms below, and the vibrations tingle through the balls of his feet. Rehearsals. The show must go on, and Phil must find somewhere else to complete his business.

CHAPTER 10

It's four in the afternoon, and I'm back at my desk in Chichester. There are many enquiries to be made, but only one of me to do them. I've been thinking about this malicious fan of Mariana's. *The Real Bard*. I've trawled the Internet for variations of the username but found nothing connected to Mariana. The Bard was William Shakespeare. The real Shakespeare? I think this is another dead end.

I get an alert on my mobile and see Grace Garcia has transferred money for expenses into my business account. This shows me she's serious. I call her with an update and tell her I need to look around her mother's office.

'I can meet you there tomorrow morning, Mr Fortis,' she says. 'How did your trip to London go?'

'I've come back with more questions than answers. I need to find out what your mother was researching. That's why I need to see her office.'

'I hope it wasn't a wasted journey.'

'Not at all,' I say. 'I met two jokers in Soho who were

trying to stop me from looking into your case. Who did you tell I was seeing your mother's agent today?'

There's a pause on the other end of the phone while she thinks. 'Only Maddy.'

'Did you tell Spencer?'

'Well, yes. We talked about it. Why?' She sounds nervous now.

'Nothing to worry about, Grace,' I say. 'It's nothing I can't handle.'

'What do you mean, they tried to stop you?'

'I can handle it. Please don't worry.'

After we've finished our call, I think about what that second man with the knife said to me, the mysterious Jethro Matisse—the one who is *everywhere*. Who have I upset? Who else knows that I've taken on Grace Garcia as my client?

I need a coffee. A real coffee. I'm feeling restless about something. Maybe it's those two fools trying to kill me earlier. That was rude. I doubt they'll be much use to their employer for six months, at least.

I decide to walk to the coffee shop with my iPad. The lock clicks shut on my office door, and I head north for about two hundred yards along South Street. It's a small coffee shop I like, family-owned, that does a great latte and a selection of muffins. I order a coffee and find a table facing the window. *Never have your back against the window.* It's a mantra they taught us early on. I remember a guy who was pulled backwards through broken glass. He was never the same again.

Searching the Internet for anything on Jethro Matisse is proving fruitless. There's nothing apart from Matisse, the French artist. I could ask Gary Bates to check him out for me. There's no clue to say where Matisse is from. *Everywhere,* apparently. Perhaps the man with the sticking-out ears and the hole in his leg lied to me. Matisse could be a name he's made up.

Am I working on this case for Grace Garcia, or am I doing it for myself? I thought I'd buried my connection to Mariana long ago. So why did she come to my door? I could have turned around when I picked up that pizza, and I would have been none the wiser. This is hard.

Halfway through my coffee, the woman with the red hair and green eyes—the Audi driver—walks by the cafe, glancing in, pretending not to notice me. I slowly sip the rest of my drink, waiting another ten minutes. She passes by again, holding a mobile phone to her ear and glancing in one more time to see where I am. Now I'm intrigued. What store does she manage, and why is she taking photos of my house? She could be an estate agent looking for clients. I smile to myself.

I leave the coffee shop and follow her. She's heading south and crosses the road. She's walking towards my office but then turns right onto Avenue de Chartres, towards the multistorey car park again. Maybe I am too suspicious. She's attractive and bound to catch my eye. I'm on the corner of South Street, watching her walk away, but then she takes a sharp left towards the back of my office block. I cross the road and run to where she turned. Where is she? There's a flash of red beside my Volvo. I head to my car, and I'm in the afternoon shadows of the surrounding buildings. A sound of rustling is coming from outside the back door to the office, and I find her. She's wearing yellow washing-up gloves and going through my rubbish bin. She has shredded paper in her hands, and it's spreading everywhere.

'Afternoon,' I say as I stand behind her. 'What are you doing in my rubbish bins? Are you hungry?'

She's startled and wide-eyed. 'Not you again!'

'And why are you taking photos of my house?'

'Photos? What are you talking about? Now, leave me alone, or I'll call the police.'

'*You* call the police? You're the one rifling through my bins!'

'Are these your bins?'

'Nice try,' I say. 'Which store do you work in?'

Now she's angry. 'I said I will call the police.'

I snatch the handbag from her shoulder.

'Give that back!'

I move her out of the way and unlock the back door. She's trying to grab the bag from me. I step through the door, shutting her outside. She's banging, but I ignore her.

'That's my bag!' she shouts. 'I'm calling the police!'

The banging stops, and all goes quiet. I'm waiting by the front door now, ready for her to appear. A couple of minutes later, and here she is. She grabs the door handle and tries to yank it open. Then she hammers her fist on the glass. I wave her bag in front of me and smile at her, eyebrows raised.

She's fuming for a few moments until she sees me playing with the latch on the bag. I taunt her with it. She goes pale when I open the bag, and she presses her palms flat against the glass and watches me. Inside, I find a canister of pepper spray and an ID card on a lanyard. It's a National Union of Journalists press card telling me she's a bona fide newsgatherer. Her name is Ella Munro. I dangle the lanyard over my finger, and she rolls her eyes. She is good at this.

I unlock the door and hold it open for her. 'Coffee? It's from a pod, but I have custard creams, too.'

Her shoulders slump, defeated. 'Can I have my bag back now, please?'

The canister of pepper spray is now on my desk. 'That's a

Section Five Firearm. You'll get yourself arrested if the police find that on you.'

'It's for self-defence.'

'Still illegal.'

I make a coffee, white, no sugar, and hand her an open packet of custard creams. She checks her handbag and takes the coffee. I make sure I move out of lobbing distance of the hot liquid.

'Ella Munro. Why are you interested in me? It's not for my good looks.'

'You're not that bad-looking,' she says.

'Thanks. Makes me feel loads better.'

'Max Fortis, the private detective who helps his clients for free.'

'Not all of them,' I say.

She takes a deep breath and reels out what she knows about me. 'You inherited a huge fortune from your uncle, Arthur Taylor Fortis, the technology magnate who made millions in the Internet boom of the 1990s. Then he made a whole lot more money from selling high-tech security systems to foreign governments.'

'Did you meet my uncle? He liked younger women.'

She sits back and sips her coffee, looking more relaxed. She's got great teeth. 'Arthur Fortis sold up, taking his fortune with him. But nine months ago, he suddenly became ill and died a few weeks later, and he left it all to you.'

'Correct. Well done. Why are you taking photos of my house?'

She blushes. 'I'm doing a piece on you. The philanthropist detective. I think many people will be interested in that.'

'Why didn't you just ask me?' I say.

'Ask you? Because you wouldn't want to talk to me.'

'True. Who's going to buy this story from you?'

'Someone will.'

'You hope.'

'I hope.'

'How did you hear about me?' I say.

'You helped a friend of mine, Gemma. She was in trouble but didn't realise how much private detectives cost.'

'Ah, yes, Gemma, the estate agent.'

'You helped her for free. She told me about your business terms, and it fascinated me.'

'You wouldn't have found anything in my rubbish,' I say. 'I shred everything.'

'So I discovered. Sorry about the mess.'

A burst of ideas runs through my head. 'Let's say you finish this story about me and sell it. Think about how much you are likely to get for it.'

She's puzzled, stroking her hair behind one ear. 'What are you getting at, Mr Fortis?'

'Do you have a figure in your head?'

'Of course,' she says.

'That will get you by for a few months until you write your next story. Am I right?'

'That's how it works. I'm freelance.'

'You're writing a story about a nobody—me. It's not enough. Let me hire you.'

She laughs. 'What?'

'You're a good investigator. I need someone to help me with a case.'

'I'm a journalist, Mr Fortis, not a private detective.'

'I'm interested in your skill set. I'll pay you a good contract rate—a fixed fee to finish the job.' I grab a Post-it note and write down a figure. I pass it to her. 'Half now, half when we've done.'

'Is this for real?' She studies the note for a while, calculates something, and bites her bottom lip. 'That's more than I earn in a year. It's tempting.'

'Plus expenses.'

Her eyes flash, and she swallows. She's trying to speak, but nothing comes out until she composes herself. 'What's the catch?'

'You work for me. Only on this case.'

'Mr Fortis—'

'Max.'

'Max.' She sounds hesitant. 'I know you're single and extremely wealthy. Dashing even.'

'Dashing? Thank you.'

She rolls her eyes. 'This isn't about anything else, is it? You aren't expecting any *extra* services from me?'

I feel it like a kick to my stomach. 'No, Ella! And you obviously don't know everything about me.'

'You're not single?'

'No,' I say.

'Sorry, I thought you were. I didn't realise.' There's an embarrassed silence. 'I'm *Mrs* Munro, by the way—a widow. What's her name? Or *his* name, of course!'

'I keep that part of my life private, Ella.'

'Sure.'

I change the subject. 'I can get my solicitor to draft the contract if you are interested.'

'With respect, you know nothing about me.'

'I've seen enough. Are you interested in my offer or not?'

'Can I think about it?' she says.

'Of course. I'll give you until the end of the week. Ella,

there's no funny business here. This is legitimate, and I need help. Some of the things I do can be dangerous, but I won't ask you to get involved in any of that.'

She nods and gathers her bag to her stomach, nonplussed by our conversation. As she leaves my office, I'm happy with that result, but I wonder if Carrie would be, too.

The evening sunlight washes lilac over the sea. Lights are coming on around the city, and the nightlife is stirring. Purple downlighters set under the eaves of the Obsidian Rooms switch on, pouring their vulgar light into Phil Marlowe's office.

Mikita stands before him, his eyes focused on his shining black shoes. Frank Pinto's huge form is with him, standing like a school prefect, bringing a naughty boy to the headmaster.

Phil has heard the news from Mikita. The task he had organised was an abysmal failure. Phil ponders what to do, his hands clenching and unclenching, stretching the lines of scabbed scratches along his wrists, cracking the skin on his red knuckles. An image from his past flashes in his mind's eye. He remembers the state of his father's hands when he returned home from work. He was meant to wear gloves to protect him from the fibreglass they used on the boats, but he often didn't. His hands would be red and blotchy when he walked in, where the fibres had cut into his scaley, thick skin. His father had powerful hands, and he used those hands to punish Phil—or whatever Phil called himself then—he had almost forgotten. It was most Friday nights. His parents would return home drunk from a night out. Hiding from his father only made it worse. Those red, blotchy hands punched his arms, slapped his face, and held him down whilst robbing him of any childhood he had left. All punishment for imagined crimes. For daring to look at his father the wrong way, for speaking out of turn.

Phil sits up, rubs his hands, and flexes his fingers. 'I question what you call reliable, Mikita.' He tries to take a sip of some steaming sweet coffee, but it scalds his mouth, burning his tongue.

'They were good in the past, boss,' says Mikita, shifting from foot to foot. 'Maybe the task is bigger than we first thought.'

'You could be right, my friend. What do you think, Frank?'

Pinto shakes his head.

'Oh,' says Phil. 'Frank disagrees with you! Frank thinks the task I set was perfectly reasonable. Perfectly achievable. That's because I think about the tasks I ask my employees to do. I don't ask for the impossible, Mikita.'

'No, boss,' says Mikita. 'It was too hard for them. They'll be out of action for months.'

Phil shrugs. 'It's coming out of your wages. I warned you.'

'Yes, boss, you did.'

'Frank here is a busy man. He can't keep picking up your unfinished business.'

'No, boss.'

Phil taps his fingers on the desk and takes a sharp intake of breath through his nose.

'How's the family?'

Mikita glances at Pinto. 'They're all good, boss. My daughter has a place at school. My wife is good too. This was my fault, boss. No one else should suffer for it.'

'Absolutely! Another baby on the way, I hear.'

'Yes, boss. My wife's six months gone.'

'That's superb news! I bet you're a good father.'

'I try, boss.'

'I like that in a man,' says Phil. 'Don't you, Frank?'

'Yes, boss,' says Pinto. 'Very much.'

Phil picks up the hot coffee, and Mikita steps back. 'You're faultlessly loyal to me, so it's nothing worse this time.' Phil smiles. 'You're lucky, and so is your family. You should demand loyalty, too.'

Phil puts his hand into his jacket pocket and pulls out a roll of cash. He throws it to Pinto, who catches it.

'Frank,' says Phil, 'buy Mikita's daughter a gift for starting school. We should celebrate this.'

'Thank you, boss,' says Mikita. 'You are very generous!'

Phil blows his coffee and takes a sip. 'I wish my father was like you, Mikita. Love your daughter and give her what she needs. Now go. I'm busy.'

Mikita is happy to go, leaving Pinto alone with Phil.

Pinto faces the window and sighs. 'Why did you poke a sleeping tiger?'

'What?' Phil doesn't like the question.

'You want to expand the business,' says Pinto, 'and you've stirred up something that will ultimately stand in your way. From what you've told me about Fortis, he's dangerous. He has connections.'

'That's nothing to do with you, Frank. I don't pay you to question me.'

Pinto turns to Phil. 'I'm just looking out for you, boss. That's all.'

CHAPTER 11

I park beside a VW Polo, facing the way I came into the lane. I've found Mariana Garcia's home in a village south of Arundel called Lyminster. Blink, and you'll miss it. The locals pronounce Lyminster '*limb*', not '*lime*'. I reckon the house was built in the early 1800s. Some would describe it as a chocolate-box cottage. It's surrounded by a low flint wall and has stone eagles engraved above the door frame. It's in a lane leading to an Anglo-Saxon church, complete with a legend of a water dragon called a *knucker.*

The air is damp and mixed with the sweet smoke from a faraway bonfire. I hear the rasping of rooks, and they're lined up along the roof, watching me as I approach. I allow myself a whimsical thought, imagining them as Lacey's spies.

Grace Garcia opens the front door of her mother's house. She's in ripped jeans and a T-shirt, and her face is without make-up. Although pale, she has a natural beauty that doesn't need it. She leads me through a dark oak hallway into a light study with thick walls and small windows. This is where her mother wrote her novels. It's a busy, eccentric space. Books are balanced in jagged piles on the floor, arrangements of dried flowers hang on the walls, and a ball of green twine and a pair of secateurs are left absentmindedly on a shelf. It has a view over a mature garden. Something pleasing to look over when she created. Two black cats dart into the room, take one look at me, and then run out again.

Grace seems overwhelmed by everything. Going through the last years of her mother's work must be daunting. I take in the atmosphere of the room. It's like Mariana Garcia is still alive in here. I can almost see her ghost sitting at the desk.

'Her computer is in the drawer,' says Grace. 'I don't think there's a password. I'm not even sure it's connected to the Internet.'

'Thank you,' I say. 'I'm sorry, Grace. I realise this must be painful for you.'

'It's okay. I'd guessed you would want to look around. I don't know what to do with it all. Her fans may want some of it. This room, the space she created here, was where she was most content. The happiest I've ever known her to be.'

'I need to ask you something. Does the name Jethro Matisse mean anything to you?'

She frowns. 'No. Should it?'

'It's a name I've come across in my investigation. I wasn't sure if there was a connection. Did your mother talk to you about her latest project? I believe she had written a book proposal for Maddy.'

Grace leans back onto the desk and shakes her head. 'She was always secretive about her work until the first draft was complete. Sometimes, she'd share her writing with me to get my feedback, but there was nothing new I know of. It was probably still in that developmental phase.'

'Did she ever discuss any research she was doing?'

'I vaguely remember she was excited about something. But she went off the idea a few weeks ago.'

'Why?'

She shrugs. 'I don't know. She never spoke about it again.'

The door opens. It's the boyfriend again—Spencer, trying to dodge the two cats. 'Grace, don't forget about the appointment with the solicitor.'

He gives me a sideways glance.

'Oh, gosh!' says Grace. 'Yes. Thank you, Spencer. Mr Fortis, please forgive me, but I must return to Chichester for a meeting. Spencer said he would stay here with you.'

'Did he?' I say. 'That's kind of you, Spencer.' This will be interesting.

Grace rushes out to her car, and I'm left alone with Spencer in the old house. He leaves the room, keeping out of my way while I search Mariana's study. I'm looking for any evidence of a new novel or any clue as to why someone would want to kill her.

I sit at the desk and remove a MacBook computer from the drawer. There's still a hint of Mariana's perfume in the drawer space. I feel like I'm intruding into a dead woman's world. A memory of long, slender feet running along the brass curves of a bedframe intrudes on my thoughts. I stop that thought right there. Then I think of Carrie. She would love this place. She always wanted a house in the country.

Grace was right. The computer doesn't have a password enabled. Mariana's filing makes everything easy to find. All her manuscripts are on here, including folders containing images, locations, scans of pages from reference books, and letters. They are all inside a published novels folder. I search for anything that could be a new proposal, but there's nothing. Maybe she deleted it. Now I check her emails—nothing.

Nothing at all in any of the folders. Someone has deleted them all.

Spencer walks in. He's wearing Levi's, white socks, Nikes, and a tight blue T-shirt like he's in a fashion shoot. He watches me as he leans against the wall. I glance up at him and see a confident smirk on his face and the gel in his hair shining in the sunlight. Is he doing a hair product commercial?

'What is it you're looking for?' he says.

'Information,' I say. I won't tell him anything.

'What information?'

I smile and shrug at him. 'You tell me.'

'There's nothing of interest on there for you,' he says.

He must be even more stupid than he looks.

'How do you know?'

'I just do.' He walks up to the desk.

'Did you delete it all?' I say.

He feigns being offended. 'I don't have a clue what you're talking about.'

I stand and put the MacBook on the chair behind me. He's still watching me as I go through the rest of Mariana's desk drawers.

'Did you get on with Mariana?' I say.

He smirks again. 'Really well.'

I find a journal and leaf through it until I find the last entries. It's then I notice Mariana has torn out three of the pages. I assume it was Mariana—maybe it wasn't her. I drop the journal on top of the computer on the chair.

'But she was unhappy about you marrying her daughter. I wonder why?'

He blinks. 'Academic now, don't you think?'

'Why was she unhappy?' I say. 'Didn't she trust you? Or was there another reason?'

He doesn't answer me, and he continues to smirk. What is it with all the smirking? Everyone's doing it.

I dig into the back of the bottom drawer and find a shirt button. It has broken blue threads still attached like someone has ripped it off. I hold it in my thumb and forefinger and show Spencer.

'A small memento?' He folds his arms across his chest to intimidate me. 'Have you told Grace you were sleeping with her mother?'

His face reddens. 'You need to drop this case, Fortis. It has nothing to do with you.'

'Now you've said that, it has everything to do with me. Grace hired me to find out the truth behind her mother's death. I'm very thorough, Spencer. *Very* thorough.'

'If you value your health, Fortis, then walk away now. Otherwise, you'll be leaving here in the trunk of my car.'

It's my turn to smirk, and I look through the rest of the paperwork on her desk. There's nothing here of interest: fan letters, daily word counts, reminders to buy cat food. Spencer steps closer to the desk, and sunlight reflects off a bunch of keys hanging off the loop of his jeans.

'What's in it for you?' I say.

'It's time to leave, Fortis.' He's clenching his fists, raising his shoulders, and puffing up his neck. I'm starting to think he doesn't like me. He thinks he can take me. What is it with people who think that? Perhaps I should hand out my CV to potential assailants so they know what they are dealing with.

I return his glare. 'So, your plan is to marry Grace and get a share of the dead author's fortune? Did you kill Mariana?'

If you're going to attack someone, doing it over a desktop is a bad idea. A terrible idea. He lunges towards me. The intention is to grab my shirt and haul me over the desk. But that's a stupid idea. I slide my left foot back and twist so my right shoulder is forward. I sweep his grabbing hand away. I'm not keen on clutching his sticky, gelled mop of hair. I've never needed gel for my hair—it has its own natural bounce. My other hand reaches around the back of his neck, and I use his forward momentum to drag him onto the desktop. You can lose your fine motor skills with all the adrenaline in a fight. That's why I practice daily. He's lost his. I stun him with a blow to the side of his neck—one of my favourite things to do—and grab his keys from his belt loop. He'll stay unconscious for about twenty seconds, so I take the computer and journal and return to the Volvo. By the time he's recovered, I'll be gone.

Halfway back to the office, along the dual carriageway, I throw Spencer's car keys into the central reservation.

Ella's mother stops on the footpath and takes deep breaths while holding Ella's arm. She smiles at her daughter and squeezes her hand. They've reached the Roman Palace—halfway. After a brief pause, they turn around and begin walking back to the house together. Ella insists her mother takes a walk with her for twenty minutes a day—it was what the doctor had suggested until she's fit again.

Her mother's face turns to concern. 'But you don't know what he's like, Ella,' she says.

'I know he's rich, Mum. He does some of his work for free or charges people what they can afford. He used to be a police officer in London, and he's been a private detective for six months. He told me he's not single, but he keeps it private. No kids.'

'He's gay, then,' says her mother.

Ella rolls her eyes. 'I don't care if he is or not. But I don't think he is.'

'He might have one of those pleasure rooms. Like in those naughty books.'

'Mum!' Ella gasps. 'What books have you been reading?' She laughs. 'It doesn't matter, even if he has. I'm not getting involved with him that way. It's just that the money is amazing. I can clear my debt in weeks. Get my own place again.'

'Oh.' Ella's mother stops.

'Don't look like that, Mum.' Ella strokes her arm. 'This was only ever going to be short-term. Simon left me with nothing, and you've been wonderful.'

'Where will you go?'

'Not far! I'll still be close. I can see you most days, especially while you're recovering.'

'What about your dream of being a journalist? Won't you be throwing that away?'

'No. It's a one-off contract, and I'm still using my investigative skills. I can come back to it whenever I want. I need that money, Mum.'

They continue their walk, crossing the road to go through the Fishbourne playing fields, greeting dog walkers, and enjoying the early autumn sunshine. Clouds are moving over them from the horizon.

'As long as he doesn't try any funny business with you, Ella. You're a pretty girl. You've got nice features. I don't want him taking advantage.'

'Nice features?' Ella laughs again. 'I'll keep my features to myself. I promise.'

'So, you've decided then? Are you sure you've read through the legal side properly?'

'I have,' says Ella. 'It's all legitimate. His solicitor sent me the paperwork last night. He didn't hang around.'

The wind picks up, and mother and daughter draw closer together. They walk past the social club and onto Blackboy Lane, over the railway gates.

'It's been two years since we lost him, Mum,' says Ella.

'Doesn't seem possible, dear.'

The sky darkens.

'I think he'd be proud of me. Don't you think?'

'Of course he would. He was your husband. He loved you more than anything. And you did him proud, especially towards the end.'

Ella nods and takes a deep breath. 'I did, didn't I, and I think he would approve of me taking this job. His last words to me were, *be brave, live your best life*. Being brave doesn't mean I'm not afraid. Every day, I'm afraid to face the world without him.'

'I know, sweetheart. But you will find a way. You'll find a way to live a different best life.'

Ella clears her throat. 'I'm going to call Mr Fortis and tell him.'

'If you're certain, my love. Only if you're certain.'

'I am, Mum.'

CHAPTER 12

That smirk should have been wiped off Spencer's face by now. I imagine him storming around as he searches for his keys, cursing me. Who is he going to call now, I wonder? It may have been his call that got me followed through Soho. There was no one else apart from Grace and the agent who knew I was going. Spencer will want a showdown with me sometime soon. He doesn't enjoy being humiliated.

I'm still no closer to having any substantial leads. I have the name *Jethro Matisse*, Mariana's computer and notebook with torn-out pages, and possibly Spencer. Do I search for a suspect to find a motive, or the motive to find a suspect? There's a shortage of both options at the moment.

I text Gary for any updates, and he replies, telling me to *piss off*—he's on rest days. We arrange a lunch date for tomorrow instead. I hate having no leads. I need something to get my teeth into.

It isn't until I've sat at my desk with a coffee that I notice a shadow at my office window. I'm surprised by who it is. I didn't think she would want to see me again. Approaching the glass, we stare at each other. It appears she's come by herself this time. She offers me the thinnest of smiles. I'm guessing she's come in peace. I unlock the front door and pull it open.

'Janice.'

'Max.'

'Just passing?' I say.

'I'm eighty miles out of my way to be just passing,' says Commander Janice Lacey. She's not wearing brown today—more of a rusty red colour.

'Come in,' I say to the woman with a wardrobe full of trouser suits.

I allow her inside and lock the door again. She's licking her lips and fidgeting with her collar. I want her to feel nervous until I'm sure she's come with an olive branch.

'I feel our last meeting didn't go too well,' she says.

I point at a chair, and she takes a seat. 'Bringing your goons with you didn't help,' I say. 'What do you want? I've said all I want to say about why I left.'

She casts her eyes around my office. I think she likes the beige, but I could be wrong—she's difficult to read.

'I've been talking to some of your ex-colleagues.'

'Don't believe everything you hear about me. It could be true.'

'You're a multimillionaire, I understand. Several hundred million.' She smiles. 'That's why you left us.'

'It wasn't only about the money.'

'It doesn't matter, even if it were. It's all you had to say, and I would have understood. If it were me, I'd have bought my own private castle by now and locked myself away from the world. Yet, you…' and she points at me, 'are still working. You're doing *this*. Why? You must have your reasons, I suppose. And you do it for free. Very noble of you.'

'Well,' I say, 'I'm glad I have your approval. I want to work. I didn't earn that money. I don't feel it's mine.'

'Nevertheless, it is yours. And I take it you're not about to sell secrets to the Russians or the Chinese? You don't need the money, right?'

'I was never a traitor.'

'No. You weren't.' Lacey shrugs. 'So why work at all?'

'I need to keep busy.'

'I would have employed you,' she says.

'I want to do some good, and I want to work for myself.'

'I admire you, Max. At the same time, I think you're crazy.'

'Can we call it a truce, then?' I say.

'I think we can. But I also come with an offer. One I had to get Home Office approval for.'

'Good grief, Janice!'

'No, it's not like that. This is about you helping me, and me helping you. A symbiotic relationship.'

'Go on.'

She smiles at my interest and sits forward. She's one of these people who would look a lot better without glasses.

'You don't have access to intelligence anymore,' she says. 'Not legally, anyway. You can't even get vehicle details other than when someone's MOT is due. In your new line of work, knowing if someone has a criminal record would be good. Don't you think?'

'Of course,' I say.

'Well, I can help you with that, as long as it's for a legitimate investigation with criminal elements. Not something like an adultery case or a lost dog. I can even cover up your indiscretions for you.'

'My indiscretions?'

'For example, if you, let's say, seriously injure someone in an alleyway in Chinatown, happen to stab a knife into their leg. That sort of thing.' She does that weird smile again.

'How did you know that was me? I was sure I had covered my tracks. Those men tried to kill me.'

'That may well be true. Both those men have convictions for violence as long as your inside leg. I've managed to keep the investigation away from you, Max.'

There's more than a whiff of blackmail with this. 'What do you want in return?'

'I'd like you to use your skills to help me occasionally, like I said. I'll even pay you for them. Not that money means anything to you anymore.'

'Why me? You have hundreds of agents you could use.'

'True. None like you, though, and you have the advantage of not being one of us anymore. If anyone does a background check on you, they won't find us at the end of it. Plus, you underestimate your capabilities, Max.'

'Okay, I'll think about it. But you won't draw me back into the unit again. I have another commitment I must stick to.'

'Really? And what would that be?'

'You must know by now what it is.'

'Ah, yes, your wife,' she says. 'Fair enough. There's something I need to talk to you about regarding Carrie, but I don't think now is a good time. It can wait.'

'Well, changing the subject, I'm hiring someone to help me for the short term.'

'Good. If they are working on any of our projects, they'll need to be informed they are covered by the Official Secrets Act. But that's your business again, not mine.'

'Do you have something for me now?'

'Not yet, but soon.' She glances at the packages on my desk and notices the address.

'Those men who wanted to kill me,' I say, 'one of them mentioned a name I need tracing.'

'You see, this will be a useful arrangement. What's the name?'

'Jethro Matisse. Does that ring a bell? Something to do with organised crime.'

'I'll ask for you. Do you have an age?'

'No, only a name.'

'An unusual name, which helps.' Lacey smiles. She glances around the office once again. 'You could get a nicer place than this, Max. It's dull in here.'

'You're not the first person to say that. I'm working on it.'

Lacey stands and sticks out her hand to me. 'That went better, I think.'

We shake.

'It did. You just had to be nice.'

I let her out of the front door and watch her walk away. I'm hoping I got the better end of that deal. The thought of working with The Firm again makes me twitch a little. It was a battle to leave the first time. Could I work with Lacey? She seems direct enough and willing to compromise with me. She wasn't sure of me to start with. Saw me as a possible threat. She said she spoke to my ex-colleagues, but none of them knew I inherited that money. Not unless she's talking about Gary. She would've had to go way back if she found Gary.

Returning to my desk, I pick up the sealed packages containing Mariana's computer and her notepad journal. They are going to a forensics company that works for the police. Hopefully, something there can shed more light on this case.

My phone rings, and it's Ella Munro. Perhaps this is a yes from her.

'Ella. Do you have a reply for me?'

'Hi. I'm calling to say I'm accepting the job.'

'That's great. Can you start Monday?'

'Sure.'

'I've got a case that I need help with. I'll get all the paperwork sent off to my legal man.'

'You mean a solicitor?'

'Yes, Charlie is a solicitor, now you come to mention it.'

'What's the dress code for Monday?'

'Anything but tartan. I don't like tartan.'

'What's wrong with tartan? Men in kilts look great.'

'Keep your sporran fetish to yourself, Ella. No, wear what you want. We'll be starting in a new office on Monday, and you can help me set up. I'll send you the address—it's not far from you, and it's a bit brighter than this place.'

'That's a relief. Your office is dire.'

'Thanks! I'm looking forward to working with you too. No tartan.'

Janie wakes up hungry and thirsty. She was dreaming of her sister at home, playing with their mother outside the front of her house, under a rich canopy of Bo trees. Janie was calling out to them, but they couldn't hear her. She was bound and gagged by ropes while they laughed and sang together.

She dries her eyes and tries to see around her. Although there is daylight outside, it's always dark inside. The gaps in the boarded window frames let in slivers of light, but barely enough to see.

There are fourteen beds in the old factory. At least they have beds now, away from the rats and mice that scurry for crumbs. There used to be fourteen girls to fill them, but now two beds are empty. Janie can't remember when she and her sister were brought here. Maybe three months ago, or it could be six.

She's forced herself to stop crying. It was the only way they would give her food and water. She is mentally strong like her sister was. Janie knows how to survive, and she will survive this and escape back home.

She speaks English, which helps. She sometimes pretends to the men she doesn't. That way, they don't talk to her, and she doesn't have to listen. The men pay extra if they damage her, and most don't want to do that. They do what they do, and then the woman lets her go to the nice room for a shower, fresh clothes, and something to eat. Bread and meat, pasta and cheese, juice and apples. Some of the food they give her, she's never eaten before. When it's safe—and she must never be caught—she secretly hides a few items inside her clean clothes and brings them back to the unit for those who have not eaten.

Janie peers over at the girl next to her in Kamlai's bed. She's asleep now, still in her makeup. Sleep is the best place they can be, so when the girl cries, Janie sings to her until her eyes close and her breathing softens. They've become friends, but they don't understand each other. The girl is European, maybe Albanian. Janie is Thai. Her friend is pale and weak. There may be another empty bed soon. Janie gives her food, but it doesn't make her better. Her heart and soul are broken.

There are two skinny teenage boys here now with black skin. They're treated well most of the time, but they steal food from the girls and mock them. The boys come and go—some are kind, and others aren't.

Soon, the daylight will be over, and the bus will return. They wake them all, take the healthy ones for the night, and assign their clients. When they have finished, they will eat again. No work means no food. So Janie must do as she is told and hopes the men will be kind. She prays for her mother and brothers. Then she turns over to sleep until evening.

CHAPTER 13

Grace wakes up alone in her flat on Thursday morning after an awful night's sleep. Her bed feels cold and empty, and the flat is silent, apart from the hum of the boiler. She and Spencer had argued all yesterday afternoon and evening. He'd lost his car keys and had a tantrum. He said some terrible things to her. She had been restless all night, wondering what she should do next.

She misses his kindness and humour. His tenderness too. When he gives her his attention, he makes her feel as if the whole world revolves around her. He has often picked her up from work with roses and surprised her with a dinner date. But that's all changed. Now she wonders what has taken hold of him, and if he's in some kind of trouble. He won't talk about it.

She gets up and showers, dresses in comfortable clothes, and has a mouthful of toast. She keeps checking her mobile, but he hasn't left a message.

There's a gentle tap on the front door, and her heart jumps. His door key to the flat was on his key ring, which he's claiming Max Fortis stole. She knows it's him at the door. This is something he'd do—there will be flowers, too. She peers through the spyhole, and he's there holding a bunch of red roses, straightening his tie.

'I thought you had work,' she says through the door.

'I've called in sick. I want to spend the day with you. I'm sorry, okay? We Ryans are famous for our passion. We care for our women. We protect them.'

'*Your* women? For God's sake, Spencer.'

'I didn't mean it like that. Look, can I come in? I want to apologise.'

Grace opens the front door, and Spencer comes in, holding out the roses to her. She ignores them. 'You said some cruel things. I've never seen you like that before.'

'It's Fortis. He brings out the worst in me. I swear he attacked me! He's dangerous, Grace. He knows you've got money, and he's trying to find a way into you.'

'Like you did?'

'Hey! Don't be like that. I'm worried about you. About us. We're getting married, remember? Why don't we make some wedding plans today? Put something down in the diary, pay some deposits.'

'Wedding plans? I've been trying to get you to make plans with me for months. Are you being serious?'

'I am. I promise. You can have anything you want. Even a church, if you insist.'

'That's generous of you, but in case you've forgotten, someone murdered my mother, and I'm still not in the mood for wedding plans.'

'You can't be serious, surely? She wasn't murdered! She was depressed, Grace! She even sent a message to her agent.'

'Mr Fortis agrees with me.'

'There's that bloody Fortis again!'

She walks into the kitchen, and Spencer follows. He slaps the flowers down onto the counter.

'Why are you so keen to side with Fortis all the time?' he says.

'I'm not taking sides!'

Grace takes a glass vase from a cupboard and fills it with water. She goes to a drawer and finds scissors to trim the rose stalks.

'He was a bent cop,' he says. 'That's why he left.'

'No, he wasn't.'

'He was. I can prove it. When I walked into your mother's study, I caught him pocketing some of her ornaments. The man's a thief! I don't trust him, so neither should you.'

'Stealing her ornaments?' she laughs. 'That's ridiculous!'

'Are you calling me a liar?'

She can see he's getting heated again.

'No. I just think you're mistaken. You've got some kind of weird grudge against him. It's childish.' She trims the stems and puts them into the vase. 'Come on, Spencer. I thought you wanted to apologise to me. All you're doing is getting wound up again.'

He takes her by the shoulders and pulls her around to face him. 'I love you, Grace. You know that. I fell in love with you from the beginning. I want to marry you, buy a big house, and have messy little kids running around our feet. That's all I want.'

Grace slams down the scissors and turns to face him. 'Why did my mother say no to you? You never told me. She wouldn't give me a reason, either. She told me to ask you.'

He turns his head away and sighs. 'She was worried you wouldn't be enough for me.'

'I wouldn't be enough for you? That's bullshit!'

'It's true. That's why I couldn't tell you. She knew the kind of man I was, my ambition, my desire for bigger things. She wondered if you had that same ambition.'

She shakes her head. 'I don't believe you. She would never have said that.'

'I told her you did. I told her you would rise to the challenge.'

'Get over yourself, Spencer. You're a pathetic liar! I've been thinking about it all night. Is it only the money you want? I'm not even sure you really love me anymore.'

Spencer groans. 'This is ridiculous!'

'So, what's your plan? Marry me for my money? Then you can divorce me and take half of everything I own.'

His hand sweeps the vase off the surface. It smashes into thousands of shards, water and roses everywhere.

'You bitch! You want to sleep with Fortis! As soon as you saw him, I bet you pulled down your knickers and begged him for it.' He grips her shoulder hard.

'Get off me! You're hurting me!' She pulls away and shakes him off. 'Get out of my flat. It's over! Do you hear me? Over!'

Spencer goes to the door. 'I'm sorry, Grace! Please! I'm sorry!'

'Get out!'

Grace slams the door behind him. She is shaking. She puts the door chain on and listens to his footsteps on the stairs as he leaves.

Spencer is cold, sitting on the bench by the play area. He's sent a text to Mikita, who will call him back. His eyes follow the gentle curve of the ground, forming the shape of a bowl. It's the site of a Roman amphitheatre, but if it weren't for an information sign, no one would ever realise.

He answers his mobile.

'What is it, Spencer?' says Mikita.

'Fortis isn't going away,' says Spencer. 'He's a bigger problem than I first thought. Grace and me had a fight. She wants me to leave.'

'Then leave.' Mikita's accent is thick and slow. 'Why is Fortis still working for Grace?'

'I can't get rid of him. He's like a turd I've trodden on. His stench goes with me everywhere.'

'The boss has had enough. Get out of there. Fortis must be onto you by now. If he puts pressure on you, you'll talk.'

'He won't put pressure on me! I can handle him.'

'Have you found your car keys yet, Spencer?' Mikita laughs. 'Fortis is a professional. He doesn't have shit for brains like you. He'll eat you for breakfast and spit you out again. The boss is being generous to you. Get out now.'

'Grace is a bitch. She owes me. I want that money! I'll force her to give it to me if I have to.'

Mikita sighs into the phone, cursing in his native language. 'If the boss hears you talking like that, he will rip your face off, piece by piece. Believe me.'

Spencer stands and paces around the perimeter of the slides and swings. He kicks the small gate, cracking the wooden frame and breaking the latch. 'I've had enough of working for him now. I'm going away, and I'll do exactly what I want.'

Mikita tuts. 'You are a bigger fool than I thought. If you lay a hand on Grace, you will pay with your life. I promise you that.'

Spencer kicks out again, snapping a hinge. He sighs,

defeated. 'I'll wait until she's gone, and I'll get my things. I've just pocketed her spare key from the hallway.'

'Good. I'm glad you've seen sense. As far as you quitting, then that's up to you. Just make sure you convince the boss that your lips are sealed. Do you understand me?'

'I get it. I'm not stupid.'

'Don't let me down, Spencer. I'm serious, or you'll regret you were even born.'

Mikita ends the call. Spencer sits back down on the bench and thinks of Grace once more. They could have made it work if it wasn't for the interference from Matisse. Now he could lose everything he's worked for. Why should he do that? He leans forward and buries his face in his hands, regretting the day he walked into the Obsidian Rooms.

CHAPTER 14

After signing legal papers regarding the new office, I meet Gary Bates for lunch in the Bishop's Palace Gardens. We're sitting beneath a giant sequoia tree, reminiscing about the people we used to know when we worked together.

I need to make up the calories from my work in the dojo. This case means I am putting extra hours into training to stay sharp and focused. Gary, though, doesn't have that excuse for his calorie intake as he tucks into a second round of sandwiches. He looks rough today, and I don't think he's shaven for two days.

'You're nearly the same age as me, Gary,' I say. 'You'll drive yourself into an early grave if you eat like that every day.'

'I'm hungry!' he says with a mouthful of an all-day breakfast sandwich. 'I burn off my calories with worry, and I'm always going up and down the stairs in the nick.'

'When was the last time you had to chase anyone?' I ask.

'Chase someone! God, no. Why would I want to do that? That's what PCs are for.'

He looks at a group of college students sitting on the grass around a blanket. The girls are laughing amongst themselves.

'They're at least fifteen years younger than you,' I say.

'Come on, mate! Anything else you want to criticise me about?'

'No, that's all.' I laugh. 'How's it going?'

'It's shite.' His face shows it. 'Relentless pressure from the boss. I don't get the time to do a proper job on anything, and duties won't give me the annual leave I want. I've had enough. The job isn't what it used to be.'

'Under that overweight exterior, Gary, you're a good man, even if you are leching at eighteen-year-olds.'

Gary screws up the sandwich packet in his hand. 'I'm not a lech! I thought I smelled cannabis.'

'Come and work for me,' I say.

He laughs. 'Thanks, Max. I needed cheering up.'

'I'm serious. You'd be a real asset to me.'

'That's kind of you, but I can't do anything else.'

He lowers his head. 'Someone was asking questions about you a couple of days ago. Somebody important. I had to tell them what I knew about you. I'm really sorry, Max.'

'That someone was Commander Lacey. I realised she must have spoken to you when I saw her yesterday. It's okay. I don't blame you. In fact, it made things easier for me.'

He smiles. 'She almost fell over when I told her about you inheriting the money. They don't get why you've set up as a private detective. Neither do I, if I'm honest.'

'I know you don't, but you'll get used to it.'

'How are you getting on with the case?' he says.

'I need help with it. I've got someone else joining me for a while.'

'Who?'

I tell him about Ella Munro and her antics to get a story on me. Then I give him the details about Lacey's offer. He's intrigued.

'It will give you an advantage over other private dicks.'

'I'll see what she delivers first,' I say. 'But it will add an interesting dimension to what I do.'

Gary sees a bar of chocolate on the bench, and he pretends he's not interested, brushing the crumbs off his jacket.

'Do you have news for me?' I ask.

Gary shakes his head.

'How about Garcia's phone? Any messages, GPS information?'

'There's been a problem, so the results are delayed. Anyway, I shouldn't be telling you anything.'

'True, but you will keep me updated, won't you?' I get up to leave. 'I have to meet a client now.'

He nods and thanks me for the sandwiches. I leave the chocolate beside him.

'The job offer still stands,' I say.

'That's nice of you, but I am set in my ways in this job.'

'Gary, what do you love doing more than anything?'

He doesn't answer straightaway, and a shadow falls over his face. 'I've forgotten, Max. I don't know what makes me happy anymore.'

'Then it's time to quit this shit job. Find out what that thing is you love before it's too late.'

I walk away, letting him ponder that thought. He's a nice guy, and I hate seeing him so miserable.

Leaving Gary behind in the gardens, I take the longer way around the cathedral, through the cloisters, in time to hear a single chime from the Bell Tower. I've only been inside the cathedral once, and that was to arrest someone for vexing a vicar. It's a real offence. It didn't please the custody sergeant when I brought him in.

Young people are enjoying the autumnal sunshine on the cathedral green—more students on a lunch break. A group is playing music with a young woman on guitar. Someone will complain about them breaking bylaws, no doubt. This is Chichester, after all.

I find Grace looking out for me at The Cross. She's in a long, dark orange coat, and her hand is fiddling with the strap of her shoulder bag. Now that I'm closer, her anxiety is obvious.

'Mr Fortis!' she blurts out as soon as she sees me. 'I'm scared of Spencer. I can't go on like this.' Her eyes are wet.

'What's happened?' I say.

'Ever since yesterday, he's been in a foul mood. Throwing things, breaking things. First, he's lost his car keys, and then he told me you're ripping me off, and I shouldn't trust you. He said he'd caught you stealing some of my mother's ornaments. We've just had a fight. He's furious with you about something. I've told him to leave.'

'Let's get a coffee,' I say.

Grace seems frozen to the spot, her legs unable to move. Her eyes focus on me again when I lead her by the hand. We go to my favourite coffee shop and order. She is sluggish, and her eyes are heavy. As she removes her coat, her jumper slips off her shoulder, revealing a red bra strap. Beneath the strap is a large purple bruise. She covers her shoulder again when she sees me looking.

'Did Spencer do that to you?' I say.

'He was angry.'

People are turning around, so we lower our voices.

'I don't need to steal your mother's ornaments. I have

plenty of my late uncle's crap cluttering up the house. Too fussy for my taste.'

'Why is he so angry with you?' she says. 'He's only just met you.'

'I accused him of something, and he didn't deny it. He doesn't like people telling him he's in the wrong.'

'No, he doesn't.'

'Are you planning to marry him?'

'Why?'

'It's not what your mother would have wanted,' I say.

'What do you mean?'

'This won't be pleasant to hear.'

She lifts her chin and fixes her eyes on mine. 'Go on.'

I reach into my pocket, pull out the button I found inside her mother's desk, and slide it across the table. 'Recognise this?'

'A button?' She picks it up and examines it, pulling at the threads. There's something in her eyes. 'It's like the ones on Spencer's shirt. The one I bought him for Christmas. It wasn't cheap. He said he'd lost it. Where did you find it?'

'It was inside one of your mother's desk drawers,' I say.

Grace frowns. 'What was it doing in there?' She inspects the button more closely. 'The button's broken. Someone's pulled it off.'

I nod. 'They have.'

Her eyes go wide in horror and fill with tears. She shakes her head, flaring her nostrils.

'No!' she says. 'She wouldn't do that to me. She loved me. She would *never* do that to me!'

'I asked him, Grace. He didn't deny it. Then he attacked me.'

'Spencer? Why would he do that to me?'

'Greed? Lust? Power? The usual reasons, I guess.'

She's wide-eyed and breathless. She sits forward and puts her hands on her chest. I take her left hand and squeeze it until it hurts. It distracts her.

'Slow your breathing,' I say. 'Deep breaths. Don't let him do this to you. You are a strong woman.' I let go.

She wipes her eyes on a tissue and glares at me, the bearer of bad news.

'Do you want some space?'

'No. It's okay. I'll deal with him,' she says. It was cold and definite. I wouldn't want to be on the receiving end of that heap of trouble.

'If he hurt you, then talk to the police. I believe he's violent, but I don't think he killed your mother. However, he may have an idea who did. He wants me to drop your case.'

'Go and see him, Mr Fortis, and get him to talk. Do you think he's connected with this man called Matisse you were talking about?'

'It's a possibility.'

'Then get him to talk. I'm going home now to remove everything of his from my flat.'

'Do you need a hand? It may help me find who he's connected with.'

'That would be good, thank you.'

She wraps her shaking hands around her cup, and we sit in silence for several minutes. I watch people walk past, waiting for her to compose herself. Then Grace's phone buzzes. The display tells me it's Spencer calling her. She's wondering what to do.

'Leave it,' I say. 'You're angry. Don't do anything angry. You'll regret it later.'

Spencer gives up on the call, and she writes a text she won't let me see.

'We can track each other,' she says. 'We have an app on our phones.'

'Does he keep his location app turned on? I bet he doesn't.'

'No. He said he couldn't because of work.'

'He uses it to track you. Delete the app.'

She does it there and then.

We leave the coffee shop, and she checks I have her address. She says she needs to get herself together first and wants me to give her half an hour. Then I can meet her at her flat in Chichester.

I make good use of the time and head to my office. Once I've spoken with the estate agent, I make my way to the east side of the city in St Pancras. I take a right turn and then right again, parking behind Grace's VW Polo. It's still ticking as it cools in front of her flat.

She doesn't answer when I press the door buzzer. I recheck the address on my phone contacts list. It's the address she gave me. I try it again—no answer. I call her number. Still no answer.

Trying another flat on the same floor, I speak to a woman on the intercom. She's happy to let me in through the main entrance. I climb two flights of stairs and knock on Grace's door. Again, no answer.

A door opposite opens a few inches with a chain attached.

'Are you the police?' an elderly woman asks me.

'No, I'm a friend,' I say.

'There was a horrible noise from inside there,' she says. 'Screaming and hollering.'

'When?'

'A few minutes ago. I was going to call the police.'

'Call the police now!' I say. 'Tell them everything you heard.' I barge at the door a few times, but it's reinforced.

'No need for that, dear,' says the woman. 'She gave me a spare key.' She passes it to me through the gap, and I open Grace's front door.

Spencer is in the hallway. He's startled when he sees me, looking flushed, and his clothes are dishevelled. His head is hanging low, and he's panting.

'What the hell are you doing here, Fortis?'

'Where's Grace?'

There's a shout from behind a door. 'Help me! He's trying to kill me.' The door has a lock, so it must be the bathroom.

Spencer's clenching his bloody fists. There's a dent in the door. He pulls back his shoulders and steps towards me.

'You've had it coming, Fortis,' he says.

He bounces on his feet and bends his knees a little. Talk about telling me what he's going to do. I doubt this so-called cage fighter can beat a sack of potatoes.

'Sit down, Spencer,' I say. 'The police are on their way.'

Here it comes. I raise my hands and pull in my elbows. He's cocky—it's a front kick to my chest. I rotate and dodge left. He hasn't protected his face. An open palm strike to his nose flips his head backwards, and he crashes through the doorway into the kitchen and lands on his back. His broken nose gushes blood, and he's dazed, crying in pain. Sirens are approaching.

I tap on the bathroom door. 'Grace, it's me. It's okay. He won't come near you now.'

Grace opens the door. Her left eye is closed, her cheek is red and swollen, blood is dripping from her split lip, and there are purple thumbprints on her neck. The neighbour is at the door, filming everything on her phone.

'Make yourself useful,' I say to her. 'Take care of Grace.'

Grace moves over to the neighbour, who takes her into her flat. I stand over Spencer, who's trying to sit up with his hand to his bloody face.

'What have you done to me?' he says, spitting out blood.

'You're a disgusting piece of shit. The worst kind of coward.'

His ribs crack as I land a sharp kick in his side. I would have done it again, but two police officers appear at the door—one has a Taser drawn.

'Grace is with the neighbour,' I tell them. 'She needs to go to the hospital. He does as well.'

———

Paramedics are checking Grace's injuries. She's feeling the pain now the adrenaline is easing off. She has defence wounds, and more seriously, the punch to her face may have cracked a cheekbone.

I watch the police arrest Spencer for domestic GBH and for threats to kill. They take him away to the local hospital for assessment. Grace will follow once it's safe for her to do so.

Her flat is in a terrible state. Broken glass and furniture are scattered everywhere. Spencer has smashed up the kitchen, ripping off the cupboard doors. He has serious anger issues. The bedroom's been turned upside down like someone's burgled it—clothes scattered across the floor and drawers flung onto the bed.

I find some paperwork pinned onto a notice board in the kitchen, so I look through it while the police take statements from Grace and the neighbour. There's a bill for mooring fees in Emsworth, a few miles from here—paid for by Grace. I uncover an old security pass for a nightclub in Portsmouth called *The Obsidian Rooms*. Spencer must have had a job there once.

It's my turn to give a statement to a PC, and he's being careful to record the details of the fight between Spencer and me. Soon after I sign the statement, that young DS from Chichester Station appears. DS Chambers interviewed me last month and has tried to pin Garcia's murder on me ever since. He's talking with the uniformed officers and glancing up at me. He's reading my statement and frowning.

The DS stands in front of me, sizing me up.

'Mr Fortis,' he says. 'Spencer Ryan's not too well. You say in your statement that you defended yourself against him.'

'He was using me as kickboxing practice,' I say.

'What were you doing here?'

I tell him Grace has hired me to investigate Mariana's death, and the DS wants everything I have on Spencer Ryan. It's nothing they couldn't find out for themselves if they'd bothered to look at someone else apart from me.

'Why do you think he killed Mariana Garcia?' he says. 'All you're doing is interfering in someone else's business. It's a domestic—let the police handle it.'

'I don't think he killed her,' I say. 'He's too stupid. Are you telling me I should have waited for the police? He was going to kill her!'

'Fortunately for you, you have a witness supporting self-defence.' He glances behind him at the elderly neighbour in the stairwell. 'I'm still inclined to nick you. You must leave this to the real police now, Mr Fortis. We'll take care of Grace from here.'

'Real police?' I step towards him. 'Do you think I'm some kind of wannabe policeman, sergeant? I was locking up terrorists and credible threats to our democracy while you were still at home, wetting your bed. With a face like yours, I expect you still do. *Real police*, my arse.'

He flushes with anger and mumbles an insult at me under his breath as I leave, but I don't turn around. Returning to the car, I feel pressure coming over me. It feels like the atmosphere this afternoon has become dark and heavy, pushing into the backs of my eyes. I mustn't let my anger take hold.

Why didn't I insist on going back to the flat with Grace? I let her make herself vulnerable. I should have known better.

I sit inside my car for a few minutes, put on a Gregory Porter CD, and let my temper cool. I need to take a break. Turn the failures into lessons—that's what my mother taught me. Thinking of failures reminds me of something I need to do. I should call Ima and Leon.

After a few rings, Leon picks up.

'Hi, Leon,' I say. 'I'm going to see Carrie. I'll be back late.'

'Okay, Max,' he says. 'Make sure you get something to eat before you go in. You need to look after yourself.'

'Thanks. Not been a good day today.'

'I'm sorry to hear that. Keep yourself safe. We'll be here when you get back.'

After the call, I leave for Haslemere to visit Holly Grange, a private hospital. The sun will set in twenty minutes, so I take the road to Midhurst, following an old Morris Minor on a single-lane carriageway all the way there.

CHAPTER 15

I spent ninety minutes in the gym this morning, so now I'm famished and ready for breakfast. I head to the kitchen and find Ima cooking me bacon, eggs, and avocado on sourdough bread toast. She's lost in thought, humming to herself. I watch her and smile. She's a beautiful woman. She'd been talking on the phone to her cousins in Paris.

'How are they?' I ask her.

'All fine,' she says. 'The children are fine. Everything is fine. But how about you? How did it go last night?'

'Not fine. Just the same.' I shrug.

'At least you still go. It's all you can do.'

'But why do I do it?'

She brings over a coffee and sits with me at the breakfast bar. 'Some trace of hope, maybe?'

'There is no hope. It doesn't look good now.'

'I'm sorry, Max. When the time comes, you will know what to do. You always have done.' She rubs my arm and smiles. 'What's happening with the move?'

'Monday.'

'That's when that girl starts,' she says.

'Ella. She can help me set up. I'm concerned about what I'm bringing her into with all that's happened recently. This isn't searching for a lost relative. I've had people try to kill me.'

'Can she handle herself if things get difficult?'

'She's feisty, but I'm not sure. I need to talk to her.'

'You should. How long is the lease on the new office?'

'There isn't one. I bought the whole thing—the leasehold, too. It's a nice place.'

'That was quick!'

'I've got people in there now painting and laying carpet. I might as well make use of this money.'

Ima shakes her head and laughs. She's always surprised at how quickly I act when I decide to do something.

'How are your investigations?' she says.

'I'm struggling. I'm no closer to figuring out who this Jethro Matisse is.'

'You'll work it out,' she says. 'You are smart.'

I eat breakfast, and Ima watches me as she leans against the counter.

'You know we miss Carrie, too, Max.'

I nod. 'It seems like yesterday when it all...'

'I know. Your uncle was full of regret. Knowing you're going to die makes you take a long, hard look at yourself.'

'Is that what he did, Ima, or was it a guilty conscience?'

'Changing his will was the only thing he could think of doing to make it up to you.'

'It turns out we never knew each other at all.'

My phone rings. It's Gary, so I take the call in the conservatory.

'Any news?' I say.

'Spencer Ryan's still in hospital,' he says. 'Broken ribs, broken cheekbones, facial injury. You did a good job on him. Grace's statement backs you up, too.'

'I'll send him a get-well card.'

'I called you at home last night. Leon said you were out.' There's silence for a few seconds. 'How is she, Max? How's Carrie?'

I never know what to say when people ask me. I'd rather not say anything at all. 'The same.' There's a pause I want to fill. 'How is Grace?'

'She's okay. No serious damage apart from the bruising. God knows what he would have done to her if you hadn't turned up. She's staying at a friend's house.'

'Max,' he says, lowering his voice. 'DS Chambers is floundering with this case. The senior investigating officer has been on his back. Try not to upset him. I don't want to have to nick you for something he's trying to fit your face to. He talked about arresting you for GBH on Spencer Ryan, citing excessive force.'

'Seriously?'

'Seriously. I'm giving you a heads-up. That's all.'

'Don't worry, I'll keep out of his way.'

Someone's calling for him, and he has to go. I return to Ima in the kitchen and find Leon with her. He's carrying a bag of goldfish.

'I won't ask,' I say.

'Restocking the pond,' he says. 'Bloody heron got three of them. I'm putting a net over it.'

'Of course. Well, have fun. I'm going to talk to Ella now. I hope I don't scare her off.'

'Wait,' says Ima. 'Ella could get some training here. Teach her the basics.'

'That would be good, Max,' says Leon. 'She might need it one day. We both know a trainer who would be perfect for the job.'

'Yes, we do,' I say.

DC Gary Bates has followed DS Chambers into a side office away from CID. It's dark in there, and Gary gets the feeling that something shady is going on with this meeting. He wonders if it was the way Chambers asked him or how he looked over his shoulder. Chambers points to the door, and Gary closes it behind him.

Gary tries to think what this could be about. Is it a disciplinary matter, or is he behind with his e-learning? What's he going to be bollocked for this time? Chambers sits behind the empty desk, and Gary sits in front of him, hands down by his sides. Chambers places his mobile phone on the desk halfway between them, checking he has turned up the volume.

'I'm expecting a call from Forensics,' says Chambers. 'You may want to hear it, too.'

'Okay, Sarge,' says Gary. Still none the wiser. Forensics? Was there something he had contaminated? An exhibit he had forgotten to label and sign?

'I want to talk about Max Fortis. The so-called private detective.'

Gary sinks into his chair. 'He's *so-called* because he *is* a private detective, Sarge.'

Chambers grunts. 'You're a friend of his.'

'We go back a long way, yes, but we're not close, close.'

'Is it true he was in the Met?'

'Yes, Sarge,' says Gary. He frowns, still trying to figure out where this is going.

'Some big shot, was he? Royal protection? MI5?'

'Yes, Sarge. That and other things.'

'Surely, if he were in MI5, he wouldn't tell people, would he?'

'He told you?' Gary's wondering why he's having to defend Max. Why is this man so obsessed with him?

'Yes,' says Chambers, 'during an interview.' Chambers locks his fingers together and watches his phone screen.

Gary nods. 'Maybe he felt being in a police station and talking to a DS was a safe place to reveal that. It should be a safe place, shouldn't it?'

'Maybe, Gary. Has he ever asked you to do checks on the Police National Computer for him? Or perhaps look up intelligence logs?'

'Shit, Sarge. No! He's never asked for that.' Gary blushes a little.

'Has he ever asked you to interfere with evidence?'

'Do I need a Federation rep in here? Because it's really starting to feel like I do.'

Chambers raises his hand and shakes his head. 'No, Gary. This is off the record.'

'Really off the record?'

Chambers nods.

'Well, off the record, I think you're a little shit who's gunning for someone to cover up your own inadequacies. *Sarge*. Off the record.'

Chambers flushes red. 'So that's how it is.'

'That's how it is,' says Gary, folding his arms.

'Since you're being frank with me, let me be frank with you.' Chambers sits forward. 'I don't trust you any further than

I could throw you. And there's a lot of you to throw anywhere. I reckon you've tampered with evidence to get your friend off the hook. I reckon he killed Mariana Garcia and likely framed Spencer Ryan for it.'

'Where's your evidence?'

'Oh, I have evidence. I've sent it off to Forensics. I have Max Fortis's DNA on Garcia's body.'

Gary feels his heart racing. 'How?'

'I'm not telling you how.' Chambers sits back and slides his mouth into a sly grin. 'They found pubic hair caught inside an item of Garcia's clothing. I'm certain it belongs to Fortis.'

'Then put it to him in an interview,' says Gary. He feels himself sweating under his collar.

'I will. I'm waiting for the confirmation call now, and you'll be here when it comes in.'

'This is total bollocks. You're trying to fit him up.'

'Not at all. I wouldn't do such a thing. The evidence stands, Gary. Forensics are going to call at any moment and tell me the DNA is a match for Fortis.'

'Why are you so certain? Where did you find the hair?'

DS Chambers's mobile phone rings. Gary can see it's the forensics lab calling and shakes his head. He feels like smacking the DS over the head with it. What can he do to fight this? Chambers answers the mobile and puts the call on speakerphone.

'This is DS Chambers, Chichester CID.'

There's a sound of rustling paper, and then someone clears their throat. 'DS Chambers, we spoke earlier.'

'Yes, do you have those results for me?'

'The pubic hair with the follicles.'

'Yes.'

'It isn't recent, DS Chambers. Quite degraded, in fact.'

Chambers face reddens. 'What do you mean, degraded?'

'Precisely that. It's several years old.'

'But it matches the comparison DNA, yes?' The pitch of Chambers's voice has gone up.

'Well. There is no comparison for the details given. It doesn't exist. Not on the DNA database or the police database. Is the person still an officer?'

'He was six months ago.'

'Interesting. It could have been destroyed by then, or it could have been restricted. Either way, it's not really the point. That hair could have been around for years. It wasn't in contact with the victim recently, certainly not around the time of the victim's death. I believe the pathologist said there was no evidence of any sexual assault or recent coitus. The sample isn't from a reliable source. Sorry if that's not what you wanted to hear, DS Chambers.'

Chambers ends the call and slams down the phone onto the desk. 'Shit!' He hunches over his hands and stares at the smashed phone screen.

Gary lifts his shoulders and smiles. 'Will that be all, Sarge? I have some *honest* policing to do back at my desk.'

Ella Munro lives in Fishbourne, a village a couple of miles west of Chichester and the next village east of Bosham, and I'm making my way there now.

Fishbourne, known for its Roman Palace, brings back memories of a rainy day spent there as a child with my school when my father was posted in the UK. It's situated north of the reed beds and a creek that leads into Chichester Harbour. Ella is staying with her mother in a house off Blackboy Lane, down a horseshoe-shaped road. These are expensive houses with driveways and double garages. My paternal grandmother lived here when I was a boy. A tall, kind lady who smelled of honey, elegant and dignified.

I find Ella's house and ring the doorbell. A woman in her sixties answers the door and squints at me with a question.

'I'm Max Fortis. Is Ella here?'

I get shown into the rear garden, where I find Ella on her knees, clearing out flower beds. She's wearing jeans and a baggy T-shirt, and her hair is tied into a scruffy knot. Quite endearing.

'Max?' she says. I guess she's surprised.

'Digging the dirt again?'

'Oh, yes.' She blushes and stands with a small, muddy fork in her hand.

'It's about Monday,' I say. I stand closer to her as her mother tries to listen in from the kitchen. 'It's still on, but I wanted to tell you something.'

'Okay?'

'I'm involved with a case that's getting messy.'

She smiles. 'How messy?'

'Bad people are hurting other people.'

'I'm not a child, Max,' she says. 'Talk to me like an adult.'

'I'm sorry. Someone has been murdered. It's not a pleasant thing to deal with.'

'Oh.' She's standing still.

'And a few days ago, two men tried to kill me in London. Someone doesn't want me working on this case. They're somehow linked to someone called Jethro Matisse. I don't know who he is yet. It sounds like he runs an organised crime gang, and he's the one giving out the orders to kill other people.'

'Really bad people, then.'

'Yes.'

We stare at each other for what feels like ages.

'Tea, Mr Fortis?' calls her mother from the kitchen.

'Do you have coffee?' I reply.

'Yes. How do you like it?' says her mother.

I'm still waiting for a reaction from Ella. There's something about her that makes me want to protect her. I don't want to get her involved in all this, and I'm trying to put her off.

'Mum asked how you like your coffee,' says Ella.

I turn and smile. 'Lots of milk, strong, one sugar, please.'

I turn back to Ella. 'Well?'

'Well, what?' she says with a smile.

'It's dangerous, as in deadly dangerous. If they find out you work for me, then you could get hurt. I can look after myself, but I can't look after you, too.'

'That's a bit macho-chauvinistic, isn't it?' she says with a crease on her forehead. She taps the prongs of the fork against her palm.

'Not at all! These people are serious, Ella. I don't want you to come to any harm.'

'I can look after myself, thank you very much.'

'Can you?'

'I can.'

'Well, that's great,' I say, now a little annoyed. We stare at each other again. 'Okay, then. I'll see you Monday morning.'

'See you Monday.'

'Right.'

I turn and leave, meeting Ella's mother on the way out with a coffee. Taking the cup, I down the coffee and hand it back to her. It was a little hot, but I didn't show it.

'Sorry, Mrs Munro. I have to go.' Then, when I reach the car, I realise she can't be Mrs Munro, too.

As I drive away, I think about Ella's reaction, and I smile to myself. I'm going to the office now to move out all my files. I don't want to waste any time on Monday.

CHAPTER 16

A new day, a new week, a new office. I spent Saturday with Leon, moving the last of the office furniture and building shelves. He offered to help, which meant I could get straight to work today.

Now, I'm trying to get used to the smell of fresh paint, the bright lights in the ceiling, and the happy-go-lucky decor. It was my choice, so I can't complain—a knee-jerk reaction against beige.

The office is about fifty yards from Bosham Station, so it's still accessible by train. It was a shop closed by multiple Covid lockdowns and needed some renovation. It's on a good-sized piece of land, including a garden behind. Leon has declined to look after it, as he already has enough to deal with. So, I've hired another gardener—a man and his son with Down syndrome.

There's a flat above the office, spacious and open, now decorated in greys and whites. It used to be someone's home, but it's now a temporary stopover if I need it. The broadband is going live later this morning, so I'm installing the coffee machine and filling up the cupboards in the kitchen.

The front door rattles as Ella comes in. She's open-mouthed at her new place of work. Under her coat, she's wearing a red and green tartan skirt and a dark-green jumper.

'It's amazing!' she says. 'So much better than the old place. Very bright.'

She walks through the main office and pops her head into a smaller side room to be used for confidential interviews. She runs her finger over the top of the iMacs and moves into the bathroom and the kitchen.

'You even have a shower,' she says.

'If ever you need it. I also have one in the apartment upstairs.'

'And a dishwasher! I could live here.'

I laugh. 'Do you want a coffee? The machine works now.'

We spend the morning getting used to the new office and installing software on the computers. Ella makes a few calls for me, and then I brief her on the Mariana Garcia case. She goes through the file and finds the photos I took from Houghton Bridge.

'I know this bridge,' she says. 'It's not as old as it looks.'

'So I heard,' I say.

'That poor woman. Imagine ending up in there. How did she climb up that wall?'

'I doubt she did.'

She continues looking through the file. 'How did she get there if she wanted to kill herself? Did the taxi take her?'

'There's no trace of the taxi. None of the Chichester cab companies knew anything about the pick-up.'

'It could have been a Portsmouth or Havant cab.'

'I checked. It's a dead end.'

'Then the driver did it as a private job,' she says.

I nod. 'I wondered that. It's a major sticking point for the police. They thought I'd made it up.'

'Do they think you killed her?'

'Apart from the taxi driver, I was the last known person to see Mariana alive.'

Ella continues through the file. 'What does the CCTV show?'

'There was no CCTV working near the magistrates' courts.'

'No, on the road to the bridge.'

'There's nothing on the bridge. And the pub CCTV only covers their entrance and car park.'

Ella does this funny thing with her mouth, pursing her lips to the left and right. 'But what about at the holiday cottages along the road?' She's expecting an answer.

I have to say it. 'What holiday cottages?'

'Further up the hill. I wrote an article for the owners last year. They showed me around. They have CCTV. I think it covers the road.' All I can do is stare at her, and she smiles. 'You didn't ask?'

'Obviously not.'

'I'll get onto that for you, Mr Fortis,' she says with a sarcastic grin.

'Thank you, Mrs Munro. And I'll get the coffee.'

'I didn't realise these old cars were so comfortable,' says Ella, stretching out in the Volvo seat.

We're coming down the hill into Houghton, towards Amberley. Ella called the owners of the holiday cottages and arranged an appointment. She's playing with the electric seat now, trying to adjust it for her legroom. Carrie was the last person to do that. She's a few inches shorter than Ella.

'How old is this car?' she says.

'1998.'

'Twenty-five years old, and she's still like new inside. I see why you like her.'

'I look after her. She was a chance find, low mileage, great condition, and owned by an old gentleman from Goodwood House.'

'I'm not being funny or anything, but you can afford a much better car than this.'

'I've got an expensive car, but I enjoy driving this one.'

'What expensive car is that?'

'It's red. That's all I'm saying.'

Ella wants to see the bridge, and where they found Mariana's body. So I drive further onto the Traveller's Rest car park, and we walk together onto the bridge. We find the recess in the wall where Mariana left her bag and shoes. There is still residue from the forensic marks on the stonework. Someone has placed a single red rose here, wrapped in cellophane. Ella picks it up, and there is a message on the card. The ink has run, but she can read it.

'*With much sadness. D.*'

'Who's D?' I say.

'A lover?'

'No. I don't think so.'

'How do you know?' she says. 'It could be.'

I point south to the first bend in the river after the bridge. Ella stands close to me to see where I'm pointing. Her hair flies into my face, so she smiles and holds it against her ear. She steps forward and places her hands on the top of the stonework to push herself up. She lifts her leg but remembers she's wearing a skirt.

'What are you doing?' I say.

'She was wearing a skirt when they pulled her out of the water. She would have had to lift it and heave herself over the top. I can't do it.'

'Precisely,' I say, 'and nicely demonstrated. She had to have either had help or someone lifted her onto the wall and pushed her in when she was unconscious.'

Ella looks along the length of the bridge. 'Could she have walked along the wall from the end?'

'No. She left her shoes here, anyway.'

'Then someone must have murdered her. It's obvious. Especially with the date rape drug in her bloodstream. I've seen enough.'

We head back to the car, and I drive the Volvo back up the hill. As we are about to pass the George and Dragon pub, we come across some buildings on the left side of the road.

'Is this the place?' I ask.

'Yes. Just here.'

I brake hard and pull into a gravel courtyard surrounded by brick cottages. A tall, well-dressed man in his fifties comes out to meet us. He greets Ella like she's a long-lost friend.

'So lovely to meet you again, Ella. And you're looking so well. That article you wrote did wonders for us. We're fully booked for two years.'

'That's great, Peter.' Ella turns to me. 'Can I introduce you to Max Fortis?'

'Mr Fortis, so pleased to meet you,' he says. He's jolly, well-spoken, and has a firm grip for such thin wrists.

'Thank you, Peter,' I say. 'You still have the CCTV from the night in question?'

'Yes, Mr Fortis. We keep all CCTV for three months.'

He leads us through a side gate into an ancillary building housing a boiler, cleaning materials, and a small room with a computer and a telephone. It's pretty cramped in here, but we can all fit in. Peter sits on the only chair and fires up the CCTV software. I'm standing shoulder-to-shoulder with Ella, pressed against the wall.

'It was from sometime before midnight that Friday,' I say, 'to about one in the morning on Saturday.'

'Yes, I have it,' says Peter.

I'm resisting the urge to take over the controls as he umms and aahs over what he has to do. He enters some dates and times into the software, and a grid of CCTV camera images appears. He's worked it out without my help.

'Camera eight, Peter,' says Ella, pointing to the screen. 'That's got a good view of the road.'

Camera eight fills the screen, and after a few minutes, a car appears. Its bright headlights bleach the image until it passes. It's a Skoda, an elderly driver. I can see what the problem's going to be straight away. Headlights blank out the registration plates of any passing vehicle.

We continue to watch motorbikes and other unlikely candidates go by. Nothing comes back the other way. Then, at 23:52 hours, there's a white Transit van with blue lettering on the side. It's slow-moving. The driver is looking left and right, peering into the darkness. A large man, his face in shadow, sits beside him. A baseball cap obscures the driver's face, but a glint below the peak reveals glasses, and he has a beard.

'Can you take that back five seconds, Peter?' I say. 'Then move it forward half-speed.'

We watch the van again. The number plate is unreadable, but the lettering on the side is clear.

'*Excellent Impressions Cleaning Portsmouth*,' says Ella. 'Pause it there, Peter.'

She takes a few photos of the hazy, frozen image on her mobile. There are no vehicles behind it or coming the other way. We let the recording play on and then speed it up until we see something happening. At 00:02 hours, the van returns past the camera. The number plate is too dirty to read.

'That's all the traffic between those times,' says Peter.

'Did the police take copies of this?' I say.

'They haven't even looked at it.'

I shake my head and ask Peter to copy the recording onto my memory stick for me. While he and Ella have a catch-up session, I study the still image of the van, but I still can't make out the two men.

After Ella and Peter's little chat, we jump back into the Volvo, and I ease it out of the courtyard.

'That's a good start,' I say.

'I've earned my wages today,' Ella says, smiling.

'You have. But my warning about these people stands. It's office work only unless you're with me.'

'Oh, you mean the *bad people*.' She laughs to herself.

'Yes.' We take a route north of the city to bypass the usual congestion around Chichester. Glancing over to Ella, I remember what Ima and Leon spoke to me about on Friday. 'Have you ever taken self-defence lessons?'

She's surprised by the question. 'No. I usually shout at people or bat my eyelids.'

'This is serious, Ella. Would you know what to do in a fight or if someone threatened you?'

'I've never needed self-defence lessons, Max. I'm a reporter. My interviews don't usually end in fights.'

'Tomorrow, I'll take you to my house. I have a dojo there. It's part of my gym.'

'You have your own personal gym?'

'Yes. Don't you?' I laugh.

'When you say dojo, it's not a euphemism, is it?' she says.

'For what?'

'A pleasure room.' She laughs.

'What the hell is that?'

I brake a little too hard.

'It's just something my mother said. Don't worry.'

I glance at her, raising my eyebrows. 'I won't ask.'

'And do you have a butler?'

'Leon tells people he's my butler. But he's family.'

We pass through Lavant and cut through Hunters Race towards Bosham.

'Do I need to come wearing gym clothes?' she says.

'Not unless you're going to wear them for work.'

'I try not to. You're going to teach me some killer self-defence moves?'

'Not me. My trainer is.'

'Trainer? I am honoured.'

'You don't know how honoured you are.'

CHAPTER 17

The broadband in the office has been activated, and the phones are up and running. As curious locals pass by, they can't resist the temptation to stop and stare. Some kids just off the train from school press their faces against the window, intrigued to get a glimpse of what a private detective looks like.

Ella's researching on the Companies House website and making phone calls. I've put up a large whiteboard on the wall, and now I'm headlining what we have so far.

Excellent Impressions Cleaning, the name on the side of the van, is at the top of the list, alongside Jethro Matisse and Spencer Ryan. Are they connected? What had Mariana discovered in her research for her book? One of the other things I discounted was Grace herself. Had she known about her mother's affair with Spencer? It's all questions and no answers at the moment.

Ella puts down the phone and makes some notes.

'What have you got?' I say.

'Excellent Impressions Cleaning Portsmouth, according to Companies House, isn't a limited company.' Ella pushes back her hair and brings up her notes to her face. 'They have a website saying they're a cleaning service for hotels and guest houses. The phone number on their website is for a mobile, and it says to call for more information. They have lots of positive reviews on Google and Facebook.'

'Any photos of faces?'

'They're stock images of hotel rooms and people—convincing enough. They're contract cleaners. I called them, withholding my number. I spoke to a man called Dennis, asking what area they covered and for a quote to clean a small hotel. He said I was out of their area.'

'I must get you a company mobile,' I say. 'You can't use your own. What about an address for them?'

'They're based in Portsmouth, and it's a Portsmouth post office box.'

'It's worth investigating further. The company could be a cover for something else.'

'Sounds exciting!' Ella sits forward and smiles. 'We need to find a hotel that uses their services.'

'There are loads of hotels in Portsmouth,' I say.

'I looked up some of the people on Facebook who reviewed them. Nothing of any value, which smells of fake accounts.'

'It's a potential lead,' I say.

'I could call some hotels and ask if they know them.'

'We'll put it on the list of tasks. Good job.'

She reviews her notes and looks up with a question. 'What happened to Garcia's computer?'

'I sent it with her journal to a forensics company to see if they can recover the data. That will be with us soon, but the results from the journal came back today.'

'That's the one you found in her study,' she says. 'How will that help us if pages are missing?'

'Look,' I say.

I pick up a notepad and place it on Ella's desk. I draw a silly face with long, spikey hair and write *Ella* underneath it in ballpoint pen.

'Classically trained, I see,' she says.

Tearing the page off the notepad, I screw it up and throw it into a bin.

'I'm hoping there's a writing imprint from the torn-out pages left on the next blank page. They use an electrostatic detection device to show the imprint.'

'If you say so,' she says.

'I do say so.' I grab one of the pencils from her desk and shade over the next page in the notepad. My drawing of Ella reappears. 'The surface of the next sheet of paper is compressed where I pushed down on the pen.'

'Nice,' she says. 'I love secret spy stuff.'

I print two copies of an attachment sent to me by the forensics company and give a copy to Ella. The attachment is a scan of the processed journal. The image is a photographic negative. The page appears dark grey, and the leftover imprint is white. I can make out numbers, letters, and doodles made by Mariana.

'So,' I say. 'I'm assuming Mariana wrote something on here that Spencer didn't want to be found. Perhaps something that implicates him.'

Ella studies the grey sheet of paper. 'What exactly are we looking for?'

'Anything.' I throw her a dry marker pen. 'Have a look, then write up anything you can make out on the board.'

I'm not sure how long we've spent doing this. The page is full of indistinct marks and letters. Ella and I are sitting in silence, staring at the whiteboard. It's a puzzle that's absorbed us for over an hour. We've found the same phrases, and she has made out some I couldn't. Our eyes are tired, so when we've had enough, we walk away and get a coffee.

Ella breaks out the custard creams and keeps glancing at me. I'm ready for a question.

'Why here?' she says.

'Bosham? The building was for sale, and it was close to my house. It's also close to the train station. I figured it would be easier for clients to get to me.'

'Being close to a train station doesn't matter. They'd find you anywhere if they really wanted you.'

'Not everyone has a car.'

Ella shrugs. 'How long have you lived in Bosham?'

'About nine months,' I say.

'Before that?'

'I rented a house in Bognor Regis. Easy to get to London by train.'

'You and trains,' she says with a chuckle. 'Are you a secret trainspotter on the quiet?'

'I can't fool you for long. I usually stayed in London with colleagues during the week and paid them a small rent.'

'Why didn't you move to London?'

She's got that journalist head on again. There's a change in the way she speaks to me—an intensity about it.

'I have commitments here.'

'What commitments? Sorry, I'll shut up. It's second nature.'

I nod. I can understand that. You have to change how you see things as a journalist. You can't take things at face value. It's like being a copper.

'Let's see if we can make any sense of these words,' I say. I realise I'm enjoying working with her. It's helpful to bounce ideas back and forth.

We go back to the whiteboard and look over the notes we've made. Some of them make no sense out of context. We discount the phrases Mariana had experimented with for her writing, like *hollow spaces* and *eerie emptiness*. We found one section at the bottom of the page that was most interesting to us.

'This is it,' says Ella. She's pointing to the text she's written on the board. '*Must stop S. What am I going to tell Grace? Call the police?*'

'Maybe she felt guilty about sleeping with Spencer,' I say. 'Perhaps he threatened her.'

'And what about this? *Dinner with Daniel,*' she says. There's a mobile number next to it, then a date, time, and location. '*Seven-fifteen on Friday, 25th August—Grants, North Street. S knows!*'

'That's the Friday I saw her. The night she was killed. Who was it she met?'

'Daniel?'

'Yes, but who is he?' I say.

'There was a D on that note with the rose we found on the bridge. Perhaps Daniel was an old friend.'

'*S knows*. I assume that's Spencer. I'll visit Grants Restaurant and ask some questions. Why don't you look through any contacts Mariana had on social media with anyone called Daniel.'

'Yep.'

'I won't be long. Don't open the door to anyone.'

'No, Dad.'

At The Cross in Chichester, street traders are pushing their trolleys and selling their greasy hotdogs and doughnuts. Others sell scarves and hats, and there's a man flogging bubble toys, blowing large, sticky bubbles into the air that are hard to dodge as you pass by.

The city centre hasn't been the same since the pandemic. Some of the big-name stores have gone, and more restaurants and coffee shops have opened in their place. I wonder how they survive.

I stop to listen to two buskers—a girl and a boy in their late teens. They're talented, playing guitars and singing Oasis songs with a twist of soul. They make eye contact with each other, and the boy smiles. After dropping some cash into a guitar case, I move on.

I walk past the noisy fruit sellers and continue onto North Street. I remember when I used to do foot patrol here, looking out for shoplifters and stopping people riding bikes. It was so much more straightforward, then. The public loves visible policing.

I find Grants Restaurant, one of Chichester's more upmarket eateries. You can tell by the tall white pillars and the cursive font on the gold lettering above the doors. I step inside, and I'm met by a young woman wearing an ivory-coloured blouse sitting behind a podium with a computer screen built in, ready to check my reservation on the list.

'How can I help you?' she says with a smile. She has the largest blue eyes.

'Good afternoon. My name is Max Fortis. I'm a private detective.'

'Have you booked for afternoon tea?' she says, looking down her list.

'No, I'm enquiring about a dinner reservation a client of mine made back in August.' That's not the whole truth, but it's close enough.

She's confused. 'Sorry, sir?'

'I am making enquiries about an incident involving my client. I believe she ate here on the 25th of August.'

She's uncertain about what to do. 'I'm going to have to talk to my manager.'

'That's what I was hoping.' I give her my cheesiest smile and check her embossed name badge. 'Thank you, Kate.'

She leaves her post, and a short man in a suit returns a few moments later. I have never understood why short men don't like me, and I haven't found one yet who does. This one's not going to be an exception. Vertical envy? The size of my feet?

'How can I help you, sir?' he says, frowning.

Now I check his name badge. 'Good afternoon, Mark.' I explain again who I am and what I'm doing here.

'I can't possibly give you that information, Mr Fortis.' He leans forward like he's about to tell me a secret. 'And there's one very good reason why Mariana Garcia cannot be your client.'

My white lie has bitten me. 'She's dead,' I say, 'but I'm acting for her daughter.'

'I see.' He sniffs. 'You want to know who our guest was with?'

'Yes. Was the table booked in her name or someone else's?'

The manager goes behind the podium and pushes a few

keys on a keyboard. 'August 25th. Ah yes. I see. Hmm.' His little head snaps up. 'I can't tell you.'

'I'm investigating Mariana's death,' I say. 'It would very much help if you would tell me.' I'm trying to remain patient.

'You are a private detective, sir. A civilian like me. You are not a police officer. Now, unless you wish to book a table…'

'Well, as a matter of fact, I do,' I say. 'That's the other reason I've come here.'

He sighs. 'Very well.'

He raises an eyebrow, and Kate returns. He must have magic eyebrows.

'You would like to book a table, Mr Fortis,' she says.

'Yes, please, Kate. Your manager is a barrel of laughs.'

She smiles and remains professional. 'When for?'

'Tonight, sometime after nine.'

'For how many?'

'Twenty. It's an unexpected birthday party. My brother is visiting us for once. It's a miracle, really. We want to celebrate with him.'

'Gosh, twenty?' She blushes and gets a little flustered. 'Goodness!'

'Yes, can you do it?'

'Well, I will need to check with the kitchen, Mr Fortis. Do you mind bearing with me again?'

'No, not at all. Take as long as you like. You've been so helpful already.'

Kate smiles and disappears again, and I slip behind the podium and check the screen. I locate the navigation buttons and look back through their bookings diary until late August. Searching through the names on the list, I find Garcia. The table's not booked in her name, but there's a note about her being a special guest. I grab my phone from my pocket and snap a photo. There's a name on there I recognise.

I hear Kate returning, and I make it back to the other side of the podium with seconds to spare.

'Sorry, Mr Fortis,' says Kate, 'we need more notice for twenty.'

I reach into my wallet, draw out a ten-pound note, and hand it to her.

'Thanks for trying, Kate. Perhaps next time.'

I walk away and study the photo I've taken. Now we have the name of the man Mariana Garcia was with four hours before her death. The phone number is the same as that written in the journal. Did he help Mariana with her research? Was it a romantic date? Was there something he told her that was a problem for Jethro Matisse?

I need to talk to Grace, who's staying in Emsworth, not far from my new office. I'll take Ella with me, as it would be good for them to meet.

Twenty minutes later, I'm back in the office to find Ella with earbuds in, singing along to a track playing on her phone. She has a great voice.

'Daniel Cole,' I say to her.

She's startled and a little embarrassed. She takes out the earbuds.

'Sorry. His name's Daniel Cole?'

'I found his name and phone number on the restaurant's booking list. That's where she was before I saw her on that Friday night outside the law courts.'

'Did he give her the GHB, hoping to take her home and rape her?'

'When I spoke to Mariana, she seemed aware of everything

happening around her. How long does GHB take before it starts working?'

Ella shrugs and types something into Google.

'Lots of words ending with *ation*,' she says and reads one of the search results aloud. 'It says here, fifteen to twenty minutes. It causes disorientation, sudden intoxication, hallucinations, loss of coordination, memory loss, impaired speech, nausea, agitation, and unconsciousness.'

'She didn't display any of those things.'

She taps the end of the pen on her lips and checks her notes. 'What's your plan, and what do you want me to do?'

'Grab your coat and come with me. I've called Grace and have arranged to update her. We can ask her what she knows about Cole.'

I wipe down the whiteboard and grab my keys.

CHAPTER 18

Emsworth is about ten minutes away. As we drive west, I glance at Ella, who seems lost in thought. Her gaze is fixed on the light shimmering on the high tide in Bosham Harbour. She clutches a key fob with a photograph of a man and strokes it with her thumb. Her nails are manicured in dark green with gold sparkles. I force myself to keep my eyes on the road.

'How's your first day going so far?' I say.

She's trying to process what I asked her.

'Oh, yes. Great,' she says. 'I'm enjoying the mystery, but then I remember real people are involved. It must be so hard for Grace to lose her mother like that.'

I agree, and then she turns away again. I'm not sure she heard me. As we arrive in Emsworth, Ella sits up and reads me the address. I take a left beside the Mill Pond, and soon after, we find the house.

The girl Grace is staying with answers the door and takes us to her. She's an old school friend, a nurse, and has been caring for her since the attack by Spencer. She leaves us to speak with Grace alone, busying herself in the kitchen.

I can't help feeling like a fraud. I already know who Daniel Cole is, although I've never met the man. He was a friend whom Mariana and her husband had known for years. I haven't told Ella as it would open up a subject I can't discuss.

Grace is sitting in her friend's conservatory. The early October light is still warm enough to make it pleasant in here, overlooking a stepped garden and Emsworth Mill Pond a little further beyond. Grace doesn't look so great, but the swelling around her eye has gone down, at least.

'It's only cosmetic,' Grace says to Ella. She's seen the concern on her face. 'It's good to meet you.'

'Ella's helping me with your case,' I say. 'It doesn't look like the police are getting any further with it.'

'I know. It's very disappointing.' She picks up a cup of tea and takes a sip through a straw. 'How far have you got?'

I update Grace about the CCTV from the holiday lets near Houghton Bridge and the information from her mother's journal.

'Does the name Daniel Cole mean anything to you?' asks Ella.

'He was an old friend of my father's,' says Grace. 'My mother used to talk about him, and he would often visit.' She gazes into the distance like she's trying to remember something. 'He took us to a park once. I was young. He was kind and drove a nice car. I think he was in the army or something like that. That's all I remember about him.'

'Your mother had a meal with him at a restaurant the night she was killed,' I say.

'Really? She didn't tell me she was meeting him.'

'So they maintained their friendship after your father died?'

'She never spoke about him after that.'

'What can you remember about that time?' asks Ella.

'It wasn't that long ago. Six years. She grieved publicly, but privately, I think she was relieved. He wasn't good to her.'

'We have a phone number for Daniel Cole,' I say. 'Are you okay if we contact him? It's important.'

'Yes, sure. He has nothing to do with me.'

'Do you mind me asking you about Spencer?' I say.

'Go on.'

'When did you meet him?'

'It was summer last year. I was with my mother in Harrogate. A crime writers' weekend. He was delivering a car for someone in the town and decided to look around the convention. He saw us and started talking to us. He seemed charming then. Very different from the person you saw.'

'I can't imagine him reading crime fiction,' I say. 'I can't imagine him reading anything if I'm honest.'

'He never spoke about books after that. He took me out on a few dates. He was good-looking, polite, and kind. He liked my mother... well, I can guess how much he was into her now.'

There's an awkward silence.

'You're brave, Grace,' says Ella. She takes her hand. 'You're going to get through this, and you're going to be stronger for it.'

That's something I can't do with female clients. I'm glad Ella is with me. I would have liked to have said the same thing.

We leave a few minutes later and head back to the office in Bosham. Ella is still quiet, staring out the window and twirling her red hair with her finger.

'Are you okay?' I ask.

She turns with a smile and an intake of breath. 'Yes, sure. I don't get monsters like Spencer Ryan. He was seeking Mariana from the start.'

'Precisely,' I say. 'That's why we need to talk to him, too.'

'How are you going to do that? You beat the crap out of him, by all accounts.'

'Do you blame me?'

'I would have joined in.'

We're approaching the roundabout near the office. 'I'll drop you off. Can you try calling Daniel Cole? See if he will speak to us.'

'Yes, sure,' she says. 'Where are you going?'

'I'm going to the hospital to talk to Spencer—it's worth a try.'

I pull up outside the office and check that she has her key. She goes to get out of the car.

'Ella?' She stops and smiles. I hesitate and want to ask her what's wrong, but it's not my place. 'I appreciate what you've done today. You can chill out this evening.'

'Thanks. I'm not sure I'm going to chill, but I'll open a bottle of wine. Do you ever stop to think about how much you'd love to share what happened today with someone? My mother will be interested, of course, but it will end with a lecture about something. I miss my husband, Max. He was my best friend. I used to tell him everything.'

I nod. 'I can understand that.'

'Can you?'

'Yes, but I'm lucky now. I have two people at home who are great listeners. They're looking forward to meeting you tomorrow.'

'It's your trainer I'm most scared of,' says Ella.

'Good, so you should be. I'd best get on. If I'm not back

before you go, lock up, and I'll see you tomorrow—my house for fun and games.'

St Richard's Hospital appears to be busy with the police this afternoon. Three marked cars and a crime scene investigator van are in front of Reception. The CSI van is the thing I'm puzzled by the most.

There's no point in me asking where Spencer Ryan is at Reception. It may raise eyebrows. He either has a police guard, or they've bailed him until he's recovered. My guess is the maxillofacial surgery ward—Walderton. He would need his face rebuilt after what I did to him. I make my way through to the other side of the hospital. It's a fair walk through the long, straight corridors of glossy floors and gentle slopes—I should have used the other car park. As I'm passing by, I try the Emergency Floor, checking the names on the whiteboard. He was in there, but not now. One of the nurses tells me where he's been moved to, and I was right.

Approaching the maxillofacial ward, I stop when I see a line of police tape and a police officer standing as scene guard. She's on her mobile and doesn't see me approaching.

'What's happened?' I ask. 'I'm visiting a friend on the ward.'

'There's been an incident, sir,' she says.

'I can see that. What?'

'The ward will be open soon. It's only the toilet we've sealed off.'

A CSI is stepping out of a doorway.

'Someone's been murdered,' I say. 'Is DC Bates working today?'

'I can't say, sir,' she says.

Then I spot him. He's wearing protective clothing and talking on his mobile. I wait behind the tape until he sees me. He's surprised and walks towards me, looking around him as if he doesn't want to be seen with me. He ducks under the crime scene tape and signs out on the scene log.

'Over here,' he says, to take me away from the crime scene and hide around the corner.

'What's happened, Gary?'

'Spencer Ryan's dead. He was in the toilet, and someone shot him.'

'When?'

'Shortly after ten o'clock this morning. Mate, you're going to need an alibi. I'm telling you now. I know this wasn't you, but the DS wants to talk to you. He's popped out. I can't be seen talking to you. He's desperate to pin something on you. I don't know what's got into him. He's even willing to fit you up.'

'I don't do pest control with guns,' I say. 'I was in Houghton. Looking at CCTV.'

'What CCTV?'

'The one we both missed. There was a van, Gary. On the bridge.'

'Shit! Really?' We can hear people talking close by. He scans the corridor. 'Look, I've got to go. Go home, mate. Don't let DS Chambers see you. Why are you here, anyway?'

'I wanted to talk to Spencer.'

'Are you crazy? Did you realise how that would look?'

'I had a few questions for him. This is a gangland killing, Gary.'

He agrees. 'You'd better get out of here. Please, Max.' Then he walks away and signs back into the crime scene.

I don't stay. I'm not in the mood to argue with that DS again. I walk back the way I came and send a text message to Ella about what's happened. She doesn't reply. She's probably gone home.

Phil Marlowe and Frank Pinto sit at the bar, watching the evening's entertainment. The air is hot, thick, and pounding. Frank downs another shot and sniggers at the men making fools of themselves at the front of the stage.

'I hate having to let staff go,' says Marlowe as an aside. 'He's disappointed me time and time again. I couldn't trust him anymore.'

'Don't feel bad about it, boss,' says Pinto. 'Don't let these people bother you. He had it coming.'

Marlowe turns away from the red and purple stage lights. The music is getting louder. 'You're right, Frank,' he says. 'I feel bad because I care too much. I inherited my mother's genes. My father was an evil shit. I'm glad I didn't take after him.'

'Mikita did you proud this morning, boss.'

'Yes, he did. No fuss, no mess. And I forgot to tell you that Mikita has some information about an old friend of ours. Judas says he wants to make amends for his sins.'

'Cole? I thought he was long gone,' says Pinto. 'He's a dangerous son of a bitch. We can't trust him.'

'Well, you know what my family thought of him. He's got someone coming to see him on Wednesday. A reporter. They want to do a story about Miri.'

'How did the reporter make the connection between Cole and Mariana?'

'Think about it, Frank. Who do you think she's working for?'

'Shit! Fortis?'

'Cole is dangerous,' says Marlowe. 'Who knows what he'll say. It makes me so sad, considering our history together. He was one of my dearest friends until he betrayed me.'

'Was it you who removed his ear?'

'We had a disagreement. I defended my honour, Frank. You would have done the same. He had trouble wearing sunglasses after that.' Marlowe laughs. 'I believe he wears a prosthetic one nowadays—shame. Never came near my family again. *Ear* today, gone tomorrow.'

'We can kill two birds with one stone,' says Pinto. He lifts his hand to the bar staff for another shot. 'I'll apply some persuasion—encourage him in his repentance.'

'Thanks, Frank. Hopefully, that will just leave the one sinner to deal with.'

There's a loud cheer, and a man has climbed up on the stage, making a grab for the girls. They are running around, trying to get away from him. He's stretching out his arms with handfuls of cash for them.

'Excuse me for a moment, boss,' says Pinto.

He pushes his way to the stage, dragging the man and his cash backwards with one hand. Pinto removes him through a side door, relieves him of his money, and kicks him onto the street. Pinto returns laughing and shows Marlowe the money.

'Good job, Frank,' says Marlowe, raising a glass.

'Don't worry about Cole, boss,' says Pinto. 'He won't say anything to anyone.'

The minibus is here, and the evening drizzle falls in streaks across its headlights. The factory door unlocks with a rusty screech. Dennis and a woman Janie doesn't know take them one at a time into the minibus. There are five of them working tonight. Four of them take their seats, leaving one behind, Janie's Albanian friend. She's staying put, refusing to move. She stands in her coat, shrugging off Dennis's fat hands. He shoves her forward.

'Get on!' he shouts.

There's no point yelling at her, thinks Janie. She doesn't speak English.

'Get on!' Dennis raises his hand to strike her.

The girl puts her head down and walks towards the minibus. She looks up at Janie, and their eyes meet. At that moment, Janie sees a look that says goodbye. Then the girl runs. She passes the minibus and heads out onto the bleak industrial estate. She runs like a caged animal, freed from its captors, into a forest of steel and concrete, wire cages, piles of tyres, and broken cars. She hesitates, deciding which way to go. The woman runs after her. Janie sits forward, willing her friend on, twisting and turning in her chair to get a better view. Her friend runs again, and soon Janie loses her in the darkness.

There's no sound but the rain drumming on the minibus's roof and windows. The air tastes of steel and grease. Darkness fills the forest beyond the headlights. Janie can't bear not knowing.

Dennis blocks the open minibus door with his large body, folding his arms. He's peering out into the shadows ahead of him.

Where would she go, thinks Janie? A village, a kind family, a good mother? Anywhere but here. Janie knows the sea is near. There could be a boat that will take her friend away. May the spirits light her way home.

Then, a dark shape appears. It's heading towards them. It's the woman. She's alone. Her friend has gone. Janie smiles, and the girls shriek with delight. She made it. She's escaped!

The woman stops beside the minibus. She's out of breath, gasping for air. She doubles over to catch her breath. Rain and sweat drip off her.

'How are we going to explain this?' says Dennis.

The woman stands upright again and smiles. 'Get a bag. You're going to have to help me. I can't lift her on my own.'

CHAPTER 19

Ella stops her Audi in front of the tall iron gates and finds a security buzzer on one of the posts. She smiles at the camera. Despite what Max told her, she's wearing joggers, a T-shirt, and trainers.

The small speaker crackles, and someone speaks.

'It's Ella Munro for Max.'

The gates open without a sound, and she returns to her car and parks it on the edge of the pea-shingle driveway. She slings her bag over her shoulder and walks towards the front door, turning as she takes in the curved walls and the expensive-looking glass you can't see through from the outside. A manicured lawn runs in a semi-circle around the driveway, and a crescent of flower borders cleared for autumn. The house screams money and luxury.

The door opens, and Max is there to greet her. 'Morning. Coffee?'

'No, I'm fine—and speechless. This place!'

'But you've seen it before,' says Max.

'Not this close.'

'Come in.'

'Thanks.'

She studies him momentarily. He's in a pair of faded jeans and a tight T-shirt. If this is a way to show her what great shape he's in, then it's working. She doesn't want to let him know. She's happy to look and enjoy. He must be somewhere between six-two and six-four. He probably spends hours in the gym, looking at those broad shoulders and biceps. He's well-groomed, with trimmed black stubble that matches his arched eyebrows and thick hair. Handsome, his brown eyes reveal strength and intelligence. They hide something, too. He only lets people know what he wants them to know. She reckons he's a man of many secrets.

'Come through to the kitchen,' he says. 'I want to introduce you to my family.'

The hallway is tall and bright in polished stone, opening onto a wide, curved staircase. Coming off the hallway are several spacious rooms with high ceilings. A door is open to a library packed full of books in dark wood shelving, and another to a dining room overlooking a vast lawn lined with trees and borders. She can see the harbour water through a gap in the trees beside an old-fashioned boathouse on the shore.

She comes to the kitchen and tries not to let her jaw drop. She loves the space and the clean lines that give it an Art Deco feel. Sitting at the breakfast bar is a couple in their sixties. Both are slim and tall, with black hair streaked with lines of grey. The man is handsome, with olive skin, a short salt-and-pepper beard, and bright blue eyes. He's wearing a pair of reading glasses and peering over the top of a newspaper. The woman is elegant, like a ballerina, and has tied her hair back into a ponytail. Her skin is soft, and she has the same Mediterranean complexion as the man. Her smile is broad, and her deep brown eyes are welcoming.

'This is Ima and Leon,' says Max. 'My family.'

Leon offers a welcoming smile. 'He pays us to like him.'

The woman laughs, so Ella knows it's safe to laugh, too.

'Lovely to meet you,' says the woman. Ella detects an accent in both of their voices. 'Leon and I are married. So, I'm his boss.'

'Of course,' says Ella. 'Ima is a lovely name.'

'Thank you.' She chuckles to herself. 'Call me Shira. Everyone, apart from Max, calls me Shira. That's the name my father and mother gave me.'

'Shira it is then,' says Ella.

She smiles and thinks these are the kind of people she could easily get to like. There's a dignity, warmth, and gentleness about them.

'I'm glad to see you're not in your gym gear,' says Max with more than a hint of sarcasm.

'I'm here to learn some self-defence,' Ella tells Shira. 'He's going to let me loose on his personal trainer.'

'Gosh, what an honour!' says Leon. 'That's an experience you'll never forget.'

'I'll take you through to the dojo,' says Max. 'I've set everything up for your lesson.'

Ella feels a twinge of nervous excitement and follows Max back through the house.

'How do you not want to stay here all day? It's a lovely house.'

'My uncle had three homes. This one, one in Paris, and one in the Canary Islands. I'm in the process of selling the other two.'

'Paris! God, Max! Why sell a house in Paris? It's my favourite city in the world.'

'I don't live in Paris. I'm considering buying a cottage in Scotland, but I don't want to take a home away from a community. Holiday homes can be a curse like that.'

'A man of principle, too.'

'It's about time I had some principles,' he says.

As they pass the one-way windows, they both turn to see two men in suits stepping out of a white BMW parked outside the front gates. They press the gate buzzer.

Ella stops and wonders if one of them is her new trainer.

'Is there only one trainer?' she asks Max.

'Yes. Only one,' he says, puzzled.

He pushes a double door to enter a gymnasium that is larger than Ella's mother's house. Blue padded mats cover part of the floor, separated by thin, moveable screens hanging from the ceiling.

'Welcome to my pleasure room,' he says with a wink. 'Would you mind waiting in here for a moment? I'll see what those men want.'

'Sure.'

Max leaves the gym, and Ella takes the opportunity to sneak a look around. Some angry-looking orange dummies are against the walls, designed to be punched and kicked. She laughs at how they resemble a man she once knew before she met Simon. What would Simon have made of all of this? She imagines him standing in the corner, laughing at her.

'Go on, girl!' he'd say. 'Make the most of it.'

There are shelves of free weights, a line of running machines, bikes, and a cross-trainer in front of large projection screens. She climbs onto the cross-trainer and pulls on the levers, almost losing her balance and stumbling as she comes off. She moves to the padded mat area and bounces on the mats, pretending to punch and kick someone.

'Interesting moves, Ella,' says Shira.

Ella blushes. 'Sorry. I was playing.'

'Shall we start?'

Ella sees Shira is now wearing jogging bottoms and a loose T-shirt.

'You're the trainer?'

'That's me,' says Shira. 'Don't worry. I've done it before.'

'Sorry! I didn't mean to be rude.'

'I used to get that reaction all the time from the soldiers.'

'You trained soldiers?'

'I was in the IDF, the Israel Defense Forces—Sayeret Matkal, the General Staff Reconnaissance Unit. I taught a self-defence method called Krav Maga. That's what you are learning the basics of today.'

Ella feels stupid. 'I've not done anything like this before.'

'It's okay. I hadn't before I started. Krav Maga means contact combat. It's for self-defence in the real world, using your instinctive reactions to help you. You're going to work hard today. And you will want to come back for more, I promise.'

'Will I?' says Ella.

'Yes, because you will understand this will save your life one day.'

The detectives walk into the house with a confident swagger. Their faces are grim, and they're wearing sharp, grey suits. They don't look like Chichester detectives. I lead them into the reception room that overlooks the rear garden. It's my favourite space inside the house. It's tranquil here, and you can hear the wind in the trees and the water against the shoreline. The detectives sit opposite me on a sofa. The senior officer is older than me, and his eyes give away years of experience.

'I'm Detective Inspector Reeves. This is Detective Constable Masters.' He tells me they've come from Brighton, sent by the senior investigating officer for the Garcia murder case. So, they have sidestepped DS Chambers on this one.

'Is this about Spencer Ryan?' I say.

'That's partly correct, Mr Fortis,' says DI Reeves.

'Where's DS Chambers?'

'He's tied up with other things. This investigation has grown somewhat now. We're trying to see what the connection is with the Garcia case. We know your background, Mr Fortis. Commander Lacey from the Met has been in contact with us.'

'Okay. So, why are you talking to me?'

'This isn't an interview. I work for the Professional Compliance Intelligence Division.'

'That's like Professional Standards on steroids,' I say.

Reeves smiles. 'I've heard that description before. It's not inaccurate. We're coming to you off the record, as they say. The SIO for the Garcia case has asked me to look into DS Chambers's involvement and his methods. We've been made aware of certain quality issues. DS Chambers doesn't know we are doing this, and I trust you won't say anything about this conversation to him.'

Someone has reported Chambers's antics—probably Gary.

'Quality issues?' I say. 'Does that include him trying to pin Garcia's murder on me?'

'Yes, most of it is about you. We've found that someone has been tampering with the continuity of evidence. The Scenes of Crime Manager raised concerns about a sample DS

Chambers wanted testing. Then one of his team reported an incident of threats against you.'

'Chambers isn't doing this on his own. Someone's compromised him.'

'That's our conclusion and why we are here. We want Chambers to lead us to whoever is using him.'

'Okay. How can I help?'

'You can help by doing nothing for the moment regarding DS Chambers. Let him bumble his way through this investigation. We know you are also trying to find Mariana Garcia's murderer. Under the circumstances, we would usually ask you to stop. But after talking to Commander Lacey, she's of the opinion your work should continue.'

'Is she? I am honoured.'

The men's faces are still set like stone. It must be hard to keep that going for so long. I wonder what they do for fun on the weekends?

'One hypothesis,' says DI Reeves, 'is there is a connection to an organised crime gang. And just so you know, we are aware of Mariana Garcia's past.'

'Spencer Ryan was subject to a hit,' I say.

'No doubt,' says Reeves. 'You are on the same track as us in your investigation. If you come across anything that leads you to identify who's running this gang, then we would like you to speak with us or your old unit chief, Commander Lacey. And most importantly, we want you to share it with DS Chambers.'

I laugh. 'You want to flush him out? See who he goes running to?'

'Precisely. He will warn someone that you are onto him.'

I like the plan, and of course, I will agree with it. But I'm also cautious. Who am I working for here? Does this put Grace or Gary in danger?

'What evidence has he tampered with?'

'Mariana's phone. He tried to stop the forensic analysis. He also obtained some intimate body samples of yours and claimed the pathology team found them inside Mariana's underwear.'

'Shit! I'm not sure where he would have got intimate samples from.'

'That's not our concern at the moment,' says DI Reeves.

That's a relief.

'What about her phone messages?'

'Digital Forensics is re-examining the mobile. We have asked them to copy the results to DC Gary Bates. He's aware of our involvement. He was the one who highlighted the original concerns to the SIO.'

Reeves pulls out his mobile phone and finds something he wants to show me. 'DC Bates sent us a WhatsApp message he received from Chambers. It underlines his precarious state of mind.' Reeves finds some reading glasses in his jacket and reads the message to me. '*Look at him! Look at his place. Like he's some supercop, flashing his biceps. I bet he had it handed to him on a plate all his life. Born into money. Meanwhile, people like me have to work hard, scrimp and save for everything, only to be screwed over by bent coppers like him! I'm going to find something on Fortis, even if I have to serve it up myself.*'

'Nice,' I say. 'I sense a bit of resentment there.' Reeves's facade slips as he chuckles a little and then turns serious again. I shrug. 'I feel sorry for the guy. He doesn't get me at all.'

'You don't have to defend yourself to me, Mr Fortis,' says Reeves.

'No. I want to say it. I know how this place looks, but none of it is real. None of it is me. My mother and father were poor. We lived abroad for most of my childhood. Didn't have a choice, moving from city to city. My mother did the best for us. The Taliban killed my father in Afghanistan soon after the Twin Towers attack in New York. He was an elite soldier. This place belonged to my uncle, and I inherited it recently. I didn't earn it or work for it. But I did work frigging hard to achieve what I achieved, DI Reeves. I didn't want my uncle's money. But I thought I could use it to do some good.'

'I'm aware of some of your story, Mr Fortis, and of those you live with, too. And I know you are more than capable of discovering Chambers's motives and the person he is leaking information to.'

'Thank you, DI Reeves.'

The DI and his quiet colleague stand. 'Good luck with your investigation. You won't hear from me again, as we want to limit our contact with you. We can't have DS Chambers finding out we are investigating him.'

Leon appears. 'I'll show you to the door,' he says to the DI.

Leon finds me in the rear reception room, staring out the window, lost in thought. 'Is everything okay?' he asks.

'I'm going to contact The Controller,' I say. 'I need some help with this. I'll also check if DI Reeves is who he says he is, and I need her to get back to me about Jethro Matisse.'

'You need to be careful of them all. Everyone has their own agenda.'

I know Leon is right. 'I will.'

'They'll want you to work for them again.'

'I've already agreed I'll help them occasionally, but that's it, nothing more. The new controller's name is Lacey. Strange woman, but has a lot of influence.'

We hear footsteps. Ima comes in as cool as a cucumber. She smiles at us and winks. Then comes Ella. She's not walking too well at all. Her hair is loose and messy, and her face is glowing. She staggers in and collapses on a sofa, eyes up at the ceiling.

'Help! I can't move,' she says.

'How's she doing?' I ask Ima.

'She needs one of my pick-you-ups,' says Ima.

'Max is in contact with The Controller again,' says Leon.

I feel like he's snitched on me.

'Max!' says Ima. 'You said you wouldn't go back there.'

'I know,' I say. 'But I've thought about it. I'm going to need some intel on this case. This could benefit them and me. Don't worry. I'm not returning as an agent. It's symbiosis.'

'I hope this new controller is nothing like the last one. Why can't they leave you alone?'

'Who is this controller you're talking about?' says Ella.

'Ah,' says Leon. 'That's a good question.'

We all head to the kitchen and sit together at the breakfast bar. Ella enjoys the promised revitalising drink from Ima, followed by a hot, smoky chicken salad with a spicy peanut dipping sauce. Ella has asked for the recipe, but it's Ima's secret, and she is good at keeping secrets—she's a professional.

'This tastes so good, Shira!' Ima smiles, and Ella is talking with her mouth full. 'I can't believe I hurt so much.' She's animated after her morning's training. 'Some things Shira taught me are so simple. Things I'd never thought of before.' She puts her hand to her mouth. 'Sorry, Max. I'm gabbling.'

'It's okay. And it's important. If you're willing to learn, I'm sure Ima will be happy to teach you more.'

'Really? This is amazing! Ima, Shira is amazing.'

'Thank you, Ella,' says Ima. 'You are one of my most appreciative students ever. Max wasn't so appreciative all those years ago.'

'You trained Max?' asks Ella.

'Of course she did,' I say, 'and she enjoyed whooping my backside—day in, day out.'

'Not so easy now,' says Ima.

Ella puts down her fork, and I can tell she has a lot of questions. I think she's realized there's a lot more to us than first appears. There's only so much I can say, but I have to say something if she's going to work with me.

'You want to know who The Controller is,' I say and take a breath. 'The Official Secrets Act covers what I'm about to say to you. So, you have been warned, and I have witnesses.'

'You sound like my old college lecturer,' says Ella.

Ima and Leon are mocking me with grim faces and nodding.

'Okay,' I say. 'After I trained officers in Protection Command—'

'What's that?'

'They provide close protection for the Royals, the Prime Minister, and others with critical jobs. After that, I was seconded to the Met's Counter Terrorism Command and worked closely with MI5 on counter-espionage. I investigated compromised government officials and infiltrated terrorist cells. Ima and Leon worked in this unit, too. Even my uncle got himself enlisted in spying for the UK.'

'A real family affair,' says Ella.

'Yes, you could say that. However, my wife wasn't

involved. For various reasons, foreign agents targeted Ima and Leon, and it became dangerous for them. When my uncle retired, they came and lived with him here for safety. He had this place fortified.'

'But you stayed in the job.'

'I did,' I say. 'To answer your question, the Unit Commander runs my old unit. We call them controllers—it's a long story. They're sometimes from the military, sometimes from the police. The current controller is a woman called Janice Lacey. She's a Met Police commander.'

'Sounds very cloak and dagger.'

'It was. Our work meant we could act above the law. It was controversial, but we had to sometimes. Some people are so dangerous to this country that they must be neutralized or made to disappear.'

'That sounds terrifying,' says Ella.

'It makes a whole lot of paperwork. It's a responsibility that breaks some people, and it would be easy to be unaccountable for our actions. But Ima and Leon ensured that didn't happen.'

Ella mulls that information over for a moment. 'That's quite a background. And now you're a private detective.'

'I'm glad to be out of it.'

'That's a considerable career change. Okay, Mr Private Detective,' she says, 'what do we do now?'

'That's easy. I'm going to find Daniel Cole and question him. His last known address was in Portsmouth.'

'He's in Bordon, Hampshire,' says Ella.

'What? You've found him?'

'Sorry, I meant to say, but I got caught up with Shira. I called that number last night and told him what had happened to Mariana. He already knew. It was Cole who put that rose on the bridge. There was a lot he wanted to tell me, but he was extremely cautious about speaking over the phone. He said he knew Matisse and wanted to get it off his chest before it was too late.'

'That's good, Ella.'

'I think I should speak to him,' she says. 'He's anxious about being found and wouldn't talk to just anyone. He trusts me. I told him we were trying to find out who killed his friend, and he told me he knew who killed her.'

'Is that what he said? Did he tell you?'

'No. He wanted to talk to me in person.'

'Why is he in Bordon?'

'He was stationed there once in the army,' she says. 'He's going to be moving again next week—Scotland. So we have to be quick.'

'I can meet with him tomorrow,' I say.

'He doesn't want to meet you. Only me. He trusts me.'

'I don't like it.'

'I can kill a man just by blinking at him now. I'll be fine.'

'That's in the last lesson,' says Ima.

'Well, I'll be close by, then,' I say. 'That's non-negotiable.'

'He won't talk if he thinks I've broken my promise.'

'You promised him?'

'It's the only way he'd talk to me! Come on, Max. I'm a journalist. I know these things.'

I glance at Leon and shake my head. She's taken this out of my control, so I will have to trust her.

'It's no good looking at me, Max,' he says. 'You hired her.'

'Okay, fine. But remember this, Ella. They've killed Spencer Ryan and Mariana Garcia. This looks more and more like an organised crime gang.'

Ella raises an eyebrow at me. 'I suppose if you're hiding somewhere nearby, that will be okay.'

'Don't forget, if things start going crazy, you wanted this, Ella,' I say.

'I do want this. And now I'm ready to continue my lesson.'

Ima smiles. 'Good girl. It's knives next.'

CHAPTER 20

Ella is on her way to meet Daniel Cole in Bordon, and Max is taking her, acting as her backup in case things get hairy. He drives them in his Volvo for the thirty-minute journey north along the A3, cutting through the Downs. They turn off and take a left towards Bordon, once an army town surrounded by firing ranges. Those firing ranges are still there, but the rest of Bordon is now a hub of rapid development and new-build houses.

Ella's trying not to moan about her aches and pains after yesterday's training. In her head, she's been going through the moves she learned from Shira, all based on her instinctive reactions to danger—her flinch reflex. She did a lot of flinching yesterday.

Shira is an enigma. She had told Ella she was a gymnast in her teens, and Ella can still see it in the way she moves. She has a scar along her arm and a tattoo written in Hebrew. There's an intriguing story there that's waiting to be told one day. And Ella wants to know why Max calls her Ima, but it's too soon to ask. She has another burning question she wants to ask him first, and as they pass the firing ranges, Ella glances at Max and plucks up the courage.

'Yesterday,' she says, 'you mentioned your wife. Tell me to keep my nose out, but what happened to her? She clearly doesn't live with you anymore.'

'Keep your nose out,' he says. But then he glances at her and smiles.

'Sorry.'

'It's okay. I wasn't serious.' Max takes a breath. 'I don't want to read any of this in one of your articles.'

'Of course.'

'Before I left the job, there was a serious data breach. Some idiot left a backup device on a train. It had many agents' encrypted contact details stored on it. And the details of their families.'

'I think I remember something about that,' says Ella, briefly touching his arm. 'It hit the news headlines.'

'It did—but only some of it.' Max takes a turning off a peanut-shaped roundabout into Bordon. 'The person who found the lost device sold it to a newspaper. Except, unknown to them, it wasn't a newspaper. It was a foreign agent they sold it to. It's not hard to guess which country that was. They decrypted the contents of the data. Before we realised it, they'd set about assassinating our people. Alarm bells rang everywhere.'

'Shit! No wonder they kept this secret.'

'Yes, exactly,' he says. 'One evening nine months ago, they targeted me. There was a warning, but it came too late for my uncle and Carrie, my wife. It should have been me. Someone had coated the front door handle of our house with a nerve agent. We'd been out for the evening with my uncle and invited him back home for a nightcap. My phone rang, and I took the call in the car while Carrie and my uncle went inside. The Controller at the time called to warn me, but I was too late. It didn't kill Carrie, but it put her in a coma, and she hasn't woken up since. My uncle died soon afterwards at home. It was a slow and painful death. Ima and Leon looked after him.'

Ella slowly shakes her head. 'I'm so sorry. That's awful. I can't imagine how that made you feel.'

Max shrugs. 'I inherited my uncle's home and fortune, and I lost interest in my work and left. The Job wouldn't leave me alone. They demanded an explanation why I'd resigned.'

'It was obvious, surely?' says Ella.

'Simple things like that aren't obvious to some,' he says. 'Let's just say we had a falling out. The previous controller lost his job because of it.'

'I remember seeing a photo of your uncle in a newspaper. He was famous in his day, but I'm not sure anyone would remember him now.'

'Probably for the best. We weren't particularly close.'

'But your poor wife. Will Carrie ever wake up?' asks Ella.

Max shrugs. 'The doctors say it's unlikely. They're keeping her alive and making her comfortable, but they tell me her body could start shutting down at any moment. Could be months or a year.'

Max stops at a garage going into Bordon. They've parked in the customer parking area to finalise a plan before going to Cole's flat.

Ella goes to step out of the Volvo, but every muscle has seized. She has bruises, too—trophies awarded by Shira. She makes it out and stretches to relieve the tightness, and Max gets out with her and moves around to her side of the car.

'Let's go through this,' he says.

Ella nods. 'If it makes you feel better.'

'It does.'

Max talks through with her what she's going to ask Cole, but she won't be told how to get the information out of him. She's good at her job and makes sure Max knows it, too.

'Remember,' says Max, 'if things get tricky, just leave. Don't hesitate.'

'Yes, boss,' she says.

'You don't have your pepper spray now, so look after yourself.'

'You sound like my mother.'

'Did your mother buy you that pepper spray?'

After they finish their briefing, they continue their journey. Ascending a hill, they take a right at a roundabout onto Chalet Hill. The road descends past a small parade of shops on the right. Max parks his Volvo out of sight of Cole's flat.

Ella puts on her reporter's lanyard, and Max rolls his eyes.

'That's why he's talking to you, is it? He thinks you're a journalist?'

'I *am* a journalist!'

Ella leaves Max behind. She realises he's like her—a control freak. She walks twenty yards towards a block of red-brick flats and presses the buzzer for a flat on the second floor. There's no reply, but she hears the echo of a door opening from inside. Then the front door opens.

Standing before her is an enormous man—over six feet tall. He's in his late forties, haggard-looking, bald, with a goatee. He's wearing a vest top, accentuating his tattooed, bull-like arms. Yet this behemoth of a man has bright, intelligent eyes. He's the worst kind of thug, thinks Ella. An intelligent thug. His eyes probe Ella as soon as he sees her. He's measuring her, evaluating her, looking behind her. He waits for Ella to speak first.

'I'm Ella,' she says.

'Where's your car?' He's suspicious.

'By the shops.'

He grunts. 'Come in.'

He punches a timed light switch and leads the way up a musty-smelling stairwell until they reach his flat. The light switches off as he pushes the door open. The stench of stale smoke and bleach hits the back of Ella's throat. The flat reeks of it. She will reek of it, too, by the time she leaves.

Cole points to an empty chair in the front room. It's the only one that's not broken. It's messy in here. The walls are smeared, stains mark the thin carpet, and patches of black mould thrive above the windows and in the corners of the room. He has a huge TV, a pile of fishing magazines on the table, and wet clothes drying over radiators.

'I'm devastated, Ella,' he says at last. 'Mariana had a good spirit.' Those words didn't seem to fit him. 'She was kind. I had no idea she felt so desperate. I thought Fortis was coming with you.'

'That's not what you wanted, Mr Cole.'

'Yes, I'm sorry. I'm out of sorts. I forgot.'

Ella smiles. 'So, you were close to Mariana?'

'Very good friends. She was a writer like you.'

'I don't write fiction.'

He shrugs and looks around at the mess everywhere. 'How did you make the connection to me?'

'Mariana's daughter told us about you. And you booked a table at the restaurant.'

'What restaurant?'

'Grants, in Chichester. Don't you remember?'

'Of course I do!' he snaps. 'What do you want to know?'

'I'm writing an article on Mariana.'

'For what reason?' His blue eyes narrow.

'But we discussed all this on the phone, Mr Cole. The police believe Mariana's death was suicide. I told you I'm looking into whether someone murdered her. Then you said you knew who it was.'

'I think the police know better than you, my love. Anyway, who would want to murder Mariana?'

'I hoped you were going to tell me. We know the evidence is doubtful.'

'Is it?'

'Yes, it is, actually.' Ella can feel her hackles rising. Cole was far more helpful on the phone. 'Her agent said she was researching a new crime novel when she… died.'

'And?'

'Did she talk to you about her research?'

'She asked for my opinions about things.'

Ella brings out a notepad. 'Have you read any of her novels?'

'Not interested in novels, to be honest. Fishing is my thing.'

'Good fishing in Scotland?'

'Scotland?' He's looking out of the window, drumming his fingers. 'Look, I want to talk to Fortis.'

'It's just me, Mr Cole. That's all you're getting today. You told me you would be happy to talk to me. Have you changed your mind?'

He grunts and checks his watch. 'Well, I'm not so sure now. This isn't easy for me.'

Ella sighs in frustration. 'You said you would talk to me about Jethro Matisse.'

He sits forward, and his chair creaks. 'I don't think I did. I've never heard of him.'

'Has someone got to you, Mr Cole? I protect all my sources. No matter what they tell me. So, go ahead and tell me if you want to.'

———

I'm still waiting. Ella's been with Cole for half an hour, and I'm getting edgy. I've been watching the passing traffic driving up and down the hill. Kids bunking off school early smoke on a wall opposite me.

I keep a close eye on a tatty white transit as it drifts past. Three men get out and unload boxes at a kebab shop. A pickup has driven by twice now. Where is she?

Then I see her. She's walking with her head down, sniffing her top. Cole must be a smoker. Judging by the scowl, she's not happy.

'I stink,' she says as she gets in. And she does.

As soon as she's buckled up, I start the engine and slip the gearstick into drive.

I glance at her. 'How was it?'

She growls in frustration. 'A waste of bloody time! Absolutely nothing.' Ella sighs, exasperated.

'What do you mean, nothing?'

'Cole told me he and Mariana met to catch up. It was all general. No names, no details. He was terse and defensive. He now says he's never heard of Jethro Matisse! Someone must have got to him, Max. Warned him against talking to me. It's like he wasn't the same man I spoke to on the phone. And he was huge! Built like an ox. Cole's nothing like I thought he would be. I can't imagine anyone frightening him.'

My irritation grows. 'How can he give you nothing? He was one of the last leads we had!'

'He didn't have anything, Max! He's a lowlife shitbag. I don't know what Mariana saw in him. Mind you, she went for Spencer Ryan.'

'Are you telling me we've wasted our time?'

'Eliminated a line of enquiry, I call it,' she says. 'There's no point having a go at me.'

I pull over the car at a bus stop. 'I should go back and talk to him.'

Ella disagrees. 'No, Max! It's not worth it.'

'People have died, Ella! I'll beat it out of him if I have to.'

'Will you? He's about twice the size of you! And if that's how you get information out of people, you can do it on your own. I'm as frustrated as you are.'

I drive off again. Ella folds her arms and stares out the side window. I'm too angry to talk.

We get onto the dual carriageway, the A3 heading south, and I'm driving in lane one behind a pickup truck. It could be the one that passed me by earlier. I'm trying to weigh our options, and Ella is looking at that small photo on her keyring. I glance down at the image of a blonde-haired man smiling back at her. Then she turns away again, moving her head back and forth to see in the wing mirror. I spot a blue van following us in the rearview mirror. It's too close.

'What's that van doing?' she says.

I signal right and accelerate to overtake the pickup, but a car, an old Ford saloon, overtakes the van behind us and moves onto the side of us. We're boxed in. I glance over, but the tinted windows hide the driver. This is bad. The road cuts through the hills and bends to the right. There's no hard shoulder. We're still trapped. I hit the horn, but the car holds its position. The blue van behind gets closer, and the pickup slows.

'It's a hit!' I say to Ella. 'Brace yourself!'

I edge the Volvo right and brake. They want me to stop, but I'm watching the Ford, waiting for my moment. I brake more, and we feel a tap on my rear bumper. The Ford is a little ahead of us, and I have his rear wheel arch against my front. I steer right and floor the accelerator, catching the Ford and spinning its backend. We pass him, and he hits the blue van behind us. It spins out and flips onto its side. The pickup gathers speed, leaving the carnage behind it. Though my Volvo is faster, I want him to follow me.

'You okay, Ella?' I say.

She's still gripping the door handle. 'I'm good. How did they know where to find us?'

'Daniel Cole. It's the only way. The only one who knew. Listen to me carefully. These people want to kill us. Understand?'

Her eyes are wide open. 'Yes.'

'And that's not going to happen.'

She nods.

'It's going to be us or them. Remember that later.'

There's an exit ahead, and the pickup is still following. I brake hard and take the left turn, making them think I'm trying to get away. They follow.

'They may have firearms, so do exactly as I tell you.'

'Guns!'

'Yes, guns. Do exactly as I tell you. In a moment, I'm going to swing the car over to the right. You get out and duck down at the front. The engine block will stop bullets. The doors won't. Understand?'

She nods again.

The road narrows into a country road, barely wide enough for two cars to pass each other. High grassy banks are on either side of us. The pickup is catching up. It doesn't mind the rougher road.

'Get ready.'

'Okay,' she says. She's gripping the door handle hard with both hands now.

'And Ella. Don't forget to breathe. I've taught others how to do this. Trust me.'

She nods once more, taking a deep breath.

I wrench the steering wheel right, slam on the brakes, and swing open my door. The Volvo turns side on, and the pickup brakes, skidding on the gravel. Ella gets out, pushed by the sideways momentum. I'm only feet away from the pickup. If they had any sense, they would have trapped my door. I get out, and two doors fly open. I'm in front of the driver's door, and I run and kick it shut on the driver, trapping his hand. He shouts in pain, dropping a gun. The door bounces open, and I thrust the side of his head hard against the sharp corner with a crunch, piercing his skull. That's one gone. Now for man number two.

I hear a crack. I drop and roll into the side of the grass bank. He's missed me. He runs around the front, and I head around the back. It's a chase game until he stops and fires again. The bullet tears through the door a few inches ahead of me. He turns, looking for Ella, and shoots at the bonnet of the Volvo. While his focus is elsewhere, I get close to him. He spins around, and I'm right there in front of him. He points the gun at my head—arm's length—with one hand. But at this distance, my action is always faster than his reaction. Every time. My head jolts to the side. I snatch the barrel of the Glock with both hands and twist it up, wrenching him towards the floor. I have the gun now. His face is full of horror as I back away and point it at him.

'You messed up my car,' I say.

'Don't kill me!' he says. It's the whimper of a dog that's about to be put down.

'Why are you trying to kill us?'

'We had orders. Don't shoot! It was nothing personal.'

'I take being shot at very personally. Who gave you the orders?'

'I… I can't tell you.'

I point the gun at his leg and shoot. The bullet goes straight through his thigh, and he screams in pain, dropping him to the floor.

'You need medical assistance, my friend. You're going to bleed to death. Who sent you to kill me?'

'Help me! Please don't kill me!'

'You'll be dead soon unless you tell me.'

'Jethro! He gave the order.'

'Jethro Matisse. Where can I find him?'

'I don't know where he is. Portsmouth somewhere. We arrange things through a third party by text. Or he sends someone to meet us.'

'You can come out now, Ella,' I shout.

Her head appears above the front wheel arch, and she stands, catching sight of the dead man with a dent in the side of his head and a gun beside him. She gasps, screws up her face and turns her head away, only to see the blood dripping from the jeans of the man with the bullet hole in his leg. She cries out. It's the exit wound that's done most of the damage.

'Max!' she says, her mouth gaping at the blood. 'He's going to bleed to death!'

'True. He can join his friend in hell as far as I care.' I talk to the bleeding man again. 'Have you got a mobile?'

He nods as he's crying in pain.

'My back pocket.'

I reach over him, turn him onto his side and take the phone from his back pocket. It's a cheap burner phone. I bring up the contact list. Empty. As is the call history. There's nothing here of any value to me. I put the phone in his hand and empty the Glock's magazine somewhere out of reach. He's not going anywhere at the moment. After wiping down the gun, I toss it behind his car.

'Call yourself an ambulance. Do it before you pass out, or you won't wake up again. Perhaps you can explain to the police why your dead friend here has a gun on him. And I'd put pressure on both sides of that wound if I were you. And use your belt as a tourniquet.'

I search the dead man for a mobile. He doesn't have one. There's nothing on him at all. No wallet. No ID.

'Come on,' I say to Ella. 'Let's get out of here.'

CHAPTER 21

Leon has come to rescue us. We made it ten miles from the A3, and I chose the scenic route in case others were trying to find us. We are on a tree-lined road on Harting Hill, and views over the Sussex Downs stretch for miles below us. I forget just how green this part of the world is—so many shades.

The Volvo sputtered to the top of the hill and came to a stop an hour ago. Oil and water have sprayed everywhere under the bonnet. That bullet did some damage. There's also a dent in the front wing where I clipped the car trying to box us in. Now we are inside the Range Rover, watching the Volvo being driven away on the back of a rescue truck.

'It's not terminal, Max,' says Leon.

'No,' I say, 'but the Volvo will take a while to fix.'

'You have other options.'

'Stop!' says Ella. 'What's wrong with you? You've just killed a man and shot another in the leg. He could bleed to death. And now you're talking about your old car! Are you crazy?'

'Didn't you listen to me?' I say. 'I told you, they were there to kill us. It's that simple. What did you want me to do? Give them a stiff talking to? This is a different world than you're used to, Ella. If you want to stay in it, then you better get used to it fast.'

'The police will be after us. We're going to get arrested for murder!'

'For God's sake, calm down! They're not after us. They'll find two men. One dead with a gun in his hand, and another shot nearby. The man who's still alive won't say a thing to the police. He's most likely wanted, anyway. There's nothing to put us there. No witnesses, no cameras.'

'But someone is dead!'

My temper wears thin. I snap at her. 'Then, at least be grateful it wasn't you!'

Ella drops back into her seat and lowers her head. I glance at her and see tears falling down her cheeks.

'I can't do this,' she says. 'I'm sorry.'

Her shoulders move as she sobs.

'Shall we go?' says Leon.

I nod to him, and the Range Rover moves forward. Ella doesn't talk to me until we drop her back at her mother's house, where I step out of the car and open the door for her.

'I wish this had turned out differently,' I say.

'Me too.'

'I'll make sure you're paid. You're great at what you do, but this isn't for you. Take care, Ella.'

'And you, Max,' she says. 'Thank Shira for me.'

It's late now, and I've driven the Range Rover back to Bordon to finish my business with Cole. I made good time as the roads were clear—good people are tucking themselves into bed. I'm not a good person.

I leave the car in the same place and pass the kebab shop. Standing outside the front door, I slot a card into the gap on the door latch. There's a metallic click, and I'm inside. I switch on my torch and go up the stairwell, taking every other step with my feet against the edges of each tread. Some people use a creaky step as a warning that someone is coming.

I'm at the door of Cole's flat, and I switch off the torch. There's no way to get in without making a noise, and I don't care how huge the man is. I must do this fast. Stepping back, I aim my boot at the lock, and with a swift kick, it caves in, splintering wood as it goes. I stand outside in a ready stance.

The flat is in darkness. No sound. I take the torch again and shine it into the hallway. Nothing.

'Cole!' I shout. 'Come on out, and I'll make this easy for you.' That ought to do it.

No reply. Silence. I hear a sound behind me. An elderly man in the flat opposite is cowering behind an open door.

'It's okay, police,' I tell him.

I reach around the inside of Cole's door and find a light switch. I step in, looking left and right. I can smell bleach, and the stench of stale smoke is awful. It's not fresh, so he hasn't lit a cigarette for a while. I stay alert as I search through the flat. It's a mess. There's a bank card on the table in the front room. Has he gone out? Perhaps to score somewhere.

The phone in my pocket buzzes. It's Ella.

'The washing!' she blurts out.

'Ella? You okay?' I say. 'Where are you?'

'I'm in bed. The washing on the radiators wasn't right.'

'I'm in his flat now. He's not here.'

'You went back! Max, look at the washing on the radiators.'

I see sweatshirts and skanky underwear.

'What about it?'

'They're the wrong size. The man I met was huge.'

'Shit!'

I recheck the bathroom, then double-check the bedroom. Tucked down one side of the bed is a duvet, heavy with a mass of congealed blood. There's a cupboard in the hallway. I open it.

Curled up are the bloody remains of a naked man. My hand goes to my face to stop myself from gagging at the stench. His throat has been cut, and his contorted face stares up at me in horror. I'm still holding the phone, and Ella is calling out to me.

'I've found Cole,' I say, 'or what's left of him. He's not how you described him. He doesn't look too pleased to see me, either.'

'If that's Daniel Cole, who did I speak to?'

'Matisse, maybe?'

'Shit! I'm scared, Max. Do they know where I live?'

'Who else knows where you're staying? Anyone you worked with?'

'Not my exact address, no. Only my mum, the bank, and you.'

'Okay. You should be safe. They were expecting me with you—it's not you they want. Keep a low profile. I'm sorry, Ella.'

I end the call and head back to the top of the stairs. The elderly man is still at his door in his dressing gown.

'Listen,' I say to him. 'There's nothing to worry about. Police officers in uniform will be here soon. Go back to bed.'

I look at my phone and find the number. I must make a call.

———

'He's losing it, Frank!' Mikita is panicking on the other end of the phone.

'Did you check your bank account, Mikita?' Pinto asks.

'I know he pays me well, but this obsession he has with Fortis is going to kill us all. I was trapped in that van for half an hour.'

'You were fine! The van wasn't so good, but it's all okay.'

'Marlowe doesn't care who he wastes. Money's no use to anyone when they're dead. I've got a little girl, a family.'

'If you don't like it, go back home to Belarus.'

'Think about it, Frank. That's all I'm asking. We lost two good men tonight. Think about that.' The other end of the phone goes silent and disconnects.

That's done. Pinto can relax. He's alone in his car, staring out over the night-time view of Portsmouth from the top of Portsdown Hill. He likes this spot. The gold and amber lights of the city below have a soporific effect on him. He used to take his daughters here when they were young while their mother was in hospital. They'd play on the hill, slaying dragons and running from giants. The burger van's bigger now, and it's busier, too. Kids in their prized wheels meet in the car park, showing off their latest mods. Pinto used to do that in his Ford Escort. Happy days, then. But not now.

He hated putting one of his men out of their misery tonight. He was bleeding to death on the road anyway, and he had let Fortis escape. He's underestimated Max Fortis. He's dangerous —skilled and clever. He won't underestimate him again.

Mikita is right—the boss is rattled. He's growing more unreasonable and unpredictable each day. Pinto's half thinking of making a break for it. Perhaps go to the continent, Spain, or Portugal. He lost touch with his girls years ago, ever since he buried his wife. He could retire with the money he's saved and have a different woman every night. He would die there, never alone again.

A kid, no more than twenty, parks beside Pinto's car with his stereo thumping. When he sees Pinto's face, he turns down the music. The boy looks like the world is his oyster. A pretty young thing sits beside him, and they're laughing together. That was Frank Pinto thirty years ago. He wishes he could go back and talk to his younger self and keep him out of trouble. He and his wife could have had a different journey together. Perhaps they could have stopped the cancer sooner, and life would still be good. He misses her more than anything in this world.

He sighs with a heavy heart. He smells his hands, and the bleach is still there. He will need a shower when he gets back. He can wash the blood and shit off his clothes, too.

The boss wants him to find out where Fortis and that girl live. Are they a couple? He imagines they are. She's something special, that one. Those curves, that slender neck. The thought of her gets him thinking. Imagining. Pinto finds his mobile and calls Dennis at the hotel.

'It's Frank. Send one over to my place,' he says to Dennis. 'The Thai girl. Make sure she's clean. I don't want her minging.'

He ends the call and starts the van, heading down the hill and into the city.

CHAPTER 22

It's an hour later when I see Janice Lacey arrive in a car, parking outside Cole's flat. She's wearing a long raincoat, and I notice her bare ankles as she steps outside. Two police cars and a CSI van are already here, and crime scene tape is fluttering across the footpath. The scene guard officer is standing at the communal front door of the flats, watching the press gathering. The wind has picked up, the tape hums, and I can smell meaty kebabs wafting in the air. It's making me hungry.

When Lacey walks over to me, she has another man in a suit with her. The protection that comes with the job—not against me this time. She walks around the Range Rover with a grin on her face.

'Wait here,' she says to the muscle with a gun under his jacket. I recognise him—I trained him a few years ago.

Lacey gets in and runs her fingers along the dash.

'I thought you had an old Volvo?'

'I broke it.'

'This is nice, though. Extended wheelbase—luxury.'

'It wasn't my choice,' I say. 'I prefer the V70.'

'You pulled me away from a hot date with a cup of cocoa and an episode of Vera.' She flashes her legs at me, and I see her pyjama bottoms. She has good legs—not at all hairy. 'Go on, tell me. What's this mess all about?' She has this self-satisfied grin on her face. She has me where she wants me. I need her help.

'Jethro Matisse. Did you find anything on him?'

'We have. I was going to call you. He's a name that's been of interest to our European counterparts for weapons and people trafficking. There's been nothing to connect him with a physical person until now. Our shared intelligence says he has imported pistols, ammunition, knives, and anything easily concealed.'

'You said up until now,' I say.

'Yes, I may have a photo of him for you.'

'Ella met a huge bald man with tattoos. Is that him? She thought she was speaking with a friend of Mariana Garcia.'

'That's not Jethro Matisse. That sounds like Pinto. Frank Pinto. Matisse's Mr Fix-it and bodyguard. Your hired help has met him?'

'This afternoon,' I say, 'thinking he was Daniel Cole.'

'That's the dead man in the cupboard?'

'Yes. Cole met with my client's mother, Mariana Garcia, the night she died.'

Lacey laughs. 'You've lost me, I'm afraid. But your girl's on their radar now, too. They'll use her to get to you if you're not careful.'

I digest that for a moment. 'Ella's not working for me after today.'

'Did you upset her?' Lacey asks.

I explain what happened in the car chase—the men with guns and Ella having to hide.

'I don't blame the poor girl,' says Lacey. 'That Hampshire incident was you, was it? The police are baffled by it. Both men are dead.'

'I didn't kill both of them!'

'One had an accident with a door, and the other had a bullet in his brain. Strangely, shot through his leg, too.'

'Oh. Someone else must have found them after we left.'

'So, you need me to get you out of this mess.'

I nod and turn to face her. 'I want to know why Matisse felt so threatened by Mariana and why they tried to kill me. There's Spencer Ryan, too.'

Lacey pulls out her mobile phone and unlocks it. She passes it to me. On the screen is an image of two men taken from a security camera. It's not the best quality, but you can make them out. One of the men matches Ella's description of the large, bald man she met today. The other is a man in an expensive-looking suit. Mid-fifties, a smart haircut, and glasses. He's slim and, even from an image, comes across as confident and intelligent. I get a response from my memory as I look at his blurry face. Something is familiar about him.

'That's Jethro Matisse,' says Lacey. 'He doesn't look like a Jethro. More like a Steve or a Kurt.' Lacey sighs and watches the CSIs moving in and out of the flats.

'Is he known to us from something else?' I say.

'I don't think so.' Lacey pushes her glasses up her nose and looks again. 'Have you seen him before?'

'I don't know.' I can feel the neurons firing in my brain, but there are no connections that make any sense.

'You don't know? That's an answer I wasn't expecting. We'll run him through the AI facial recognition kit.'

'I'd go in and arrest him,' I say.

'We don't know where he is now. And you're not a warranted officer anymore, Max. There's only so much you can do. Why don't you come back? Do it properly.'

'I'm happy to stick with our original arrangement. We help each other, remember?'

She rubs her eyes. 'It was worth a try. Now, there's something else we must discuss. May I ask if your wife is still with us?'

That hit me between the legs. 'Yes, she is.'

'Must be hard. Be honest with me, Max, and you'll hate me for bringing this up.' Lacey sucks air through her teeth. 'I've been studying what happened that night in fine detail. We received the intel that Petrov's agents had targeted you four hours before your wife and uncle touched that door handle covered with the Novichok gel. The first call to you about the threat was made while you were in the restaurant with them. But, as far as I can tell, you did nothing. You said nothing. And you never touched that door handle yourself. You somehow avoided it. How do you explain that?'

'Are you accusing me of allowing the attack on my wife and uncle?'

'Not accusing, Max,' she says. 'I'm curious.'

Lacey's words have exploded in my head like a grenade. I want to obliterate her face. My hands are wet with sweat. But this is the strange thing. Lacey's looking at me like she's a priest about to absolve me of my sins. There's a chance to free myself here, to get the absolution I've been craving for the last nine months.

'You're right,' I say. 'I did get the first call in the restaurant. Carrie and my uncle were ordering. They were laughing together about something. She looked incredible that night, and everyone was looking at her. I'd recently discovered that my uncle was infatuated with her. Yes, Arthur Fortis was nearly thirty years older than her, but he didn't care. He thought his money could get him anything he wanted.'

'You believed they were having an affair.'

'I guess for my uncle, it was only about the sex. I'm not sure what it was for Carrie. But the joke was on me. They must have thought it was hilarious, thinking I didn't know. And they flaunted it in front of my face. But I knew. I knew everything.'

'Didn't Shira say anything to you?'

'The night before, I challenged Ima and Leon to find out what they knew. Leon told me what was going on. He loved my uncle but knew his weaknesses. Beautiful women were my uncle's Achilles heel.'

'Let's not beat around the bush here,' says Lacey. 'You delayed telling them about the threat. In effect, you killed your uncle and put your wife in a coma.'

I shake my head. 'No! When we returned to our place, I hesitated and stayed in the car. I thought about it, I admit. But it was only for a moment. I didn't even think Petrov's men would have put anything on the door handle, and the intel wasn't even clear when it would happen. But I got another call while they walked to the front door. Your predecessor said the men had been caught. Then I came to my senses. I ran out and called them. I shouted for them to come back. But it was too late.'

'Your hesitation, Max, I'm sorry to say, shows intent. It was your fault.'

'You got me,' I say. 'Have you recorded this conversation?'

'No. You're okay. But it puts a different slant on things.

The attack was a direct consequence of Petrov's order, but you got something very wrong, Max.'

'What did I get wrong?'

'I will tell you, but first, I want you to admit it wasn't our fault. It wasn't the unit's fault your wife is in a coma. Because I believe you still hold us responsible.'

'Shit, Janice! I've always known it was my fault! Okay?' The man outside opens the door to check on Lacey.

She snaps at him. 'Leave us alone!'

I take a breath. 'I could have done something sooner. I was so full of anger and hatred for them. They both betrayed me.'

'And that's why you don't like his money? Probably that house he left you, too.'

'Yes. My uncle changed his will before he died. It was his apology to me for what he did. Now tell me, what part did I get wrong?'

'Petrov's men were caught. Well, after some love and attention, they told us something that threw a different light on the events.' Lacey leans in towards me and covers her mouth— a habit in case cameras are on her, and someone is trying to lip-read. 'Hear me out, and don't shoot the messenger—this will be hard for you to hear. We discovered Carrie had been compromised. She agreed to pass valuable information about our operation to the Russians.'

'Don't be ridiculous!'

Lacey holds up her hands, trying to calm me down. 'I said, hear me out. She had agreed to pass on information about you, Max. You were a pain in the arse to the Russians—you know you were. Your uncle discovered Carrie's duplicitous betrayal and used it to blackmail her for sex.'

'I can't believe this!'

'We believe Carrie was going to tell you. To confess all. But Arthur Fortis persuaded her not to. As far as Petrov was concerned, Carrie had become a liability. His entire operation was in jeopardy.'

'Shit!' I see where this is going.

'The Novichok was primarily intended for Carrie, not you. If they'd got you with it, too, that would have been a bonus for Petrov. I'm sorry.' Lacey pulls out a bag from her pocket. 'Mint?'

I rest my head on the steering wheel. It's now that everything is coming back to life in me. Seized gears move. A missing piece of a puzzle has fallen into place. I sit back up and wipe my eyes.

'When did you find this out?'

'When I first started in this role, I was tasked with following up on what happened to Petrov. The Russians disowned him, and he vanished into thin air—he's still out there somewhere. I read the intelligence file and the interview transcript with his men. They told us Carrie was their target. It's why I called you to begin with. I wanted you to know the truth.'

I nod. 'That changes a few things. I need to talk to Ima and Leon.'

'You can't, Max,' she says. 'I'm sorry. This information is top secret. Need-to-know basis only. They don't need to know. Anyway, what good would it do?'

'What now, then?'

'You and I will do what we've agreed. You continue with your not-for-profit detective agency.' She smirks. 'Enjoy it. Do nice things for people. But at the same time, you help me when I need it, and I'll help you. I've got you the security clearance you need. You'll be my undercover secret weapon.'

She's got me where she wants me. I'm trapped by this, and I must agree. If I don't, then that hesitation to act when I was in the car, watching my wife and uncle heading to the house, that hesitation will be used against me.

'Will you support me in getting Matisse?'

'I expected you to ask me that. Yes, I'm happy to support you.'

'Thank you.'

'By the way, did you know I've come up with a code name for you? I love that part. I love a code name.' She smiles.

'Good grief.'

'Your code name is *Achilles*. I didn't think it was too bad until I heard what you said about your uncle. Achilles, the famous Greek warrior.'

'Could be worse.'

Lacey steps out of the car, and the man in the suit relaxes. 'You'd better go, Max. Hampshire CID is on the way. I'll speak to you soon.'

I nod. 'Thank you. It was hard to hear, but I appreciate it.'

I drive away, leaving the mess behind me, my head swimming with this nuclear warhead going off. I'm not sure what I feel right now. Is it relief, or is it fear? I pass the firing ranges and onto the main route back home.

For months, I've known Carrie was my fault, even though part of me thought they deserved it. Carrie betrayed me and our friends on so many levels. If I had stopped her that night and she was still here with me, how long would she have continued undermining me? No, what she got, she deserved. It turns out I never knew Carrie at all.

Saturday night, 7th January

I catch a glimpse of her in my rearview mirror as we pass beneath the amber streetlights. She's studying the side of his face as he sits beside me in the passenger seat. They'd been laughing together like badly behaved children in the restaurant. But now that her simpering smile has gone and her mask has dropped, something cold and fearful has taken its place.

My uncle, silver-haired, strong-jawed, and broad-shouldered, glances over his shoulder at Carrie, and I can almost taste his wine breath. There's that confident smile. The one that says he owns it all. He is a self-made man who can have anything he wants.

He turns to me. 'So, you didn't enjoy your meal.'

My nostrils flare, and I tighten my grip on the steering wheel, the leather creaking beneath my fingers.

'You barely touched it,' he says. 'Spent the whole time on your phone.'

'Work.'

'Still haven't found that off button, then.'

I take the bypass towards home, and my uncle switches on the radio. He finds a jazz station and turns it up. It's not the jazz that I like.

'Pull over,' he says. 'I need a piss.'

'Can't you wait?'

We're approaching a lay-by in the darkness.

'Just here.'

I stop, keeping the engine running, while he walks a short distance away. Carrie gets out and moves into the front seat, adjusting the legroom. Her floral perfume drifts between us. Something my uncle bought her for Christmas.

'I was feeling sick in the back,' she says.

My gaze meets hers in the dim glow of the car's interior. 'I'm not feeling great, either.'

'Do you think we can go away somewhere?'

Her eyes are pleading with me.

'Why?'

'Just you and me. Escape to the country. Somewhere away from people. Away from—'

My uncle returns and realises he must change seats.

'Like that, is it?' he says, sliding over to where Carrie sat a few moments ago. 'It's bitter out there. At least the seat is still warm.'

Ten minutes later, we pull into our road. My uncle has invited himself in for a nightcap. I squeeze into a parking space about twenty yards from our house.

He sighs with disapproval when I switch off the engine. 'Why you choose to live in such a tiny shoebox is beyond me.'

'It's what we can afford,' says Carrie. 'We don't need a big place.'

My phone rings. It's work.

'I need to take this. You go on ahead. I'll catch you up in a minute.'

I wait until they're walking to the house before I answer it. It's my boss. As he talks to me, I watch Carrie search for her keys in her bag. My uncle is beside her with his hand around her waist.

I end the call and know what I need to do. They're approaching the front door. Carrie has her key, and they face the porch. Inside my head, a frantic voice screams at me to move, to run. But I can't. I'm still, silent. What if I do nothing?

But something jolts within me. I push open my door and run towards the house.

'Stop! Carrie! Don't go in there!'

But it's too late. The front door is open, and the light from the hallway is spilling into the porch. I stand back.

Carrie is staring at me. 'What is it, Max?'

CHAPTER 23

Early morning, Thursday, 5th October

Ella can't sleep. She's tossed and turned in the darkness for the last two hours. She gets out of bed, in the bedroom she had when she was fourteen years old, and stares out her window, watching the shadows in the rear garden. She imagines that burly, bald man looking back at her from below and shudders. She's having flashbacks of Max killing that man. A life ended so violently, so abruptly. The sound of the gunshot. She wishes she hadn't seen it all now.

She opens her door and walks out onto the landing. She would do this when she was young, raiding the fridge at night for a cheese and ham feast. Her mother's bedroom door is closed, and she never hears anything when asleep. She'd started shutting the door after Ella's father died so Ella wouldn't hear her crying herself to sleep.

Ella blames herself for her part in the day's events. Why didn't she realise that wasn't Daniel Cole in the flat? It didn't even sound like him, for God's sake. She could have been killed. What if the Volvo's engine block had not stopped that bullet aimed at her? But then there's another voice inside her head. She remembers the excitement and the thrill of Max taking out the men. This is what he did for a living. He was like a secret agent, something she'd only seen in the movies. The reality was nowhere near as cool. The fear, sweat, and danger were real.

She uses the toilet and heads down the stairs. She's wide awake now. It's three in the morning and almost fully dark outside. She goes to the kitchen, pours a small glass of milk, and cuts herself a slice of cheese. She's feeling the nerves as she stands in the darkness. Will she ever be able to sleep again?

She finishes her snack and moves into the front room. The lights from all the devices on standby help her negotiate her way past the coffee table and stand in front of the window. The curtains are open, and there's a waning moon painting the rooftops of the houses opposite in silver, casting a shadow of something dark on the road. A large vehicle is parked in front of the house. Her heart beats hard. Nothing parks on the road down here. Every house has a driveway. It's a black four-by-four of some kind. It's too dark to make it out. She pushes her face closer to the window. Is there someone in there?

'Shit!'

She jumps back and feels faint. What can she do? Wake her mother? Take her out the back? No. Her mother is still too frail to run anywhere. Turn on the lights. Call the police. How long would it take them to get here? The man could smash the windows and kill them all before the police arrived. Think! Confront him. Grab a knife and the spare can of pepper spray she's hidden in the electric meter cupboard.

Ella opens the cupboard and feels around by the switches until she finds the metal can with the plastic flip lid. She's glad she ordered two of them now. She roots in the kitchen, trying not to clatter in the drawers. She doesn't want to wake her mother—not now. Not the bread knife, but the carving knife. She goes to the front door and slips trainers over her bare feet. Fear is making her hands and knees shake, and she feels sick. She must get to him first. She'll shout and scream if he attacks her. She'll wake the neighbours.

She eases the door open to look outside and lifts the catch on the pepper spray. The black shadow is still there. She counts to three under her breath, then she yanks the door open and runs out.

'Leave us alone!' She's running towards the dark shape now, the knife thrust forward in one hand. But when does she spray him? The driver's door opens, and she shrieks. 'Get away from me!'

With the other hand, she holds out the pepper spray.

'Ella!' says a hushed man's voice. 'Ella. Stop! It's me, Max.'

Ella freezes, but she's already sprayed him. She missed. Lights go on in bedrooms up and down the road.

'Max? What the hell are you doing? I could have killed you!'

'I doubt it. But it was impressive. Lower the knife, please. I come in peace.'

Ella looks up at the curtains twitching.

'Come in before someone calls the police.'

Max turns and waves at the houses opposite and follows Ella into the house.

Clarice sits up in bed and checks the clock. It's after three in the morning, and she sees Phil's silhouette against the window. He's looking out onto the street below. Nothing usually stirs out there at this time of night, only the occasional fox picking through the rubbish bags.

'Phil? What's wrong?' she says.

At first, Phil doesn't answer, but then he turns towards her, his face in shadow.

'I'm struggling to sleep tonight,' he says. 'There are a few problems at work.'

'Do you want to talk about it?'

'No.'

'You never talk about your job. I'm happy to listen.'

'I said no, Clarice. Now, go back to sleep. It's okay. I'm just worried about something.'

He turns away again, and Clarice sits up, plumping the pillow behind her back.

'Who's Jethro?'

'Jethro?'

'It's a name you said in your sleep,' she says.

'Oh, gosh! Did I? He's a client. I'm sorry, my love. I hope I didn't worry you. It's a complex account I'm working on. Nothing more than that.'

'There must be something more. You seemed pretty angry with him.'

'He's a bit of a dodgy character. He has his finger in many pies. Makes it difficult to keep track of. He pays well, though. I have to make sure I'm keeping him on the straight and narrow. Don't worry. It's all in hand.'

Clarice gets out of bed and wraps her arms around him. 'You will talk to me if you're in trouble? The whole world needs a Phil Marlowe to keep it on the straight and narrow.'

She kisses him. 'You're a good man, Phil. I'm really proud of you.'

'I'll talk to you. I promise. I'm trying to manage a project for him, and he's had problems with contractors. There's a man who's trying to cause trouble for Jethro. He's making things more difficult for me.'

'Set Juliet on him.'

Phil laughs. 'Yes, she'd give him a good talking to. Look, Clarice. Don't repeat the name Jethro to anyone. My work is confidential.'

'My lips are sealed. Now, come back to bed. I'm getting cold in here on my own.'

———

We're sitting in Ella's mother's kitchen, drinking hot chocolate and speaking in lowered voices. I hadn't expected to be here tonight, but at least I get to see Ella in pink and white pyjamas. They're flattering, tracing the curves of her body, and I find myself studying her longer than I should.

'I still don't understand what you're doing here,' she says. 'You scared the shit out of me out there.'

'I wanted to make sure no one was watching you,' I say.

'The only person watching me was you, weirdo!'

'I was checking you were okay, but I may have fallen asleep.'

Ella laughs. 'That's nice of you, but you can't live outside my mother's house forever.'

'I know.'

'And I've quit, remember?'

'Have you? I don't remember that.'

'Yes! I have.' She realises she's speaking too loud. 'I didn't expect to be shot at, Max.'

'I did warn you.'

'Well. I get it now!'

'That's why I didn't want you to go out.' I rub my face. I'm feeling groggy and can do without any more confrontation. Attempting a smile, I soften my voice. 'I could still do with your help.'

Then she tilts her head as if a thought has struck her. 'You're not in love with me, are you?'

'What? No!'

'You're stalking me.'

'No, Ella, I'm not. I'm not attracted to you in the slightest.'

She looks offended but then smiles. She was joking. 'I'm glad that's cleared up.'

'I didn't mean it like that. You're not unattractive, as it happens. I didn't want you to get hurt.'

'I'd stop digging if I were you.'

'Come and live in my house for a while. I have plenty of space.'

'You want me to move in with you?'

I didn't phrase that well. 'Not like that. It's for your protection.'

'What about my mother?' she says.

'These people aren't interested in your mother.'

Ella is studying me. I can still see suspicion in her eyes, wondering what my motivation is.

'You know Ima and Leon are there, too. It's not only you and me. I'm definitely not trying to seduce you.' Everything in my being wants to add the word *yet* to that sentence.

She nods and goes quiet, looking around at her mother's

kitchen. She stands and paces the floor for a few minutes while she thinks. Then she stops and faces me.

'I'll continue working for you. Same pay as before, but don't get me killed, okay?'

'It was you who arranged the interview with Cole,' I say.

'It was,' she says. 'I'll give you that. When shall I move in?'

'What about this afternoon?'

CHAPTER 24

I woke up around ten this morning, feeling bleary-eyed after only five hours of sleep. After the gym and a session in the dojo, I update Ima and Leon about yesterday's events—the parts I can tell them.

Ima hugs me and says something in Hebrew. 'You know you put Ella at risk yesterday.'

'I do,' I reply in English. My Hebrew isn't so good. 'I want her to stay here for a while, in case this Matisse knows about her.'

'There's plenty of room,' says Leon. 'She's a nice girl, Max. Clever.'

I ignore the look between them. My mobile rings to break the silence. It's Lacey.

'Recovered from last night?' she says.

'Just about. What is it?'

'I must show you something, but I can't send it. I need you to come here.'

'When?'

'Now, Max. It's important.'

She ends the call, and I tell Ima and Leon.

'Sounds urgent,' I say.

'Be wise, Max,' says Ima. 'She's an unknown quantity.'

'I will.'

'I can drive you,' says Leon.

'No, you two had plans for the day. I don't want to spoil them. I'll take the red car.'

'You're going to drive the red car?' Leon laughs.

I nod.

'Don't forget, she needs fuel.'

Dave, the mechanic, told me the Volvo needed a new engine, which could take a few weeks to sort. Ima and Leon need the Range Rover, so I'm left with the last thing in the garage to drive. Someone from a local dealership looks after it for us, as I've not touched it in nine months. It was my uncle's car, and he only drove it once. I inherited it and called it the red car.

I leave at once, find somewhere to fuel up, and head for London via the A3. The red car is a Ferrari 488 Pista. She has only five hundred miles on the clock, and she's a beast. While the Ferrari is an undeniably beautiful car with incredible handling, she's not a Volvo V70. It's just my preference.

I turn off the A3 at Putney and follow the north side of the Thames through Chelsea. The last part of my journey is slow, but now I'm heading into an underground car park near Thames House, Millbank.

Once inside Thames House, I must wait at security for Lacey, who's magicked a pass with my old photograph. They've resurrected my biometric data, too, which they should have destroyed when I left.

'Never forgotten,' I say to Lacey.

'What did you expect?' she says, giving me that thin-lipped

smile. She's in her brown trouser suit again. She most likely has a hot date later with Vera.

We go through two more levels of security using an iris scan, and I'm in an office facing the river. A man in a charcoal suit is already here. I recognise him—Detective Inspector Scott. He's Met Police like Lacey.

'Mr Fortis,' he says, stands, and shakes my hand.

'DI Scott,' I say.

'He's a DCI now,' says Lacey. 'Not that you care, of course. DCI Scott has been liaising with DI Reeves from PCID.'

'Is that about DS Chambers?' I say.

'Yes,' says Scott.

Lacey has a buff-coloured folder with her marked *Secret* in red.

'Max, I need to show you this. You'll understand why I couldn't put it into an email for you.' She's about to slide over the file but decides to do a preamble first. 'Seven years ago, you worked on a case involving a people trafficker who imported young adults as slaves for a mix of foreign diplomats.'

'I remember it well,' I say. I know where this is going, even if Lacey doesn't, and I can feel my heart rate accelerating. 'That was one of my first cases here. I got shot at.'

'I read that. Your efforts brought the trafficking to an end within a year, and we ended up deporting several diplomats back from whence they came. I note that some of the details have a need-to-know-only marker on them. I can't access them. I assume it's a witness protection programme.'

'It is. I can get to that presently,' I say.

Lacey nods and glances at DCI Scott. 'Very well. The man at the top of the trafficking operation lost somewhere in the region of two hundred million dollars in revenue. Do you remember his name?'

I smile. 'Andrew Harman,' I say. 'He died in a warehouse fire. He got caught torching his own place soon after I brought down his operation.' Lacey raises an eyebrow, waiting for something from me. A rush of cold sweat crawls up my body.

'The AI facial recognition software found him in that photo I showed you last night,' says Lacey. 'It's given a ninety-two per cent match.'

'That was Harman with Frank Pinto?' I say, struggling to believe the words as they leave my mouth. 'How is that possible? He looks nothing like him.' But slowly, the pieces start falling into place. 'So you're telling me he faked his own death and changed his name to Jethro Matisse.'

'It appears so. Andrew Harman had a big grudge against you.'

'A grudge!' I laugh. 'He vowed to destroy me.'

'Well, as Jethro Matisse, it's possible he's gone back into the trafficking business. We need to check that he hasn't contacted certain government ministers.'

'Which ministers?'

'Need-to-know basis, I'm afraid.' Lacey pushes the file over to me.

I open it and once more examine the photo from the CCTV image she showed me last night.

'He's changed his appearance,' I say. 'Lost forty pounds at least. He was a big man when I knew him. I wish this damn image were clearer.'

'And talking about the need to know,' says Lacey. 'I've shown you mine, now you show me yours.'

I rub my eyes, still feeling the effects of my late night. 'It's the case I'm investigating now. Andrew Harman was Mariana

Garcia's husband. Mariana was put into a witness protection program. After Harman died, they decided she should stay with it in case of reprisals.'

'Ah. I see. If Harman is still alive, then Mariana Garcia may have been murdered under his orders.' Lacey signals to DCI Scott with a gesture, prompting him to speak.

Scott sits forward and points to the first page. 'We didn't know that Harman was up to his old tricks again. But thanks to you, now we do. We've searched on the Portsmouth city-wide CCTV system, but he's likely aware of our capabilities and knows he's wanted. Given the information from Commander Lacey, we suggest Harman, aka Matisse, is targeting you for revenge. I didn't realise Mariana Garcia was connected to him —it must be in the file somewhere—but he may have used her to bring you out into the open.'

I'm struggling to understand this. 'Surely he didn't use Mariana to find me?' I stand up to clear my head. 'I'm a private detective. He could have searched for me on the Internet. It's not difficult.'

DCI Scott shrugs at Lacey, and she nods at him to continue.

'We've traced the name, Jethro Matisse,' says Scott. 'He first appeared during the pandemic in April 2020. He was supposedly importing medical PPE into Portsmouth, so he set up an operation there. It looked as clean as a whistle from the outside, and the then Health Secretary approved it. But in January 2021, traffic officers stopped a lorry on the M27 transporting a shipping container. When they opened it, they found young women from various North African countries. As usual, they had come over with the promise of work, but they were diverted into slavery. It was suspected to be connected to Matisse, but he wriggled out of it when the document trail went cold. He had covered his tracks. No one could have known his name was linked to Harman's. I thought Harman was dead. Anyway, after that, Matisse disappeared, and we haven't heard from him since.'

I stand against the wall and look out of a small, tinted window onto the River Thames below. 'When I saw Mariana Garcia sitting outside the Law Courts that Friday night, I felt she reminded me of someone I'd seen before. I ignored it then because she looked so different. Then, of course, I remembered. She was Mrs Harman.'

'Were you instrumental in bringing his wife in as a witness?' asks Scott.

'I was,' I say. 'I was the one who convinced her to testify against her husband and go into the witness protection program. Soon after we had her evidence, Harman was killed in the fire—or so we thought. Mariana was in hiding, which would have included changing her identity.'

Lacey stands and glances at her watch. 'Sorry, but I must go and report to the Home Secretary. I wish I could help you further with the Garcia case, Max. Our job here is confined to searching for any connection Harman has with government ministers.'

'Thank you,' I say. 'I think it's time to update the police investigation with this evidence, especially DS Chambers.'

'Ah, yes, DI Reeves was saying Chambers could lead us to Harman,' says Lacey. 'Bent coppers and all that. I'll leave you to work that through with DCI Scott.'

Once Lacey leaves, DCI Scott and I go through the evidence to present to DS Chambers, redacting text where necessary. This will encourage him to tell Harman something of what we know about him, but not too much. Enough for Chambers to lead us to Harman.

Afterwards, I leave Thames House and walk along the river, trying to let this sink in. Andrew Harman, Mariana's husband, isn't dead. He must be the one behind Mariana's murder. After everything I did to him, I can understand why he wants me dead, but not everything is fair in love and war. He's hiding behind the name Jethro Matisse now. But where is he? Perhaps it's time I draw him out, and I'll use DS Chambers to do it.

Arriving at Chichester Police Station two hours after leaving London, I inform the front office staff I have some important information for DS Chambers. I'm going to play this by ear, as I'm unsure how he will be with me. Leaving me stewing for twenty minutes, he finally turns up, glaring down at me as if he's far too important to talk to me.

'Something you want to say?' he asks.

'I come bearing a peace offering,' I say, 'hot from MI5.'

'Are those your wheels out the front?'

'The red car? Yes.'

'Nice. What do you want then?'

I nod at the man sitting on the chair near me who's come in to report a noisy neighbour. I don't think he should hear this.

'Come with me,' says Chambers.

The DS leads me into an office off the main corridor. I remember this little room. I had a woman throw up over me in here once. Chambers closes the door, and we sit at the small desk. I push over the buff folder to him. The word *secret* is crossed out and signed by DCI Scott. Chambers opens the folder. The photo and several redacted statements about

Andrew Harman are inside. Chambers finds the statements from Mariana Harman and some written by me.

He says nothing. He's touching his face and licking his lips. He spends some time reading through the material he has. I can hear heating pipes ticking and the low drone of people talking in the distance. It's stuffy in here, and he's perspiring, pulling down his tie, making him appear more human. Now and then, he catches me smiling at him. I'm not sure it's helping.

'Do you believe this Harman murdered his wife?' he asks.

'I do.'

'And he's calling himself Jethro Matisse. That's an unusual name. Sounds made up.'

'Do you think so?' I say, but my sarcasm is wasted on him.

Chambers stacks the sheets and puts them back into the folder. Then he picks up the phone and calls DCI Scott. I'm not sure he's listening to Scott. It's more likely he's trying to come up with a plan. It's around an hour by the time he finishes all this. Little by little, I've been watching the colour drain from his face. The small room is getting even more stuffy.

'Well, Mr Fortis,' he says, sitting back in his chair and rubbing his eyes. 'I owe you an apology. I knew nothing about this, and I've been told to leave you alone. You have a special arrangement.'

I nod and say nothing. I know better than to milk it. He's a total shit who's going to get what he deserves. I stand and offer my hand to him, which he takes, and I leave the folder with him.

CHAPTER 25

I arrive back in Bosham and put the red car in the garage. Ella's silver Audi is in the driveway. I remember little about the journey home as I mulled over my meeting with DS Chambers and the news about Andrew Harman. Did Harman want Mariana to find me? Some part of his sick plan. Once she had done that, it was time to take his revenge on her.

Harman is ruthless and cold-blooded, but worse still, he's intelligent with it. Chambers can't fully know who he is dealing with. He's being used.

'Hey,' says Ella as I walk into the kitchen. 'Me again.' Ima and Leon are here too.

I nod to her. 'Nice to see you with your clothes on. How are you feeling?'

'Tired. Mum knew nothing of your visit last night, but I had a few interesting looks from the neighbours.'

'I bet you did. You'll get yourself a reputation.'

'How did it go?' says Ima. She's concerned about my return to HQ.

'Enlightening,' I say, explaining to her what I learned about Jethro Matisse and Andrew Harman.

As I talk about my meeting with Lacey, Ima sits down and listens, trying to work this through.

'Mariana Garcia was his wife?' she says.

'Yes.'

'Why didn't you know who she was when you saw her that Friday?' asks Ella.

'She looked different from how I remember her. She may even have had surgery. She'd changed her appearance when she went into witness protection, and I'd lost track of her by then. I think she was surprised I didn't recognise her. She didn't say who she was or tell me about Harman being alive.'

'But what made her decide to come to you? You were just some police officer working on her husband's case.'

The room goes silent, and the sound of the gate buzzer startles us. DC Gary Bates is standing outside, shuffling his feet.

'I'll get him,' says Leon. He stops and smiles at us on his way to the front door. 'Ella's made a good point.'

My eyes meet Ella's. 'I don't know why she came to me.' I wonder if she can tell I'm lying. My biggest question is, how did Mariana find me? 'When I first went to talk to her, she told me to keep away! It wasn't exactly a friendly meeting.'

'Perhaps someone put her off talking to you,' says Ella. 'Or she simply changed her mind.'

'That makes sense if Harman had got to her,' I say.

Leon leads Gary to us. He doesn't notice us at first, as he's too busy gawping at the house.

'Gary,' I say, 'what brings you here?'

He finally acknowledges everyone with a wave. 'This

place is something else,' he says. 'I came by your new office, but no one was there. I have something to show you.'

'You could have rung.'

Gary has clapped his eyes on Ella and is smiling like a fool.

'I'm DC Bates,' he says to Ella. 'Call me Gary. I've known Max for many years.'

He shakes her hand, and she smiles at him, which only makes him worse.

'Gary,' I say again, 'you could have rung.'

'Not with this.' He has something in his pocket. 'I shouldn't be showing you, but... It's the last of the text messages Garcia sent on her mobile. We got it back from Digital Forensics this morning. I heard you spoke to the DS. He's been acting really strangely since.'

He hands me a couple of pages of A4 paper with printed text. Ella reads it over my shoulder.

From: Kenneth Thomson, Digital Forensics, Haywards Heath

To: DS Adam Chambers, Chichester, West Div, Sussex Police

CC: DC Gary Bates, Chichester, West Div, Sussex Police

Hi Adam

I know you told us the results on MG's texts are no longer needed, but I came across this. You may want this record for disclosure/unused material. The simplified record below shows texts between Mariana Garcia and someone in her contacts called Andrew.

I've copied in DC Bates, who was chasing up the results.

Regards,

Ken

Date: 25/08/2023 20:33

ANDREW

How was dinner?

MARIANA GARCIA

Still spying on me?

ANDREW

You promised undying love to me once.
Remember?

MARIANA GARCIA

Until DEATH us do part, is all I remember.

ANDREW

Death puts things into perspective

ANDREW

Have you checked on Grace today?

MARIANA GARCIA

Why?

ANDREW

Grace and I have a mutual friend

MARIANA GARCIA

?

ANDREW

Spencer works for me

MARIANA GARCIA

You're lying!

ANDREW

Thanks for finding Fortis for me

ANDREW

But if you talk to him, Grace dies

MARIANA GARCIA

I'm not anywhere near him!

ANDREW

Do you think I'm stupid?

ANDREW

I'm watching you now

ANDREW

One step closer to him

ANDREW

You die and Grace dies

ANDREW

Simple

MARIANA GARCIA

Leave Grace alone!

ANDREW

A taxi's coming to take you home

ANDREW

Get in it

ANDREW

Don't come back

MARIANA GARCIA

I can't get hold of Grace!

MARIANA GARCIA

Where is she?

MARIANA GARCIA

Where is Grace?

MARIANA GARCIA

Touch a hair of her head, and I will kill you myself.

ANDREW

Again? Just get in the taxi

(The last message was sent at 20:42 hours.)

'There's the reference to the taxi that took Mariana away, Gary,' I say.

Gary nods. 'But we're still none the wiser which cab firm he worked for.'

'What does Chambers say about this email?'

'Nothing,' he says. 'I haven't heard anything from him.'

'I'm not surprised.' I take the sheet of paper and read the email again. Mariana must have been desperate to talk to me. I was her way out of this, but Harman got to her. 'So Harman warned her off from speaking to me. But would he really have used Spencer to kill Grace?'

'Mariana obviously thought he would,' says Ella. 'He could have been bluffing. She must have remembered what you did to her husband. Maybe she was going to ask for your help again.'

'She must have been terrified.'

Ella nods. 'What do we do now?'

'You can continue your training with Ima,' I say. 'I think that's important. And keep Grace updated for me. I've got someone to see, and then I'm going to pack a few things for an overnight stay. I'm going over to Portsmouth tomorrow to try to flush Andrew Harman out. I'll use a different name to stay under his radar.'

'Incognito—nice,' says Gary.

'The Controller's given me a code name. Achilles. She likes it.'

Ella puts her hand to her face and laughs.

'I think it's cool,' says Gary. 'A great Greek classic, even.'

'Agents use code names,' says Ima. 'It protects their identities.'

'I reckon you like it, too, Max,' says Ella. 'Is Ima your code name, Shira?'

Shira laughs. 'It would be an unusual code name, Ella.'

'My code name is Achilles,' I say. 'I may insist you use it. Get used to it.' I wink at her.

Gary is looking a little left out. 'How about me?' he says. 'What do I do?'

'I don't care,' I say. 'You don't work for me.'

Gary laughs. 'True. I forget that sometimes.'

Ima is standing with Ella with her hand on her shoulder. I hand the sheet of paper to Ella and go to leave. 'Ima,' I say, 'try not to break her.'

———

Adam Chambers checks his watch before strolling from The Hard in Old Portsmouth and along the walls of the harbour entrance. He follows a route that takes him over the cobbles of Bath Square, into the narrow Tower Street, until he reaches The Round Tower, overlooking the walls and the sea below. Ascending the winding stone staircase inside the tower, he emerges at the top. Finding himself alone, he sits on the bench, gazing across to a tall, white column by the submarine museum in Gosport. The northeast wind has a bite to it up here, and he wraps his coat around him, checking his watch again. They're late.

The sound of leather soles on stone echoes from the stairs below, and the massive shape of Frank Pinto appears. Then comes Philip Marlowe, following behind once the coast is clear.

When Chambers first met Marlowe, he introduced himself as Jethro Matisse. Some alter ego Marlowe uses to hide behind when doing business. Matisse is a monster who hides in the shadows with a deadly reputation, using the fist of fear and violence to maintain his status in the city. Chambers isn't as afraid of him as much as Marlowe would like. If he tried any of that shit on him, he had enough on Marlowe to put him away for a long time.

Marlowe sits with Chambers, and Pinto stands over them, blocking the wind from them both.

'I don't have long,' says Chambers. 'I was followed. I think my boss suspects something.'

'Followed!' says Pinto. His anger is evident.

'Don't panic! I lost them. Led them on a wild goose chase to a pub in the country.'

'You'd better get on with it then,' says Marlowe, 'before they find you again. What's so important?'

'This.' Chambers brings out a buff-coloured folder from beneath his coat and hands it to Marlowe.

'Interesting,' says Marlowe and smiles. He opens the folder and examines the contents, reading the statements. 'They got your good side, Frank.' He shows Pinto the fuzzy CCTV image of them both.

'Are you Andrew Harman?' Chambers asks.

'Andrew Harman died in a fire,' says Marlowe.

'Just stop the crap for once!' snaps Chambers. 'I've saved your neck so many times. I deserve some respect. Are you Andrew Harman or not? How many names does one man need, for God's sake?'

'Harman was killed in a fire, sergeant.'

'Then what about this?' Chambers pulls out a printed copy of the email from Digital Forensics, showing the text messages. 'Read it!'

'Then maybe he's still alive,' says Marlowe.

'And you seriously want me to believe these messages to Mariana Garcia weren't from you?'

Marlowe smiles at Pinto. 'Why am I repeating myself to this man, Frank?'

'I don't know, boss. Maybe he's hard of hearing.'

'More's the point,' says Marlowe, 'why is Max Fortis still causing me grief? There must be enough evidence to convict him.'

'The hair samples were useless. Too old.'

'Shame. I'd kept them especially.'

'Were you shagging Harman's wife, too?'

'I think everyone was, sergeant,' says Marlowe. 'I must say, I am disappointed in you for not dealing with Fortis appropriately. Don't I pay you enough? Is that the problem?'

'You're being unreasonable.'

'Pinto says you know where Fortis lives now. Do share.'

'Don't even bother—I've been there. He's in Bosham, on the Hoe. Believe me, the place is a fortress. You'd never force your way in there.'

'How about the girl?'

'She lives with Fortis now.'

'Nice,' says Pinto.

Marlowe smiles. 'We've known each other for a while now, Adam. I hope you feel I was able to help you and your family get through your financial difficulties. I love helping people. I've always wanted to make a positive difference in this world. I want to leave it better for me having been here.'

'I am grateful for what you did for us. But this is too much.'

'I'm sorry to hear that.'

A large French ferry sails past the tower.

'I'd love to be back in France right now, or even Spain,' says Marlowe. 'Did you know I spent the last three years in the Loire Valley?'

'I can't say I did.' Chambers checks his watch again and shifts in his seat.

'Running late?'

'I need to get back to Chichester. I don't want to cause any more suspicion than I have to.'

'Well then. The problem is, what do I do with you?'

'What do you mean, *do with me*? You can't do anything with me.'

'We'll see about that. You're of no use to me anymore.'

Chambers looks up at Pinto, towering over him, and licks his lips. 'That file is a copy, Marlowe. If anything happens to me, then someone will find the originals inside my desk.'

'Is that a threat?'

'No, it's my insurance.' Chambers holds his nerve, fixing his eyes on Marlowe.

'How about we call it quits then?' says Marlowe.

'You leave me alone now. Forget you ever knew me.'

'What do you think, Frank?'

Frank Pinto doesn't answer.

'I'm walking away now,' says Chambers. 'I don't want to hear from you again.'

Chambers stands and moves away from Pinto towards the stone staircase.

'The problem is, Adam,' says Marlowe, 'it's going to be very hard to forget you. Don't you think, Frank?'

'I agree, boss,' says Pinto.

'Find someone else to cover for you,' says Chambers. 'I'm done with you.'

He stands by the top step, and Pinto moves behind him. With both hands, Pinto launches Chambers down the steps. His head cracks against the wall, and he continues his spiralling descent to the bottom. Marlowe and Pinto walk down after him. Pinto stares into Chambers's vacant eyes and sees how his head has twisted to the side.

'I bet that hurt,' says Pinto.

Now that I'm here, my heart sinks back to that low place again. It's all the smells, tubes, and wires—they get to me every time. Hospitals. They've silenced the constant beeps from the medical machines for me. The hours I've spent listening to them used to drive me nuts.

The October sunshine pours through the blinds, lighting up Carrie's room. If Carrie were conscious, I imagine she would be looking out at the tranquil view of the South Downs with me, watching the migrating geese fly south towards the wetlands. We spent many weekends trudging the South Downs Way together, picnicking under secluded trees, and making love in the balmy days of summer. They were happy times.

But Carrie is in a coma, and this is her private room, looking out onto the corridor and the nurse's station. I sit beside her bed, gently brushing the blonde hair from her face, and kiss her cheek. This will be the last kiss I give her. The very last. Sitting back, I wish she would open those eyes once more so she could see me, and I could tell her what she had done to me.

'I've been coming here for the last nine months,' I say. I often talk to her when I'm here. I've told her my most intimate thoughts. 'I don't know if you've ever been aware of it. I've been wracked with guilt for what I did. Lacey was right. I hesitated. Part of me wanted you and Arthur to die for what you did, and I felt so guilty.'

Her heart rate fluctuates between sixty-five and seventy. Her oxygen saturation is ninety-nine per cent.

'Then I heard about your deal with Petrov,' I say. 'I had to check it, of course, and I saw the evidence for myself. You betrayed me, Carrie, twice over. You would have had me killed —you aligned with Petrov, of all people. Petrov! But the hardest thing to bear was you and Arthur. You let him blackmail you, and you never came to me. I can't forgive you for that.'

Her heart rate fluctuates between seventy-five and eighty.

I take in the view from the window again. 'Was I so worthless to you that you would sell me out so easily? There was so much we could have done together. So much.'

A nurse enters and examines the readings from the machines, jotting down notes. 'Would you like me to get you anything, Mr Fortis?'

I shake my head. 'No, thank you. She's so beautiful like this. I always thought she would wake up at any moment and laugh. Like it was a big joke or something.'

'She is truly beautiful,' says the nurse. 'I'm sorry, there's nothing more we can do.'

'It's okay. What's your name?'

She smiles. 'Shona.'

'Shona, I doubt I'll be coming back again. I'll keep paying the bills, but I'll leave her to die alone now. I must move on.'

Shona looks puzzled as I walk away, passing the nurse's station, heading down the corridor, and out through the double doors.

CHAPTER 26

It's Friday morning, and the first thing I want to do is buy a small van. I can't drive around Portsmouth in a Ferrari. Leon takes me to a used car garage owned by his friend. I need something that doesn't stand out—something large enough to store things in if I have to. I pay cash for a white VW Caddy van that won't attract attention. It's decent and easy to drive.

I must find somewhere to stay, and it needs to be a hotel with large numbers of domestic staff. I'm guessing that it should be central to the business district, not far from the old dockyard would be ideal. I know a large hotel near the city centre, and it's easy enough for me to hide in plain sight there. I'll be a few minutes from some of the nightlife and the shops on Commercial Road. I can't pay for a room under a cover name, so this is where having a good solicitor who knows your business comes in. His name is Charlie Green. He booked the room through his company for me. There's a sales conference there this weekend, and I've snatched one of the last available rooms. The hotel bills Charlie, and Charlie bills me, plus twenty-five per cent. I give them Charlie's name, and he does the rest.

Hotel foyers have excited me ever since I was a kid. There's just something about them. As a teenage boy, I remember travelling with my mother, standing behind her in countless hotels, waiting to be checked in. I especially loved it when they had the clocks on the wall with the times across the world. They would put her up in five-star hotels then. She was a well-respected expert in her field, so she got the best rooms.

I check in under Richard Bright, and they tell me it's all paid for. It's a good room on the sixth floor, but not the hotel's best. I like hotel rooms. You're secluded, nobody next door wants to talk to you, and you're treated with respect—most of the time.

As I settle into my room, the lights are coming on over Portsmouth and Southsea. From my window, I watch the last rays of sunlight reflecting off the sail-like curves of the Spinnaker Tower, lit white this evening. Dockyard cranes peek over the high-rises, topped by red spots glowing from their highest points. The sun has set a juicy blood orange-red, and the stars begin to poke through a purple-blue canopy.

I don't usually feel alone, but I do tonight. It's a weird feeling, and I don't like it. Carrie is dead to me now, and I feel a black void creeping up inside me.

My phone startles me when it rings. Ella is calling me.

'Is that Achilles?' she says, sniggering.

'Ella, how are things?'

'Okay. Grace confirmed that Andrew Harman was her father. She's like, *of course, he's my father*. It would have been helpful to know this at the beginning.'

'It's okay. Well done for that.'

'Well done? It wasn't difficult.' There's a pause, and I can hear her breathing. 'Are you okay?'

'I'm fine. I've booked into a hotel, and I'll start my search tomorrow.'

'I'm not convinced you're fine, but I guess that's your business. Are you missing me, Max? Is that what it is?' She laughs again.

'God, no,' I say.

'And I don't have a smart arse telling me what to do all day.'

'You have your Shira to play with.'

'Shira is amazing and lovely. I'm seriously in love with her.'

'You'll have to join the queue.'

There's another awkward pause. 'Max, be careful, okay?'

'I will.'

Another pause. 'Do you need some company?'

I don't know what to say. There's nothing I'd like more right now. 'I'm good. I'll crash and go to bed.'

She sighs. 'Going to bed early is a sign that you're getting old. Perhaps another time.'

'Yes, another time. And thanks, Ella. I appreciate it.'

When she's gone, I think about Carrie and how things used to be when we were together. It's the intimacy I miss more than anything. I don't have that anymore. Without thinking, I put my shoes on, go to the hotel bar, and do something I haven't done for many years.

———

Janie finishes her meal, strips off her dirty clothes, and steps into the hot shower. She's alone in here. A place of sanctuary from the men and women who abuse her. She scrubs herself with the jasmine soap and washes her hair. She examines the red marks on her wrists and tries not to think about how she got them. She wishes she could stay here under the hot, clean water. Their foul stench washes away and is no longer hers.

There's a rap on the door. It's time to come out. She wraps herself in one of the hotel towels and puts her dirty clothes into a bag. She may not see them again, especially if they've been ripped. Clean underwear, jogging bottoms, and a T-shirt are hanging over the towel rail. At least she has eaten. That was her reward.

'Hurry up!' shouts the woman.

Janie is finished. She only has time to towel-dry her hair and run a brush through it. The door opens, and Janie must avert her eyes. She's not permitted to look at their faces. She nods to say she is ready to go.

The woman leads her down the hotel corridor used by the staff. Janie's flip-flops flap out a rhythm as she walks.

'Are you hurt?' asks the woman.

Janie shakes her head.

'Did he use a condom?'

Janie shakes her head. They seldom do.

'I will give you a tablet,' says the woman.

They reach a fire door, and then they emerge into the darkness. The minibus is already here. The woman points, and Janie quickly climbs in, finding a seat in the dim light. The others are here, waiting in silence as the lingering scent of jasmine fills the minibus. But there is one missing—a boy. Janie can feel the tension from the others as they tremble in their seats, averting their eyes from Janie. Something has happened.

After a few minutes, the fire door clunks open, and Dennis

pushes the boy towards the minibus. The boy is struggling to walk. He has blood on his face and his jogging bottoms. Dennis puts a towel on the seat, and the boy eases himself down, crying in pain.

'He won't be working for a few weeks,' Dennis tells the woman. 'I made them pay for the damage.'

'He needs a doctor.'

'You know as well as I do that ain't going to happen.'

'We've got antibiotics,' says the woman. 'We'll have to see how he is.'

'Let's hope, for his sake, he heals soon.' Dennis gives the woman a knowing nod.

Janie hears and sees it all. One day, she will tell someone everything that's happened. She will tell them about her sister, the friend who ran away, and she will tell them about this boy.

The minibus door slides shut with a loud clunk, and Dennis drives them back to the factory.

CHAPTER 27

The girl lying in bed beside me must be ten years younger than me. I'm not sure, as I'm having trouble focusing. I don't remember so much about the night before, but whatever happened, I'm regretting it now.

She's facing the other way, naked, and her brown hair drapes over her white pillows. Delicate pink freckles cover her shoulders and run down the back of her forearm. I can't even remember her face, which makes me sad. This isn't something I do.

I get up and find my underwear. I'm always in the gym at this time of day, so it's no wonder my muscles are getting twitchy. I put on my jeans, and the girl stirs. Her arms cover her breasts, and she rolls onto her back, frowning. Her head must hurt, too.

'Do you want some water?' I say.

She opens one eye at me, smiles, and blushes.

'Yes, please,' she says in a sleepy voice.

I get her a clean glass and fill it with water from the bathroom. The man I glimpse in the mirror isn't someone I recognise. I run my fingers through my hair and return to her. She's put on her underwear now and is gathering her clothes.

'Thanks,' she says as I pass her the water. 'It's Hannah.'

'Good morning, Hannah. I'm Richard.'

'Hey, Richard. That was a fun evening.'

'Was it? I don't remember much about it.'

'Then it must have been good.' She runs a brush through her hair. 'You have a great body, by the way.'

'Thanks. And you.'

She laughs. 'You're not the talkative type.'

'No. I've not done this for a long time.'

'I can tell.' She stands and is now dressed in the clothes she wore last night. A short red dress—not quite the same look in the morning. 'Look, I have to go. I won't give you my number because you won't call. Am I right?'

'Yes, you are.'

'That's okay. It was fun, Richard. You have gorgeous eyes, by the way. I wish my eyelashes were as long as yours. Can we swap?'

'No, it's okay. It might freak my friends out.'

'That's true.'

I watch her collect her things and put on her long coat. She checks her bag and her purse.

'Do you need money for a taxi or anything?'

'No, I'm fine. I'm only in the student accommodation. It's about two hundred metres from here. Bye, Richard.'

That hurts. She's a student, and she uses metres instead of yards. She could be more than fifteen years younger than me. Gary would have something to say about that after the hassle I gave him.

She blows me a kiss and leaves. I'm left confused. Why did I do that? I can't afford to get distracted. It's Saturday morning, and I have a lowlife to find.

After a quick shower and change, I leave the hotel. My stomach's not feeling great, and I hope the ibuprofen kicks in soon. Since I don't know how much I drank last night, I leave the van where it is and walk into the city.

Portsmouth city centre isn't how I remember it. It was full of big-name stores once, but I guess it's the same thing that's happened to Chichester. This morning, one would never know there were crowds out the night before. An army of street cleaners has already been at work. You'd only know by the patches of vomit in the gutter and shop doorways.

What am I searching for? The putrid stench of Andrew Harman. He's a dog that's returned to his own vomit. I'm looking for coercive and controlling behaviour, and from my years of experience with this crime, I know where to look. The victims often have a controller telling them where to go and what to do.

Supplying an illegal workforce is likely a pointer to slave labour. Middle England hasn't woken up to the fact that slavery still exists in this country. They think it was something that only happened hundreds of years ago.

Where do I go? That's harder to answer and tempting to think of stereotypical targets like takeaways, car washes, and fruit pickers, but the reality can be more subtle. This is in everyone's neighbourhood, hidden in plain sight.

Recollections of questioning the bar staff last night start to resurface. Nobody wanted to talk about the foreigners working at the hotel being paid next to nothing. I asked whether they knew if sex workers were being brought in. A few blanked me —they thought I was a pervert. Others didn't want to know.

That's when I started talking to Hannah. I told her I was a reporter. She was serving behind the bar and kept coming back to talk to me with another shot of bourbon. I'm never going to touch bourbon again. The men from the conference were leching over her, and she didn't feel safe.

She told me she had seen a girl brought in from the railway station once. A cleaner—Asian. Hannah said she was crying most of the time, and Hannah wasn't allowed anywhere near her to check if she was okay. They took her away in a minibus. That was a good lead.

We know Excellent Impressions Cleaning operates in hotels. That's why I've gone to one of the busiest hotels in Portsmouth.

They have to bring them into the city somehow, moving them by train, car, or even straight from the docks. Following Hannah's comments, I'm starting at the railway station—it's as good a place as any.

I'm people-watching. Portsmouth and Southsea Station is busy on a Saturday morning. It's bright inside the station building, with the light pouring through glass panels in the apex of the roof. There's a coffee shop here and a cash machine. First-year university students are milling around, still finding their feet. I think of the beautiful Hannah in my bed this morning and feel that guilt again. Ima would not be impressed with me, but I push those thoughts aside. That's why I can't afford to act like an idiot. It distracts me.

I scan the crowd, searching for girls travelling with older men and women. Girls in hoodies, their faces covered, exuding body language of fear and defeat, being ushered left and right. I'm listening out for foreign voices or no voices. When you see it, you know. When you look into their eyes, you know.

I'm watching the ticket barrier, and the hours drift by. I've been trained to do this, to sit and watch while trying not to look like a terrorist or a crazy person. Crazy person—I don't think we can use that phrase nowadays. My hangover has gone, and now I'm hungry.

I take a break and step into the coffee shop, ordering a latte and a slice of pre-packaged fruitcake. There's a free stool here, so I sit, wait, and watch.

I finish the last dregs of my coffee, and someone pricks my attention. A skinny girl, sixteen to eighteen, with greasy blonde hair, grey tracksuit bottoms, and a hoodie over her head. She's pulling at strands of hair from under her hoodie and putting the ends in her mouth. An overweight man in his fifties in a black leather jacket and sunglasses is with her. She fits the description—so does he. He's bought her a bar of chocolate, and then I watch her eat it. She devours it at once, almost inhaling it. She drops the wrapper on the floor. That could be deliberate. They're hot on litter here. They have wardens that will fine you for dropping chewing gum. Maybe it was to get someone's attention. The man bends over, picks it up, and pokes her in the back. He's not happy with her.

Now I'm following them. They queue up at a ticket machine, so I queue behind them. I try to catch the girl's eye, but her head is down. He punches in two singles to Brighton. I buy my ticket and follow them through the barrier.

I pretend to scroll through my phone as I stand behind them on the platform, waiting for them to climb onto the train. He's keeping the girl in front of him, and they don't speak. They find a seat together. She sits nearest the window, and he sits nearest the aisle. I move opposite him, and he shifts in his seat as our knees touch. He's uncomfortable and wondering why I didn't take one of the other empty seats.

'This is the train to Brighton, right?' I ask him.

'Yes,' he says. Short and sweet. He's English with a local accent.

The girl is looking down at the floor. Her arms are folded, and her hands are tucked inside the sleeves of the hoody.

'Are you and your daughter going shopping?'

He frowns at me, wondering why I'm still talking to him. 'No.'

'No?'

'She's not my daughter.'

The train jolts and begins to move. The man gets out a mobile from his leather jacket, and I catch the girl snatching a glance at me.

'I bet you'd like to go shopping,' I say to her. I sound like a creep.

'Please,' said the man, 'don't talk with her. She won't understand.'

'Really? Where is she from?'

'Please mind your own business,' he says.

'She's not your daughter. Any other relative?'

'What?' The man sits forward. 'No. Please, can you leave us alone now?'

The train has reached full speed.

'Do you want to go with this man?' I ask the girl.

She shakes her head.

'She would say that,' the man says.

'What's going on? Where are you taking her?'

'Go away!' he shouts. 'It has nothing to do with you.'

I grab him by the collar. 'If you're harming her, then it has.'

'For God's sake, I'm a social worker! I'm taking her to a children's home. She ran away. Let me show you.'

I let him get something from his pocket. It's a lanyard, *East*

Sussex Social Services. Shit! The girl laughs. It's a big joke to her.

'I'm sorry,' I say. 'I thought—'

'I know what you thought,' he says. 'Commendable, I'm sure. You assaulted me. I should call the police.'

The train slows. It's pulling into Fratton Station.

'Okay, I'm leaving. You ought to keep that lanyard on.'

'I don't want to stigmatise her. You get off here, and we'll call it quits.'

I nod, and I get off at Fratton. This is a bad day. As the Brighton train pulls away, I wonder if I've completely lost my touch.

———

I return to the hotel and head to my room to crash out on the bed. It's been made up, and the coffee and minibar have been replenished. I check my mobile, and there are no new messages. I need to do better than this if I'm going to move forward.

Something catches my eye on my bedside table. It's a small blue business card. Housekeeping must have left it there.

Room cleaned. Any concerns?
Call Housekeeping on 1607

Supplied by Excellent Impressions Cleaning

We also provide bespoke

personal services for

business travellers

The last four lines are in small print. Bespoke personal services—intriguing. I've struck lucky at last. However, is it too convenient? I've been in the city for just a day, and I've already found a lead. If this is a trap, then they know I'm here, and if that's the case, who told them? No. I'm going to give this some thought and put the card in my wallet. They have a gym at the hotel. That's where I'm heading now—it will clear my head of the last twenty-four hours.

I put a few things into a holdall and start making my way to the gym. I pass trolleys used by housekeeping services along the corridor covered in fresh, folded towels. Looking through an open doorway, used bed linen is on the floor, and fresh glasses are on the side.

A young Asian woman with her black hair in bunches steps into view, and she sees me.

'Your room will be another fifteen minutes, sir,' she says.

'That's okay,' I say. 'It's not my room. Are you all contract cleaners, or does the hotel employ you?'

She's puzzled and puts her head back a little. 'Is there a problem, sir?'

'None at all. You all do a great job. Are you all employed by the hotel?'

'Most of us are,' she says. 'A few contractors come in when it gets busy.' Her accent hints that she's local to Portsmouth.

'I had a card put in my room. Can I show you? I thought it was a little strange.'

She steps out of the room and examines the card I take out of my wallet.

'They're the contractors,' she says. 'But these *bespoke personal services*? That's a little dodgy if you ask me.' She laughs. 'If I were you, I'd speak to the duty manager. He wouldn't be happy with that.'

'Thank you. That's what I thought.'

She nods at me as I continue my journey to the gym. So, they have a contract here. That makes me feel a little easier. It appears they are targeting men staying alone at the hotel. I won't show the manager yet. I want to make some calls first.

CHAPTER 28

I dial 1607 from my room phone. The line purrs with an internal ringtone.

'Housekeeping services, Dennis speaking. How can I help you?' His voice sounds polite and cheerful.

'I've had a card placed in my room, six-zero-three, saying you provide bespoke *personal* services.'

The phone clicks and purrs again. I'm put through to another number, and a woman answers. I repeat what I said to Dennis.

'That's correct,' she says. 'What service would you like?'

'I don't know. I guess you don't mean extra polishing.'

'No, sir.'

I pretend to fumble through this, like some nervous adolescent. 'Girls?'

'Yes. What's your preference?'

'I like them young and pretty, and they must speak English. Happy to do anything I want.'

'I see.'

'Only one girl. And not quick. I want a couple of hours.'

'Okay.'

'And I want to pay in cash.'

'We only take cash. That's going to cost you four hundred for two hours. Another thousand if you damage her.'

I feel sick. 'Four hundred.'

'What time would you like her?'

'Eight o'clock? I should have the cash by then.'

'Room six-zero-three?'

'Yes.'

'You pay the cash upfront to Dennis at the door. Then he hands over the girl.'

'Great.'

'Make sure you keep this to yourself.'

The call ends, and I stand up, needing a moment to catch my breath. I'm sweating. Memories flood back to when I worked on cases like this many years ago and how dirty it made me feel. The darkness of the job, the compromises made, the ethical lines blurred—it was a stain that never entirely washed away.

I call Lacey and fill her in on the day's events. Once she stops laughing about the train episode, I tell her about my plan.

'She'll be here at eight o'clock,' I tell her. 'Can you get someone to me by then?'

'I can. Is that to stop you from killing her controller?'

'It is, and she'll need rescuing. A safe house.'

'There's a charity we deliver them to once we've got our best evidence.'

'Thanks, Janice.'

'Good job, Achilles. If you need some alone time with this man called Dennis, my woman will wait.'

'Thanks.'

After the call, I splash my face with water and look at

myself again. This type of job screws with your emotions and makes you feel isolated. I must stay professional and stick to the job at hand. My personal feelings don't matter now. That's not how it works. I'm going to have to leave the hotel after this. I have a feeling Harman's operation is focused on Portsmouth, and he'll soon be looking for me here. Hopefully, I'll find enough evidence for the local police to deal with him, but I doubt Harman will come without a fight. Knowing Harman, he'll go into hiding first, and then he'll come all guns blazing for me. What I'm about to do will send him a clear message. I'm going to tread all over his territory.

After the gym and showering, I go to the bar, which serves food. Hannah isn't here—she only works evenings. I feel like my usual self again, and I've stopped feeling ashamed. I'm taking it as a lesson learned, and I'm always learning. The news from Lacey about Carrie must have hit me harder than I thought. It's a whole new level of betrayal, which was bound to affect me. I've had to stop myself from wondering how much Ima and Leon knew. They've only ever been faithful to me. Maybe they were protecting me. Ima will always protect me.

After a plate of protein, fat, and carbs—steak and chips—I call Ella. I can hear she's outside, walking somewhere.

'I know it's Saturday,' I say, 'but I wanted to check you were okay.'

'All good, thanks. I'm out for a walk with my mum.'

'I won't interrupt—'

'No, it's okay. She's busy gossiping with a friend she's met.'

'How was your session with Ima?'

'It doesn't hurt so much today, and I'm loving it. Shira's so interesting and scary. Do you mind if I ask you something?'

'Here we go,' I say. 'Do your worst.'

'Why do you call her Ima and not Shira?'

I laugh. 'What else should I call my mother?'

'She's your mother!'

'Yes. She's my ima. It means mother or mum in Hebrew.' There's a stunned silence on the other end of the phone.

'Oh no! I asked her if ima was her code name.' I can feel her cringing from here. 'So that's why your uncle took Shira in. She was his brother's wife.'

'Well done, Sherlock.'

'No wonder you're so good...' Ella's voice fades. 'Never mind. Anyway, I talked to her about the CCTV image of the van at Houghton.'

'Okay?'

'I think this is interesting. Excellent Impressions Cleaning. Shira said something that clinched it for me. She said that in old Hebrew, Jethro means excellence, and when you think about it...'

'Matisse was a post-Impressionist artist?'

'Yes! Clever, eh!'

'Cheesy. I should have known about Jethro.'

'Jethro's not as cheesy as Achilles.' She laughs. 'It's okay. Mum can't hear me. Sorry, my *ima* can't hear me.'

She can't see me roll my eyes. 'Listen, when they made up my room, I found a business card beside my bed. I spoke to one of the regular housekeeping staff about it. It's from Excellent Impressions Cleaning. They're contracted to provide extra staff when the hotel is busy, and it's pretty bustling with a conference this weekend.'

'Okay, so they cleaned your room.'

'Not only does the card say they made up my room, but they're also offering bespoke personal services to business travellers.'

Ella sniggers. 'Who's a lucky boy then? If that's something that floats your boat.'

'Not particularly. And these people could be sex slaves, Ella.'

'Now I feel bad,' she says.

'Good. Anyway, things are moving along.'

'What are you going to do now, Achilles?'

'I'm going to pose as a client. I must talk to one of them. I've asked Commander Lacey for some backup. It's going to be a little awkward. But…'

'Do you want me to come over?' she asks.

'I really would. But it wouldn't be a good idea.'

'Why not? I'm not doing anything here.'

'Because…'

'Because?'

'You'd be too distracting for me,' I say.

Ella goes quiet for a few seconds. 'What do you mean by that?'

'I'd be worried about your safety. I'll keep you updated, and thank Ima for me. That was helpful.'

'I will definitely thank your *ima*. Look after yourself, Max. Stay focused, eh?'

As the call ends, I sigh. Yes, I must remain focused. Perhaps hiring Ella wasn't such a good idea.

CHAPTER 29

A tall woman with cropped hair called Nelly has come from HQ. I'm unsure if that's her real name, but she's a police officer—she looks ex-army. She didn't say much when she came, and she's now sitting in front of the TV after raiding the contents of the minibar.

'You get what we're doing tonight?' I ask her. 'You're fully briefed?'

Nelly nods, finishing a tub of cashews. 'I had a phone call with Commander Lacey before I rushed down here. It's all good.'

'Do you work on Lacey's team?'

'Yep. And I've heard of you. You're a bit of a legend. They still talk about you.'

I nod, not sure what to say to that. I check my watch—it's one minute to eight.

Nelly and I turn towards the door when we hear a knock. She nods at me.

'Housekeeping,' says a male voice. It's Dennis.

'Coming,' I say.

I crack the door open. Standing before me is a young girl, a skinny bag of nerves. Close behind her is an ugly, overweight man, stinking of foul body odour, trying his best to intimidate me. My guess is that the girl is Thai. She's wearing a white crop top and a short black skirt—no older than sixteen. Her eyes are on the floor at first, and when she sees how tall I am, she starts to tremble.

'Does she speak English?' I say to Dennis.

'Yes,' he says with a grunt. 'Give me the money now.'

I hand him four hundred pounds in fifties and twenties.

'What if I'm finished sooner?' I say.

He sneers at me. 'Call 1607.'

'Okay.'

'If you break her, it will cost you another thousand. Don't let her out until I come to collect her.'

'Right.'

He pushes the girl into my room, and she staggers forward, her hands held together in front of her, and biting her lip. Dennis walks away, and I close the door. The girl moves towards the bed, keeping her eyes focused on the floor.

'No. Stay there,' I say to her. 'You're going to be okay now.'

She lifts her head, and her eyes go wide in horror when she sees Nelly in the chair. Nelly turns off the TV.

I reach over to a desk chair. My bags are packed beside it. I pick up my jacket and hold it out to her.

'Put this on, and don't be afraid. We want to help you.' I'm not sure she understands what I'm saying. 'We're not going to hurt you. You are safe now.' She looks cautiously at me and then at the jacket. 'You can keep it. We're going to get you away from that man. Do you understand me?'

She shakes her head and panics. 'No! Please! He'll beat me so hard. I need to eat. I can't go with you.'

I take two steps back and crouch down to her level. She has dark rings below her eyes and she's thin, malnourished.

'My name is Max, and this woman is called Nelly. Nelly is a police officer, and there are police officers in a car outside. You have done nothing wrong. We want to help you escape and find safety. I promise we will not touch you without your permission. Put on the jacket—you can keep it.'

She tentatively takes the jacket and puts it on. It looks enormous on her, but it gives her a layer of protection.

'Good.' I smile at her. 'What is your name?'

'Daisy.'

'Is that your *real* name?'

'No. My name is Janie.'

'Janie, do you want us to take you away from that man? To go somewhere safe.'

'He will find me! They will find me!'

'No. They won't, Janie. I will find *them*, and they will never do this to you or to others again. I am going to stop them.'

Tears well up in her eyes, and she nods at us. 'Yes, please! Help me.'

'Janie, it's okay. Listen to me. Nelly and I have a plan. You will not be left alone with me. Please trust us.'

'Do you understand?' says Nelly.

She's sobbing now. 'My sister.'

'I can only start with you, Janie,' I say.

'She is dead. The men made her sick.'

'I am so sorry. I'm here to get the men who are doing this. I promise I will do my best.'

'Thank you.'

I turn to Nelly. 'We must move quickly.'

It's dark outside, and Ella waits for Leon to let Gary in through the gate and bring him into the lounge. Shira is knitting in an armchair and looks up as Gary enters. He appears pale and worried. Leon has gone to get him a coffee.

'Gary,' says Ella. 'What's wrong?'

'Where's Max? Is he still in Portsmouth?'

'He is.'

'Detective Sergeant Chambers is dead.'

Ella sits up. 'How?'

'I don't understand it, to be honest. He was found in the Round Tower in Old Portsmouth. It appears he fell, fractured his skull, and broke his neck.'

'That's awful. How likely is it he simply fell?'

'Unlikely, in my opinion. Look, I have to ask, and I feel bad about it. Do you think Max might have…'

'Pushed him? No!'

'No way!' says Shira, jerking up from her chair.

Gary rubs his eyes. 'It's just that, with the recent friction between them and everything.'

'The friction was only coming from Chambers,' says Ella. 'But I think things were pretty much resolved after Max went to see him.'

'That's what I said to the SIO, the senior investigating officer in Portsmouth CID.'

'Why was Chambers in Portsmouth?' asks Leon, handing Gary a coffee.

'I don't know. He never said he was going. We don't have a case that way—apart from Jethro Matisse, of course.'

'Could he have been trying to find Matisse?' asks Ella.

'There's nothing in the crime log about it. No, it's all fishy. He would have updated control if he were leaving the area. But we have nothing. There are no witnesses, forensics, or CCTV apart from him on The Hard, watching the boats go by. He checked his watch a few times.'

'I'm so sorry, Gary.'

'Can I talk to Max?'

'You can't tonight,' says Shira. 'He's in the middle of something important. I'll have him call you once he's back.'

'Thanks.'

'You look terrible,' says Shira. 'Have you eaten, or are you still on duty?'

'I've finished for the night. I'm going back to my flat to eat yesterday's leftover Chinese.'

'Let me make you something better for you than leftover Chinese. How about a spicy chicken stir-fry with noodles?'

Before Gary can say anything, Shira is up and out to the kitchen.

'His death seems too much of a coincidence,' says Ella.

'Chambers has got caught up in something,' says Gary. 'He kept pushing for the Garcia murder case to be written off as suicide. It was the senior investigating officer who stopped him. Then he tried to frame Max and bury Garcia's text messages. I had to call my SIO. It was my duty.'

'Max is right about you, Gary,' says Ella. 'You're a good man.'

'Cheers. He was right about you, too.'

'Oh? What did he say?'

Gary winks. 'Oh, I can't say.'

'He said you're adorable,' says Leon.

Ella laughs. 'I doubt he said that, Leon. But it was a good try.'

I move out into the corridor and listen and hear the droning of voices from a TV in the room opposite mine. It's all clear, so I walk over to the lifts—Dennis has gone. I glance up at the corners of the ceiling. There's no CCTV.

When I return to the room, Nelly is wearing her stab vest with a police-issue Glock 19M hanging from it. She smiles at me.

'Ready?' I say.

Nelly nods. 'Janie,' she says. 'Are you okay if I put my hand on your shoulder to guide you? It's so that we keep together.'

'Yes,' says Janie. Her eyes are fixed on Nelly. She looks like an Amazon warrior in all her gear.

We leave my room and head down the corridor until we reach the lifts. One of them is moving up and stopping on our floor. I ready myself, and the doors open. A man in a suit steps out, engrossed in his mobile. He doesn't even notice us as he turns the corner.

We get in the lift, and I hit the button to take us to the ground floor. The doors take ages to close, but they slide shut just as someone walks past. We head down to the sound of electronic piano music playing from the speaker. This is so bizarre.

Janie is trembling beneath my jacket and reaches out to Nelly to hold her hand. Nelly needs both her hands free, so she tells her to grab her belt instead.

'Stay close to me, Janie,' says Nelly with a smile. 'I will protect you.'

We step out of the lift, and Nelly has her hand on Janie's shoulder. We must look a strange sight as we walk through the foyer. The attention falls on Nelly, in her stab vest and gun. She speaks into her police radio.

We step outside and hear the screech of a car braking hard. It's a black BMW, an armed response vehicle. A male officer in uniform is driving, and next to him is another female officer. I turn to Janie.

'I'm going to stop them, Janie. I promise. These police officers will take care of you, and hopefully, you can go home soon.'

'Home?' she says, almost as if it's a place she'd only heard of in a dream.

The female officer gets into the back of the unmarked police car with Janie, and they go. Janie is safe.

I turn to Nelly. 'Now for Dennis,' I say.

'Try not to *break him*,' she says.

We head back to my room, meeting no one on the way. Nelly puts the TV back on, and I dial 1607 on the phone.

'All done,' I say to Dennis.

'That was quick. Still the same price, or did you damage her?'

'No, she's okay. You can come and get her. I've had enough.'

I cringe as I put the phone down.

A few minutes later, there's a tap on the door.

'I'm just going to the toilet,' says Nelly.

I nod.

I let the man in, closing the door behind me. His stench

quickly fills the room—someone really should tell him about his personal hygiene issues.

He puffs out his chest, frowns, and glances around. 'Where is she?'

'She's not here,' I say.

'What do you mean?'

'Janie is with the police.'

His face changes and is filled with rage. He lunges towards me with both hands, but I've slipped to the side and dodged him.

'Who are you?' he says.

'My name is Max Fortis, and at the end of our time here, Dennis, you will tell me three things. How many other girls are in the hotel, where you are keeping them, and where is Jethro Matisse?'

Dennis throws a sudden punch at me. I deflect it and move in on him, launching him against the wall. It's then I notice he's wearing a stab vest of his own under his jacket. It makes things a little more tricky, but nothing too challenging.

He's coming for me again, and there's something in his hand now. A knuckle-duster. Those things can kill you. He's standing in a boxing stance. He knows how to fight. Great. Where's a police officer when you need one?

He comes with two fast punches, and I block them. They're too fast to take advantage of, and he's covering himself straight-away. Now he's smiling. That's one good way to piss me off.

He moves lightly on his feet, sparring with me. He's surprisingly agile for an ugly, fat man. I don't care—he's expending energy. Fighting is draining, so I let him continue. He throws two more punches, but I duck to the right, raise my knee and extend my leg, sweeping his legs away. He lands with a heavy thud on his back, grimacing. It's knocked the stuffing out of him.

He tries to roll over, but I land my full weight on his right patella, dislocating his knee and cracking his fibula. The air turns blue, but it gets a lot worse for him as I flex his broken knee out of place.

The room is full of screaming until I stuff the end of a sheet in his mouth.

'Ah, Dennis,' I say. 'I bet that hurts. Has anyone told you that you stink?'

I push his lower leg again, flexing his fractured fibula. He's thrashing around with his arms until the pain gets too much, and he passes out for a few seconds. Then it starts again when he comes to.

'If you want this to stop, Dennis, tell me what I want to know. How many other girls are in the hotel? Where are you keeping them? Where is Jethro Matisse?' He thrashes again, so I increase the tension in his knee. 'Are you going to tell me?'

He nods, so I remove the bloody sheet from his mouth. He's bitten his tongue.

'Screw you!'

The thumb gouging his eye breaks him—more noise.

'No more girls here!' He's whimpering now. 'Stop! I beg you!'

'Stop? I bet those girls begged for it to stop. Did you help them? Where are you keeping the others?'

'Factory unit. Frances Nelson Park, Unit 10.'

'Good.' I relieve the pressure. 'And Matisse? Where is he?'

'I don't know. None of us know.'

'Us?'

'Shit. Please. Don't do this! They'll kill me.'

'Why shouldn't I kill you? You torture children and feed them to perverts.'

'We deal with Frank Pinto. He works for him.'

I let him go and stamp on his other knee for good measure. That level of pain has knocked him out.

The bathroom door unlocks. 'God, what's that awful smell?' says Nelly. 'You haven't killed him, have you?'

'No, officer. He attacked me, and I defended myself using reasonable force. Section three, Criminal Justice Act.'

'Sounds good to me,' she says. 'I'd better call him an ambulance.'

The office is hot and sweaty, soaked in purple light. Music and cheering rise from the floor as the second act gets underway. Phil is at his desk, and Pinto stands before him, waiting for the tantrum to subside.

'Shit, Frank!' Phil holds his head in his hands. 'How did this happen? Eh?'

'We don't know, boss! Palmer must have said something.'

'Palmer? He's one of yours, isn't he?'

'He is—Dennis. His wife works here.'

'Where's the loyalty? Loyalty! They swear their allegiance to us. As you have.'

'I don't know, boss. The Filth are all over the hotel. But Palmer keeps everything clean. They won't find anything. I checked myself. Hazel is the same.'

'Who the hell is Hazel?'

'She picks the girls. Matches them to the clients.'

'I hope, for your sake, Palmer is dead. And this Hazel.'

'He's in hospital. He knows the price for failure. They all do.'

'How did the police know? What's the betting Fortis is behind it?'

'There was no Fortis booked into—'

'Of course there wasn't, idiot! Do you need replacing, too, Frank? You're losing your touch.'

'I am not losing my touch,' he says through gritted teeth. 'And I've always been loyal.'

'Then why are you still here? Fix it. And send a memo. Tell everyone Jethro Matisse demands loyalty. Make sure everyone gets it.'

'Yes, boss.'

'Remember what I have in my possession, Frank? Don't let me down.'

'Yes, boss. I remember.'

Phil Marlowe kicks back his chair and stands by the window. 'Mariana learned a lesson in loyalty. She thought she could escape me. But I caught up with her in the end.'

'You did, boss.'

'Palmer's wife—bring her to me. She's going to record a message about loyalty. It's something to share with her colleagues. And get me a change of clothes. I want to see Clarice afterwards.'

CHAPTER 30

I've checked out of the hotel. It's swarming with Hampshire Constabulary's finest. Dennis is in hospital and has been arrested. They've made another arrest of the woman I spoke to on the phone who arranged the meeting. DCI Scott from the Met has come to Portsmouth, representing Lacey and supporting local police.

Scott and I are in my VW Caddy. He's listening to his police radio and following a raid that's going on near Eastern Road, one of the routes in and out of the city. Police have entered the factory unit situated in a deserted corner of Frances Nelson Park. Initial estimates are ten young adults locked inside the unit— seven females and three males. All hungry and, according to reports, desperate. One of the males has serious injuries. The noise from a nearby waste recycling centre had covered their cries for help. Specialist officers have taken them under their wing.

When I heard the information coming back from the raid, I sat back in my seat and sighed with relief. It was all worth it.

Yes, I tortured the man called Dennis. A means to an end, and nothing compared to what he had done to those innocents.

DCI Scott comes off a call to the Gold Commander running the operation.

'No links were found to Jethro Matisse or Andrew Harman in the unit,' says Scott. 'And no paperwork. We're going to need translators for those kids.'

'Questioning them will take time and patience,' I say.

'The guy who brought the girl to you, his full name's Dennis Palmer,' says Scott. 'We've seized his mobile, and we're getting it examined. In the housekeeping office, there was a list on the desk. Names of hotels across the Portsmouth area.'

'Can I have a look at the list?'

Scott smiles. 'Not officially, but as it's you.'

Scott brings out his mobile and shows me the photo of the list of hotels. I'm going through each one, trying to find a connection.

'I can see why Lacey wants to keep you in her sights,' he says.

I laugh. 'MI5—you can never leave. You're theirs for a lifetime.'

'It wasn't what I expected,' says Scott. 'I'm still a cop, and I don't get to see everything that goes on in the background. You were on the enforcement end, so I get why it wasn't easy doing that day in and day out. Most people I've met in Thames House are regular people. No flashy James Bond characters anywhere. It's a mix of nobodies you live next door to. But then there were a few like you. There aren't many people who can do that now.'

I shrug. 'I have an arrangement with Lacey. I'll help her

out from time to time. That's the most I'm going to do for them now.'

I continue to scan the list, and I wish Scott would stop talking. There are about thirty hotels listed, and I only know a few of them.

'Anything jump out at you?' says Scott.

'No,' I say and shake my head. 'Shit! We're still no closer to finding Harman. I was sure this would lead us to him.'

'You've disrupted his operation. That's a good thing. I wonder how long he will take to work out it was you.'

'Bring it on,' I say. 'Can you send me that list? I'm going to have to rethink.'

I arrive home a few minutes before midnight. Leon is waiting up for me with Ella in the lounge. Ima, asleep beside Leon, stirs when I come in.

'You've kicked the hornet's nest,' says Leon. 'They will try to find you now.'

'Harman won't know it was me yet. It will give me some time to get a plan together.'

'Max, DS Chambers is dead,' says Ella.

I stare at her. I'm tired, and what she said takes a few moments to sink in. Then she tells me about Gary's visit and how Chambers was found.

'I wonder if he spoke to Harman,' I say. 'I hope DI Reeves managed to tail him.'

'That's what Gary said,' says Ella. 'He said he knew he was being followed and lost them.'

'If that's the case, then Harman now has everything I

shared with Chambers. We were hoping Chambers would lead us to him, to draw him out of hiding.'

'Mariana's computer is back from forensics,' says Ella. 'They've recovered a pile of emails and a folder containing photos. You'll want to look at a proposal document they found. That's all we have so far. It's locked in my desk in the office.'

'That's something, at least,' I say. I crash on the sofa next to Ella. Her hair is a little wet. She must have only just got out of the shower.

'Sounds like it was still a success tonight,' says Leon.

'They recovered ten young people—kids—from the unit. They were all in a bad way—petrified. They found two more in the hotel. All from abroad. Some were students, and others were brought over with promises of work. Still no Harman. That would have been too easy.'

Ella passes me my hot chocolate and smiles. 'I'd say that was a good result, Max. One step closer.'

'How many more of them are out there?' I say. 'They found a list of hotels in Portsmouth. He could be using all of them.'

Ella crosses her legs on the sofa and turns towards me. 'I took the liberty of going over the undeleted emails. There were a couple of exchanges with Daniel Cole. Cole told Mariana she was in danger. Cole and Mariana were having an affair many years ago. I want to show you something, or do you want to read it tomorrow?'

'Go on.'

Ella produces a printed copy of an email. 'This is what Cole wrote to Garcia the night before they met for dinner.'

Ella has highlighted the text she wants me to read.

The table is booked for 8:00 p.m. Don't be late. I'll let you know where you can find him. I won't put it in an email in case there are prying eyes. He calls himself 'Jethro' now. He only lets a few people know where he is. He demands loyalty from everyone but trusts no one. He'll kill me if he finds out I told you. Are you sure you won't come to Scotland with me? Get away from him forever.

'This is so frustrating!' I say. 'He must have told Mariana where she could find Andrew Harman. Now that's gone with her.'

Ella is watching me. 'If I were to give you the address of something important, would you expect me just to tell you?'

'No,' says Ima, still sleepy. 'You would write it down and give it to him.'

'Precisely, Max's ima!' says Ella, pointing at Ima with a tired smile. 'He would have written it down, too, or she would.'

'Is it in her bag?' I say. 'Her purse? There's nothing recorded on her phone.'

'Was she wearing a coat?' says Ella. 'I'd put it in my pocket if he gave it to me as he left.'

'Her coat? Her bloody jacket! The woman at the pub, Ella. The woman at the pub stole Mariana's jacket. She's probably emptied everything out of there by now.'

'We can only try,' she says.

CHAPTER 31

It's funny the things you think about when you're driving. The 9th of October, today, would have been my father's birthday. My mother and I spent some time this morning talking about him and sharing our memories. He and my ima had been married for fifteen years when he was killed in action. I was thirteen. When I was sixteen, my mother had moved permanently to the UK, and I left home at nineteen to join the police. Ima said I was too young.

I often wonder what my father would make of me now and what he would have thought of Carrie. He was a good judge of character. Apparently, much better than I am. Everybody loved Carrie. I loved her and never knew what she saw in me. Now I know—nothing.

'You're miles away,' says Ella. 'Are you okay?'

I glance at her. She's looking chilled in the passenger seat of the Ferrari. I wasn't going to take the red car, but she whined like a child until I gave in.

'Nothing, really. I was thinking of my father and mother.

Ima remarried five years after my father died. Leon gave her a new reason to live. What was your husband's name?'

'Simon,' she says. 'Two years this year. I struggle with the idea of loving someone else.'

'Ima thought the same thing, but then she met Leon.'

The red car cruises to the top of Bury Hill, north of Arundel, until I reach a roundabout. Ella is humming something tuneful.

'You have a nice voice,' I say. 'How long were you married?'

'Seven years. Simon would have loved you. You're an all-action hero compared to him. He was a different kind of hero. The Big C got him in the end.'

'I'm sorry.'

She nods and smiles at me. I take the exit towards Amberley and Storrington.

'How are you going to get the coat from the woman?' she asks.

'I'll try reasoning with her.'

'I know how your reasoning works.'

'I'm not a monster, Ella.'

I can see she's looking at me. 'I've never seen someone kill another person before. It was quite a shock. I've thought about what you did, and I know now you had little choice.'

'I didn't get any pleasure out of it.'

'I know. I never thanked you. They would have killed you if you hadn't, and I would have been next. You saved my life.'

We descend through Houghton and past the holiday cottages, where we watched the CCTV. Within a few moments, the red car purrs over the bridge, getting curious glances from walkers as they duck out of our way. We head into the pub car park, and I park facing outwards.

It's gone eleven o'clock on a Monday morning, so the Travellers Rest isn't busy. We can see lights on inside and shadows moving at the windows.

'Ready?' I say. 'You pin her down, and I'll hit her.'

Ella laughs. 'Good cop, bad cop, is it?'

'Bad cop and worse cop. Don't worry. I'll be subtle—I promise.'

The landlady's name is Elaine Whitcliff, according to the notice above the pub door, and she's serving behind the bar when we walk in. I greet her and introduce Ella, ordering a lime and soda for her.

'You were in here a few months ago,' Whitcliff says, 'asking about the author who threw herself off the bridge.'

'You have a good memory,' I say. 'It was even more tragic than that, sadly. Turns out she was murdered.'

'I didn't realise she'd been murdered!' Whitcliff's jaw drops. 'That's awful!'

'A terrible thing. DC Bates from Chichester police came and spoke to you.'

She has a nervous twitch.

'Did he? Oh yes, I remember.'

'He asked you about a missing jacket,' I say, watching the twitch grow more intense. 'He said you told him there wasn't a jacket, but I think there's been some mistake.'

'What do you mean?' She's now scratching the palm of her hand.

'I saw the woman the evening she was murdered, and I distinctly remember her wearing a black leather jacket. She wasn't wearing the jacket when the police pulled her out of the water, was she, Ella?'

'No, Max,' Ella agrees. 'Did the search teams find it?'

'No, they didn't, which means one of two things.'

'What?' says Whitcliff. That nervous rash on her hand is getting worse.

'Either the killer removed it before killing her, or someone took it from the bridge.'

'The killer must have taken it,' says Whitcliff. She's peering up and down the bar, probably wishing she could serve someone else.

'Well, yes,' I say. 'Because you said you didn't see it.'

'Why are you telling me all this?'

'Because if someone took the jacket, they would be committing a serious criminal offence. Not only theft but also perverting the course of justice. Do you know the maximum penalty for perverting the course of justice?'

'I've no idea,' says Whitcliff, glancing behind her.

'Life imprisonment.'

'Well.' She swallows. 'That's not good.'

'Elaine,' I whisper, leaning forward. She mirrors me.

'It's okay. I know you have the jacket, but I won't tell the police.'

'Do I?'

I nod. 'We know you do.'

Her face is now a bright, sweaty pink. 'Come back here with me for a minute.'

She lifts a hatch, and we walk out behind the back of the bar. Elaine goes to a coat rack full of raincoats. She lifts one off and hands us a black leather Ralph Lauren jacket, hiding underneath. I pass it to Ella. There are zips on the breast pockets, and she searches them. Next, she moves to the inside of the jacket. There's one zipped pocket, and she feels inside. It seems like we're out of luck, but then she freezes. Her fingers pull at something. I can see a yellow Post-it note stuck to the lining, and she peels it off and puts it in her jeans pocket.

'Take the bloody jacket!' says Whitcliff. 'I don't want it anywhere near me.'

'Are you sure?' I say. 'I'm going to hand it to the police. Do you want me to tell them you found it?'

'No! Please. It's okay. Tell them someone handed it in.'

I wink at her and nod. 'Okay, Elaine. No worries. You've got my card if you need to contact me.'

Elaine is glad to see the back of us when we leave. A couple of young men are standing next to the red car, having their photographs taken. When we arrive, they make off into the pub. Before Ella gets in, she pulls out the Post-it note and reads it out.

'The Obsidian Rooms, Duchess Street, Southsea.'

'That's a nightclub,' I say. 'A nightclub with a certain kind of entertainment.'

'Strippers? Have you been there before?'

'Me?' I laugh. 'Not my thing. I'm more of a cosy pub person.'

'This could be the type of place Harman frequents,' says Ella. 'Worth a look? A bit of a risk going back into Portsmouth, though.'

'It is. They may recognise me now.'

'Why don't I go in there?'

'Too dangerous.'

'Oh, come on, Max. They don't know who I am.'

A phone call interrupts us—saved by the bell. It's Leon.

'Max, you'd better get back here now,' he says. 'There's been a fire. Someone has broken into your office.'

CHAPTER 32

When we arrived at the office in Bosham, the fire was already under control. There's a crowd here watching from the street. The police have taped off the scene, and the hoses are soaking what's left of the shell of the building. It went up quickly.

Gary is here waiting for me and has the fire service watch manager with him. There's a forensic fire investigation unit here, taking photos.

'Arson,' says Gary. 'Witnesses saw three men in black smashing the windows and throwing petrol bombs in there. Members of the public thought you were still inside.'

Ella is standing close to me. 'That lovely office! This must have been Harman,' she says.

'No doubt,' I say.

'So sorry, mate,' says Gary.

'It's okay,' I say. 'Everything is insured. There was nothing in there that can't be replaced.'

'I locked Mariana's computer away in my desk,' says Ella.

'Oh, that's unfortunate.'

'You seem remarkably cool about it, Max,' says Gary.

'What do you want me to say? It's only an office. I'll get another one. Harman has sent me a message. Maybe he thought I lived above it. Are you checking CCTV?'

'The chip shop's camera caught what happened.'

'The chip shop has a camera?' I say. 'What is this world coming to?'

'A grey pickup, number plates removed.'

'No one injured?'

'No. Scared a few pensioners waiting for their lunchtime cod and chips.'

'I'll write my own statement for you. This has to be Harman. Gary, I'll send you and your SIO what we have so far. I'm grateful they don't know where I live.'

'DS Chambers did,' says Ella.

'God, you're right. We need to be doubly careful.'

'That job you did in Portsmouth hit the headlines,' says Gary. 'You're not on someone's Christmas card list anymore.'

'I'm going back there,' I say. 'I will find him, Gary. I'm not done yet.'

'Don't go all vigilante on me, Max.'

'What do you take me for?' I notice Gary eyeing up the red car.

'Perhaps you could take me back to your place in that car of yours,' he says.

'Only has two seats,' says Ella. 'Sorry.'

We return to the car, leaving a disappointed Gary behind. As we drive towards the roundabout, I look left at the pub and down a side road. There's a blue pickup parked behind a Mini. I head off towards Fishbourne, allowing the pickup to follow us.

'Harman must have a fleet of Nissan pickups,' I say, looking in the rearview mirror.

'Are we being followed *again*?' says Ella, turning to see.

'Yes, but don't worry. I'm not looking for a fight this time. Stop turning around. I don't want them to see you. I wonder if they're trying to find out where you live.'

I drive into Fishbourne and turn left. The pickup is still two cars behind us, so I don't floor it or do anything clever. I'm leading them away. I slow down to go over a level crossing and then continue north under the shade of trees.

'We're going the scenic route, then,' she says.

'I thought you'd enjoy it.'

I take a road towards Lavant and turn into a housing estate, but I'm upping my speed this time. The pickup falls back.

I make a sharp right and right again. They're not behind us now.

'Hold on tight,' I say.

I floor it. The car lurches forward, and I'm doing sixty in a thirty in less than two seconds. Ella lets out a yelp. I brake hard and take another right. We're back on the main road, and I pull away, doing ninety now. There's no sign of the pickup. I've left them far behind. I'm returning to Bosham, and normal driving has been resumed.

'You don't seem upset about your office,' says Ella.

'I'm not.'

'Most people would be devastated.'

'No one was hurt. It's an added complication for the police, but not for me.'

'I can't imagine what it's like inside your head.'

'You don't want to know. Anyway, I didn't like it.'

'The office?'

'No. It didn't feel right.'

'God, you're so fussy!' she says.

'It was something you said. People will find me wherever I'm based. I like Old Bosham village, by the water. I may try there instead.'

'I suppose you're insured and everything. What's it like not having to worry about money?'

'I've never worried about money. Despite being paid well, Ima taught me to be content with what I have. Some people want what they can't have. My uncle was one of those.'

I drive to Old Bosham and park the red car outside a craft centre about a hundred yards from the waterfront. The red car gets a few looks, but I ignore them. Opposite the craft centre is a secondhand bookshop. I point it out to Ella. Along the side of the shop is a glass door with gold lettering that has worn away with time.

'This place was my second choice,' I say. 'I went for the other one because I'd wanted to be near a railway station. What do you think? Change the lettering, and it will be perfect. There's even a car park nearby.'

'Fortis and Munro. I like it.'

I laugh. 'I thought you wanted to continue your journalism.'

'I'm joking. Yes, I do. I think it's a nice place.'

'Anyway. We have some thinking to do. We can use my study back at the ranch.'

Leon is tidying the front garden this afternoon, keeping an eye out for strange vehicles. I put away the red car in the garage alongside Ella's Audi.

Ella and I work together, using the study as a temporary office. All my files are cloud-based, and copies of cases are digitised. I've lost nothing except the space and a good coffee machine.

I've spoken with Leon, and he's delighted to have help in the garden, so even the father-and-son gardening duo I hired won't be out of work.

Ella has been researching the Obsidian Rooms in Portsmouth. It's a niche nightclub, and its website is heavy with sexualised images and designed to titillate, featuring semi-naked young women dancing and doing acrobatics on poles. Since when were poles sexy? There are images of men laughing together, holding drinks in low-lit corners. Sordid is the word that comes to my mind. Perhaps I can't talk after my behaviour the other night.

'It's owned by Marlowe Obsidian Entertainments Limited. The director is Philip Marlowe.'

'That's a Raymond Chandler character,' I say. 'A private detective. The Big Sleep.'

'You've lost me,' says Ella.

'Never mind. Not Andrew Harman or Jethro Matisse, then?'

'No. But he may know them. It's worth a punt. I can ask.'

'On your own? That won't look weird at all.'

'I might be the kind of girl who likes that kind of show.'

'Are you?'

'Wouldn't you like to know.' She's grinning at me. 'And I'm certain you'll want to wait outside for me. You could be my dad.'

'Now it sounds really weird. Okay. But I'm not going to let you be in there for long. And don't draw attention to yourself.'

'Why do you think Harman was going after Mariana?

Surely, he wouldn't want her to know he was still alive. And then there's his hatred for you.'

'Possibly revenge for her affair with Daniel Cole.'

Ella puts the end of her pen against her lips. 'It makes no sense to me, Max. After all this time, Harman returns from the dead, and Mariana seeks you out. It's that question again— why you? Why not go to the police?' She's good. Perhaps too good. I can see it in her eyes as the truth becomes clearer to her. She stands and stares out over the garden, watching Leon while thinking aloud. 'Cole offered to take her away to Scotland, but she didn't want him. She wanted to find you. You went in to help her when she was with Harman, and you somehow convinced her to go into witness protection to testify against him.' She turns, and her eyes narrow as she points at me. 'Or is this what you want us to believe?'

'I don't follow you,' I say, but I'm sure I do.

'Something doesn't ring true, Max. The book proposal—I see it now.'

'You've read Mariana's book proposal?'

'It was you who had an affair with Mariana. Not Cole. That's why Harman really hates you.'

What can I say? I have lied to everyone since I took on this case. I knew who Mariana was from the moment she drove away in the taxi. There was nothing I could tell anyone.

'There were things I had to do when working undercover that were essential to infiltrate criminal networks.'

'And you *infiltrated* her. Infiltrated! Why did you lie to me, Max? You are such a bastard!'

'It wasn't a lie! I honestly didn't recognise her at first. She looked different from when I first knew her. She had changed her appearance for the witness protection program. It was only after she got into the taxi that I remembered her. She was

Harman's wife, and I used her to break my way into his organisation. It was a shit job, Ella, but it had to be done.' I sigh and lower my voice. I'm so tired of having to defend myself on this. No one gets it. Everyone is a bloody armchair expert. 'There are agents and police officers still doing jobs like this, even now.'

'Did you take on this case out of guilt?'

'No! I want justice for Mariana and Grace.'

'What else haven't you told me?'

'Loads of things! So many things. Because I *can't*. It wasn't an affair with Mariana or Miri, as she called herself then. She wanted to feel appreciated, and her husband couldn't do that for her.'

'And you did that by lying to her!'

I thump the desk, startling her. 'What the hell have my professional decisions and my work got to do with you! How dare you sit there in judgment over me? You know nothing about what I had to do for this country. To save hundreds of lives of children being abused and trafficked by the rich. I did it for them, and I didn't care a shit about Harman or his little family. I wanted him sent down—that's all I wanted.'

Ella flushes as I glare at her. She avoids eye contact with me as she speaks slowly. 'The proposal for Mariana's new story, the one she had sent to her agent. I emailed it to you before the fire. You may want to read it. It didn't make sense to me at the time, but it's obvious now. Someone else's point of view other than your own blinkered, short-sighted, and pigheaded point of view can be helpful sometimes.'

I can't handle this tension. I turn away and leave the office for my bedroom. Stuffing a bag with clothes and essentials, I load them into the van with some surveillance gear.

Ima and Leon are in the back garden, so I leave them a

note and text a short message to Ella, even though she's only a few feet away. I tell her under no circumstances should she go to that nightclub in Portsmouth, but to stay safe.

CHAPTER 33

Compared to the red car, the VW Caddy feels like a sedate old lady. I park her along the seafront near the Southsea promenade. There's a wide green space north of me, and the D-Day Museum to the south, along with a hulking real-life landing craft from the Second World War. My mother took me there in my teens, shortly after we moved here permanently. I remember nothing about it other than I was in love with a girl called Lauren. She was all I could think about. Ima did her best to find interesting things for us to do on her rare days off, but I spent that day sulking.

I'm sulking now. A voice in my head tells me that Ella is right, but I'm right, too. I did what had to be done, as it was expected of me. Harman's operation had to be broken.

Beside the green, the road runs east to west. It's a pleasant afternoon, and I'm tempted to walk towards the Hotwalls and Old Portsmouth to rid myself of this toxic mix of sadness and anger. Then I remember what Ella said. The book proposal I'd been searching for was recovered from Mariana's computer. I dig out my laptop from the back of the van and connect it to the Internet via my mobile. A pile of emails download, and there's one from Ella. The subject line says, *Read This - What does it mean?* I open the attached document and see it's titled '*For Maddy-Proposal Version One*'. My heart feels like it's missed a beat.

Hi Maddy,

This is the idea I was talking about. Set in the 1980s— a fishing village in Dorset.

[Begins:] Cathy lay wrapped in the warmth of slumber when Michael slipped away. It was the gentle caress of his lingering body heat beneath the covers and the faint trace of his cologne on the pillow that stirred her awake. As dawn's pale light filtered through the curtains, she ventured through her silent house, Michael's sanctuary, while Andrew, her cruel husband, was away. *[I don't want Cathy to sound too pathetic here!]* What greeted her were the hollow spaces where Michael had once been. His coat, cap, and bag had gone, leaving behind nothing but an eerie emptiness that matched her marriage to Andrew. Desperation led Cathy to scour the quayside. Her enquiries to the fishermen were met with stoic silence, their tongues bound by fear of Andrew's retribution. If they all knew of her clandestine affair with Michael, it was inevitable that Andrew knew as well.

[Development:] With each passing day, Cathy finds herself haunted by the regret of having nothing tangible to remember Michael by—no photograph, no handwritten letter, no cherished gift. Her recollection of that fateful morning exists solely as an echo of emptiness, tinged with the residue of their shared dreams from the night

before he left—*[then I reveal:]* they made plans to murder Andrew and escape the clutches of the coastal town, to begin anew *[I was thinking of somewhere romantic, like the Highlands of Scotland]*.

Michael had promised her he would take that perilous step and confront Andrew. He had infiltrated her husband's world *[a fishing fleet, where competition is fierce]* and glimpsed the true essence of the man—an embodiment of cruelty and terror, a ruthless despot who held the lives of the hardworking townsfolk in his merciless grip. *[Possibly a little OTT. I was thinking of Russell Crowe regarding his looks.]*

In the ensuing days, Cathy discovers she is pregnant —it has to be Michael's. She reluctantly concludes that Andrew must have killed Michael and cast him into the depths of the sea, joining the others who dared to defy him, those who stood in his way.

[Ends:] Cathy's heart is broken. She's filled with hatred for Andrew and a deadly rage. The fire that consumed the boatyard may not have returned Michael to her side, but it marked the irrevocable end of Andrew and, with cruel irony, took her own life, too. *[I'm going to add foreshadowing for this! You know me.]*

[Then we move to the final chapter/epilogue:] Michael returns to the village in the present day, seeking Cathy to explain why he forsook her that night, to tell her he was an 'undercover cop' working to expose Andrew. But he couldn't go through with killing him, and his bosses withdrew him suddenly from the case. But he has to live with the bitter regret that he has lost his only true love forever.

Sorry, it's a mess. No title yet. Tell me what you think.

Miri x

I close my laptop and sigh. I was never in love with her, but she must have thought I was. But it was only work. It was The Job. I'm hoping the pregnancy part of the story was only in Mariana's imagination.

―――――――

When I first started working for The Firm, they told us no one would understand what we did and why we did it. If the public had found out, there would have been an uproar. As long as they can sleep well in their beds at night, what do they care? But there were consequences for everything I did. I broke Mariana's heart without regret. She was a means to an end— collateral damage. Yet even after I treated her so cruelly, she sought me out for help. Ella's low opinion of me is correct. I am a bastard of the worst kind. No better than Andrew Harman, than my uncle, or my unfaithful wife. I don't enjoy holding up this mirror to myself because the man in the reflection is a hypocrite. Yet, I move on. I assess, I examine my options, and I act. My options are to live or die. I choose to live and learn. My actions are to find Mariana's killer and make him pay. It's a cold, callous assessment, but if I'm to move on, I must allow myself the room to be a better person.

I walk north onto the green. Ahead of me is Duchess Street. On the corner, facing the seafront, is a large Georgian house painted vulgar purple with black window shutters on the second floor. In bold, black lettering that looks like glass are the words *The Obsidian Rooms*. Obsidian is a black volcanic glass that is extremely sharp when splintered. The whole building is like a grotesque lump of obsidian.

Across the road from the club is an enclosed garden with low hedges and flower borders. There are benches inside for the elderly visitors to Southsea to sit and enjoy the views over the large expanse of grass towards the sea. I'm not sure what they would make of the view in the other direction towards The Obsidian Rooms.

This garden area is likely to be in darkness at night. There are no lights here, and it's far back from the streetlights. It would be an ideal place for drug deals and somewhere quiet to kip for the homeless. It's an ideal place for me to hide and watch the nightclub. I would be concealed here, able to watch those coming and going from the front of the club.

I return to the van and grab some of my kit. I'm wearing a hoodie and jeans. I've got a rucksack containing food, my camera, and binoculars. I wait in the van and watch the sun setting over Gosport in the west. My phone is switched off, but Ima and Leon won't worry.

As the streetlights flicker on, I return to the small garden area. It's almost in complete darkness here now. I come across a teenage boy and girl making out on one of the benches, so I talk to them, interrupting their amorous exertions. The boy gets annoyed with me, but when he sees how much taller I am than him, he backs down, and they walk away. I have the place to myself again.

I settle on a bench facing my target and bring out my camera. I've got a clear view over to the front entrance. Groups of men are already forming outside, egging each other on, and others are waiting for reinforcements before they go in. There are women too, some brought by their partners, and others arrive in noisy partying gaggles. A low thud of a bass line is coming from the doorway, and I'm glad I don't live nearby. I'm turning into a grumpy old man before my time. I detest places like this.

Another show starts when coloured lights go on and off above the doorway, revealing girls at the windows in their underwear, faking horror at being caught, making the place look like a glorified knocking shop. I'm surprised they can get away with it. It's professional designer sleaze that you wouldn't take your grandma to.

Two door staff appear. Hench guys, hair cropped close to the scalp, black puffer jackets, earpieces, body-worn video cameras. They have their security badges on show, strapped to their arms. There are two cameras over the door, complying with licensing regulations.

A man steps out to talk with the bouncers. He's in a shirt and tie. The zoom lens picks him out as a man in his forties, with short ginger hair, beard stubble, and a glint of an earring. He's giving orders but is friendly with the queue. He takes a few steps to the right to smoke a cigarette. Then he's walking around the side of the building and into Duchess Street.

I decide to follow him, dropping everything into my rucksack, and walk onto the green, avoiding the front of the club. I cross into Duchess Street, keeping the man in view. He's now standing in a large Georgian-style doorway—a side entrance to the club. I'm casual as I walk past, engrossed in my mobile as the door opens. A woman and another man in a hoodie exit the building. The man is tall, white, large build. The woman is Asian, shorter, with long black hair and a short black dress. The man with the ginger hair sees me. He's watching me, but I take no notice of him. The men pick up a long black bag by the carry handles, and the woman follows them. The bag appears awkward and heavy to carry. I cross over, keeping them at forty-five degrees to my right. I pretend to take a call and stop walking. The group of three walk on, and a car pulls up—a black Mercedes. They heave the bag into the boot, and the ginger man returns to the club. He's still watching me, so I walk further on and turn left out of view as the Mercedes drives away.

After a few minutes, I've walked around a block, and I'm back on the green, heading towards the small garden again. I'm about to set up again when I see a tall redhead with long, shapely legs in a short silver dress with high heels. She approaches the door staff, and they smile at her. I get the camera out again and zoom in on her face.

'Shit! No!'

There's nothing I can do as Ella walks into the club.

CHAPTER 34

I run to the van, ditch the rucksack and hoodie, and tidy myself up. Why is Ella doing this? How the hell is she going to ask questions about Jethro Matisse? I hope she hasn't brought her press lanyard with her.

I jog back to the club and calm myself as I approach. Harman's men might be working here, and if they recognise me at the door, everything gets much more complicated.

I have a fake ID—a driving licence. I'd prepared it for when I was Richard Bright at the hotel. I stoop and slope my shoulders. The door staff don't give me a second look— they're too busy eyeing up the girls following me in.

As I walk in, I'm hit by a wall of sound and darkness, punctured by sweeping lasers. It's heaving in here already. A DJ is performing on the side of an elevated stage, pumping up the crowd. Dancing in the centre of the stage are topless girls in ultra-small briefs, bathed in red and magenta spotlights.

There are so many people here that I'm struggling to single out anyone. It's a mass of churning bodies. Exhibitionists own the centre, and voyeurs line the edges. Despite my height, I can't see Ella. The flashing lights and pulsing lasers break my focus. It's like a war zone in here.

The bar is an obvious place to start. It's long, covering the entire length of one wall. It's a structure framed in chrome and plastic with neon lights flashing behind. The bar staff are wearing deep-red, sparkling waistcoats and bow ties. Tasteful if you work in a holiday camp.

I find a few clear inches at the bar by moving a few younger men out of the way. From here, I can see the entire length of the bar. There's a girl with short pink hair next to me. She's looking me up and down.

'Hi,' she says. She says something about how tall I am. It's all I can make out above the music. 'Buy me a drink?' That was clear. I only want to find Ella, but I oblige, not wanting to cause offence as soon as I arrive. The girl wants me to flirt with her, but I'm not interested.

Then I see Ella. She's about ten feet away, and a man's talking to her. They move away from the bar and lean against a rail near some steps that lead down onto the dance floor. I leave my new flirtatious friend behind and follow Ella at a distance, keeping out of her line of sight. Her new admirer is wearing a shirt and tie and a radio clipped to his belt. She's flirting with the staff already. I get a little closer, and I see them laughing together. She's drinking some kind of cocktail and seems to enjoy his company. She looks amazing.

Now and then, I see him zone out. He's got an earpiece in, so he has something to do with security. He's not leaving her and is enjoying her company. I edge in closer, but it's too noisy to hear. A large hand pushes against my back, and a bald man as tall as I am moves me out of the way. Following him is a man with a short beard who looks in his late forties. He's wearing glasses and has sandy-coloured hair, greying at the sides. The bulky, bald man with a goatee is protecting him. It's then I realise he's Frank Pinto. He's the man Ella met in Cole's flat. Shit! What if he recognises her?

She glances sideways at Pinto and turns away as if she's allowing her new friend and Pinto to talk. But who's the other man with them? I don't recognise him as Andrew Harman. Is that the proprietor, Philip Marlowe?

Now she's edging away, looking uncomfortable. Pinto hasn't noticed her yet. I can see his bulk is muscle, but it makes it hard for him to be agile. The man with the glasses and beard smiles at her. She pretends she's shy and turns away. But then she sees me, and her eyes light up in astonishment. I'm shaking my head at her.

'Having fun?' I hear the man in the beard ask her. Pinto still doesn't notice her. Maybe her sexy look tonight is enough of a camouflage.

'This place is amazing,' she says, shouting over the music.

'I'm glad you think so,' he says to her, all smiles. 'I'm Phil. Phil Marlowe. It's my club.' So, it is Marlowe. He's smooth and unsubtle.

'Really!' Ella is all flirty with him now.

'You're on your own.' It's a statement.

'I am. I thought a friend was coming to meet me, but he didn't turn up.'

'I would change your friends if I were you. You've been talking to Mikita,' he says. 'I've been watching you. You're gorgeous.'

'Thank you,' she says. 'You're very sweet.'

Now I'm behind this man called Marlowe, and I'm watching Pinto. Marlowe continues the charm offensive with her, and I'm studying his body language. His right hand keeps clenching, and when he starts a sentence, his chin juts forward, like there's some hidden resentment there. If he's been watching Ella, then I'm sure his bodyguard would have been watching her, too. They know who she is, so they'll assume I'm here, too.

Marlowe steps in closer to her, and I can't hear what they are saying now. She is trying to back away, and Marlowe goes to put his arm around her. Fear flashes in her eyes, and she glances my way.

I barge forward, sweeping her away from Marlowe with my right arm, moving her behind me. She screeches in surprise. Pinto's fists clench, but before he can turn, I land a pre-emptive punch hard into his kidneys. He buckles.

'Follow me!' I shout to Ella.

I'm holding onto her, dragging her with me through the crowd. Pinto and Mikita are barking orders behind me. I find a space and pull her towards the door. Her heels are slowing us down. Two of Pinto's men block our path. Thick set, glaring, arms outstretched like they're herding cows.

'Out of our way!' I say.

They move to grab us. I kick one in the knee, and he falls. The other man grabs Ella. She sweeps his arms off her and punches him in the throat. It's a good move, and he falls away in pain. We reach the doors, but they're trying to close them on us.

I push her in front of me. 'Run!'

Someone is behind me. 'Fortis!'

Ella is through the doors, but now they're closed. She's on her own out there. My back is against the locked doors, and the crowd cheers at the entertainment. In front of me is Pinto and the man Ella flirted with. What's their plan? Pinto's bulk doesn't intimidate me. The crowd parts, forming a circle around us, and their phones are out filming the spectacle. The music is cut. What are they going to do next?

'Do you really want this publicity?' I say to them. 'Don't step any closer, or you'll be counting the tiles on the hospital ceiling. You don't know what you're dealing with.'

Pinto glances at the baying crowd. In my mind, I'm daring him, wishing it to happen. My heart is pumping pure adrenaline now.

Marlowe steps out from behind Pinto. His head twitches as he ponders what to do.

'Let him out.' He bares his teeth. 'Unlock the doors and let him out.' His expression is cold. This won't work well for him. 'Another time, Mr Fortis. What do you think?'

'I'm certain of it,' I say. Then there's something in the way he looks at me that I recognise, even through the weight loss, the hair, beard and glasses. 'Andrew Harman.'

He frowns at me, and his head twitches. 'Andrew is dead, Fortis. You, of all people, should know that. Mariana burned him alive.'

There's a click behind me, and the doors open outward. I step back. Then I see Ella. Two bouncers are at her feet, crumpled on the floor in pain.

'Are you coming or what?' she says to me.

We're not out of danger yet. As I back out the door, there are now six men in suits facing me. They're wondering if they could take me. These odds are difficult. So any one of them coming forward will get themselves killed. It's a matter of survival, and I don't take prisoners.

'Let him go!' barks Marlowe. 'There will be another time soon. I promise you that.'

I can smell Ella's perfume close to me, and I feel a hand take mine.

'Let's go, Max,' she says.

I straighten up, back away, and then turn. We cross the road and walk away into the darkness as two police vans appear, their blue strobes punching into the night.

No one follows us. Adrenaline is pumping around my body, and Ella still has my hand. She knows I'm angry with her, and she forced me to go in after her. But I'm not shouting, and I'm not yelling in her face. I'm calm—it's all over, and she's safe.

As we approach the van, I check again that no one's following. I unlock the van doors, and we get in.

'Are you hurt?' I say.

'No. You?'

'No.'

We sit in silence for a few minutes. I can't look at her. She looks so good.

'Aren't you going to say anything?' she says. She's facing me now, but I'm looking ahead across the Solent and towards the lights of Ryde on the Isle of Wight.

'What's the point?'

'I'm sorry.'

'Ok.'

'Is that it?' She tilts her head, trying to get me to look at her. 'Aren't you going to shout at me? Why can't you look at me?'

'Because you look amazing. Absolutely. All I wanted to do back there was protect you. To keep you safe. I don't want to fall for you, Ella, and I'm seriously at risk of doing that if I look at you.'

A breeze from the sea rocks the van on its suspension.

'Oh,' she says. 'I wasn't expecting that.' She looks out of her window, and she's dabbing her eyes. 'I don't want that either.' She takes a deep breath. 'I'm sure the sex would be great and everything.'

'It would.'

'But my heart is still with someone else.'

'I know, and I won't try to compete with him.'

'No. Not yet. He's all I see when I wake up each morning. I'd give anything to do that one more time.'

'I wish I could remember what that felt like.'

Ella takes my hand and squeezes it.

'I'd better get out of these clothes then. I mean, I'd better change.'

We both laugh.

'Yes. Where's your car?'

'A couple of blocks away.'

'I'll take you there. Where's your car key? You don't have a bag.'

'That's a secret—need to know only.' I can tell she's grinning.

I drive Ella to her car, which is tucked away in a side street. As she opens her door, I finally look at her. Now I know I can't compete with a ghost.

'Well, at least we know who Philip Marlowe is now,' I say.

'We do,' she says. 'Do you think he's Jethro Matisse *and* Andrew Harman?'

'He must be.'

'He was such a creep.' She stares at me, trying to find the words to say. 'I'm sorry I messed up. I shouldn't have gone in there. I did it out of spite.'

'You handled yourself well tonight,' I say. 'I'll see you in the morning. I'm going to be here for a few more hours.'

'Okay. Don't do anything dangerous.'

I nod, wind up my window, and drive away.

Phil Marlowe leaves the club through the side door. It's one-thirty in the morning, the music is still pumping out, and the topless dancers are working their final set. The Obsidian Girls are hunting through the crowd for the men who are looking for a good time. Some of the girls find the lonely business travellers, taking them away to dark corners, or there are rooms above the venue if they pay more.

Marlowe finds his Mercedes outside the door. Pinto's men had borrowed it earlier to dispose of what was left of Dennis Palmer's wife. He gets in and locks the doors. Resting his head against the headrest, he lets out a sigh.

'This is it,' he says, gazing into his rearview mirror. 'I've got to finish it now.'

Checking his mobile phone, there's a message he's been waiting for. A plane in Bembridge, Isle of Wight, is available if he needs it. It can get him out of the country with four hours' notice. If the police want to take him, they won't think of trying to stop him there. They'll be all over him soon, so the timing is critical.

Marlowe senses tonight's drama was a signal, a message from Fortis to flush him out. It's time to act.

'But it's got to be on my terms,' says Marlowe, focusing on his eyes in the reflection. 'Where and when—my terms, not his.'

Leaving Southsea, he drives through Fratton, passing long lines of shops, pubs, and garages along the way. He continues through North End, passing traffic lights and a police van flashing its blues.

Marlowe reflects on the last few weeks when he had everything going for him. With Fenz gone, the business could have flourished. There was money to be made. Now, he's drumming his fingers on the steering wheel, passing under the amber streetlights, and catching himself in the mirror again.

'Fortis has screwed me once more, so he's brought this on himself.'

He has made plans that he intends to see through to the end. His first objective is to get Fortis, then he'll move the money, and finally, he'll take a one-way trip to Europe as far south as he can go. To get Fortis, he needs to find his weakness, and after tonight's fiasco, he knows exactly what that weakness is. The girl. He protected her. He went in to save her.

'Yes,' he says. 'The girl. I'll find her, and then I'll have Fortis where I want him.'

His thoughts turn to Clarice. Would she go with him and leave her family? He hopes she would. He thinks she's been good to him, but not as reliable as he had hoped. This would be the test of her loyalty to him. And if she chooses to stay?

'There are a hundred more like her,' he says. 'And I have her money—her dumb business investment. The world is full of saps like Clarice. She was only good for one thing. It would break her heart, but who gives a shit? She'll move on. Stick to the plan.'

Marlowe drives away, his thoughts kicking around inside his head. A car's headlights sweep his rearview mirror. It's a taxi. The roads are full of them this time of night. After another few minutes, Marlowe parks outside Clarice's house. She doesn't have Juliet tonight—thank God. He hates that little screech. The lights are out, and she's most likely asleep. She won't mind him waking her. He's got a lot of pent-up energy he needs to unload.

'Keep going,' I say to the taxi driver. 'Drive past slowly.'

I snap a few shots of Marlowe as he leaves his car and pulls out a door key to a house. I've got him. I could even take him out at home if I wanted.

'Where now?' says the driver.

'Back to Southsea. Great job.'

'Never done that before,' she says. 'What are you, a private detective? A reporter?'

'I can't tell you. Otherwise, I'd have to kill you.'

She laughs. 'Fair enough. What does your wife think about you doing this job? Bet she finds it sexy.'

'I don't have a wife. Or a girlfriend.'

'Boyfriend then?'

'I'm not gay.'

She's looking into my eyes in the rearview mirror. She's sweet, a little older than me, and she's attracted to me.

We head back to my van, and I pay her with a grateful tip.

'Do you sleep in your van?' she says, looking at the VW Caddy.

'I left the Ferrari in the garage.'

I yawn. It's been a hectic day. So much has happened.

The taxi driver smiles at me, tilting her head slightly. 'My house is empty if you need a place to lay your head.'

CHAPTER 35

I wake up to the sound of my mobile ringing. It's Leon.

'Hi,' I say. My voice is croaky, and I'm not sure where I am. 'Everything okay?'

'I was ringing to ask you that. It's gone eleven, and we haven't heard from you.'

'Shit! Is it? I overslept. Is Ella with you?'

'She is. She's been relaying her version of the story from last night. She handled herself well.'

'Yes, she did.'

I sit up, and the taxi driver is kneeling in her underwear at the end of the bed.

'Where are you?' says Leon.

The taxi driver sneezes.

'I'm in Portsmouth,' I say. 'I fell asleep in the van.'

'Yes, of course. Sounds like you had a busy night. Will we be seeing you shortly?'

'Yes, I'm heading back soon.'

'Good. Ella is leaving, so don't be too long.' He ends the call.

The taxi driver wants more from me, but in the cold light of day, a rainy Tuesday, I can't oblige. I have things to do.

I find out the taxi driver's name is Mel, and I tell her my name is Richard. She doesn't believe me, but that's okay. She likes it. I get dressed, and we laugh about last night.

'Let me know if you need a place to stay over again,' she says. 'And next time, bring your Ferrari.'

'Thanks,' I say.

I leave after a quick shower and a coffee. She makes good coffee. When I step outside, I remember I'm in Waterlooville, a few miles north of Portsmouth. I followed Mel in her taxi to her house, and I'm glad I did. We make no promises to see each other again, but it's something that could happen, maybe. So, I depart with a casual *see you around* kind of wave.

Driving back to Bosham, I wonder why I've done this again. Is this going to become a habit? Perhaps I should take protection with me from now on. But what about Ella? No. I can't go there. This has to stop. No more. The journey back allows me to clear my mind and refocus on the next step forward.

When I pull the Caddy into the driveway, I meet Ella as she loads up her car.

'You're not dead then,' she says in an acerbic tone.

'Hey, I fell asleep.'

We walk into the house, and Ima is cooking me bacon. She won't eat it herself but is happy to make it for me, and I'm starving.

Ella is looking me up and down. 'You have a shower in your van now, do you?'

'What is this?' I say. 'Are you my mother now?'

'No. Sorry.' She blushes. She's in jeans and a T-shirt,

somewhat different from the sparkling number she wore last night.

Ima brings me a bacon bap, and I tuck in.

'Are you moving out?' I say to Ella.

'Yes. I think I'm safe to go back to my mother's. She needs me there, to be honest. No one knows where I live, but they may find me here.'

'It was nice having you stay,' I say, wiping my fingers on a piece of kitchen towel.

'Nice? Thanks.' She smiles, but it doesn't reach her eyes. Ima and Leon leave us to talk, and Ella leans back and folds her arms. 'I spoke to someone called Mikita at the nightclub.'

'So I saw.'

'He says they have thirty or more showgirls that work there. He called them the Obsidian Girls. I think they're nothing more than sex slaves.'

'The girls in the hotel were just a sideline. I need to stop that man for good.'

'What happens now?' she asks.

'I'll contact Lacey to fill her in about Harman.' I rub my eyes and sigh. 'Matisse is Hyde to Marlowe's Dr Jekyll. He's pretty screwed up, whatever way you look at it.'

'What shall I do now?'

'Look, I think I've put you in enough danger to last a lifetime. And things are getting a little awkward between us, which is totally my fault.'

'I see.' Her eyes look sad.

'As far as this case goes, we must hand this over to the police now. I'm not a vigilante. There's enough now for a strong case against Marlowe, Harman. I'm guessing you enjoyed all of this.'

She nods. 'Very much. It had all the best parts of being an investigative journalist.'

'I can imagine. Look, about last night. I'm sorry if I embarrassed you by what I said.'

Her green eyes stare into me. 'It's okay, Max. To be honest, I'm glad you felt that way, but I'm not in that place yet. For the record, you are a good-looking man. And I regret laying into you about Mariana. It wasn't any of my business.'

'So you're leaving right now?'

She nods.

'Would you be happy to work with me again in the future? Missing dogs, unfaithful husbands?'

She shakes her head. 'Something with a little more danger involved would suit me better.'

She hugs me, and I hug her back. I don't want to let go, but she pulls away and picks up her bag.

'It's only been just over a week,' I say, 'but I'll pay you for the whole month. You are pretty good at the job, Ella. You should change careers.'

'I don't think so. My mother would kill me.'

Ima and Leon meet her in the hallway and hug her. They look sad to see her go. We say our goodbyes at the front door.

'Stay in touch,' I say.

'I will.'

When I close the door, Ima touches my arm.

'Max, have you been to see Carrie?' she says. 'There was a call from one of the doctors, and he is trying to get hold of you.'

I sigh. 'Thanks, Ima. I'll call them now.'

Clarice looks back into the house from the garden, and it sounds like Phil is still on the phone. How can she talk to him about last night? He came in like a storm, and now her emotions are strewn everywhere.

She puts the fallen leaves she's raked up from the lawn into the compost bin and washes her hands in the utility room. Working in her garden has helped her to gather her composure once more.

She hears him arguing with someone. They've betrayed him and undermined his decisions behind his back. He hates disloyalty. She tucks her hair behind her ears and ventures into her house. The air is filled with obscenities and violence as he struts around, putting people in their place. She hates it. This is her home, her sanctuary, and he's violating it like he violated her.

When he came home in the early hours, something evil possessed him. He demanded her body. He wasn't the kind and gentle man she first met. He was cruel and controlling, making her do things she didn't want to do. What had happened to him to change him like this?

When she finds him, he's staring out the lounge window, muttering to himself. She is standing in the doorway behind him when he snaps his head around, startled. He gathers his composure, and the Phil she knows returns. His face softens, and the glare in his eyes fades.

'Clarice?' he says. 'Is everything okay, my love? You look like you've seen a ghost.'

'We need to talk,' she says.

'What's wrong?'

'I'm scared.' He frowns and walks towards her, but she holds up her hands to stop him. 'No! Please. Stay where you are. Okay?'

'What's happened?'

'You. You've been arguing on the phone all morning. Your temper is scaring me, and your language is vile. And what got into you last night?'

'What are you talking about?'

'You know what I'm talking about.'

He tries to dismiss her with a laugh. 'I missed you. I wanted you.'

'You were an animal! A beast. I didn't know you, and you wouldn't stop. You hurt me, Phil!'

'Rubbish. You wanted it as much as I did. You never said no.'

'How the hell could I? You had your hand over my mouth.'

'I don't understand.'

'And neither do I. What happened to you?'

'Nothing, Clarice. I'm fine.'

'Who is this Fortis you keep shouting about on the phone? Sounds like you want to kill him. What's going on?'

'I don't know what you're talking about. You must have misheard.'

He goes to walk out of the room, but she won't let him, blocking the doorway.

'I didn't mishear anything. I expect the neighbours didn't either.'

He puts his hands to his head and sighs. 'Why did you have to hear that? Fortis is the man who's trying to ruin me. He's making threats against me. He's threatened to kill me.'

'It sounds like it's the other way around, Phil. What are you involved with? It's that club, isn't it. What are they making you do?'

'Nothing. I own it.' Phil laughs. 'It's all mine.'

'Stop it! It's not funny.'

'I'm not joking. I own the Obsidian Rooms.'

'Don't be bloody ridiculous! What's happened to you, and why are you being so cruel?'

'I'm not. I'm being honest with you.'

She points her finger at him. 'And who is Andrew Harman?'

Phil jerks his head. 'How do you know about Andrew?'

'I found an open letter to him beside the bed. I thought it was one of mine.'

'Did you read it?'

'Not all of it. It's from an MP.'

'That's meant to be private!' Phil drops into an armchair. 'Andrew's dead, Clarice. He died years ago.'

'It's not my fault about the letter,' she says. 'I picked it up by accident.'

'You've been tetchy all day about something. A real grump. Do you think I'm having an affair? Is that it?'

Clarice shakes her head. 'No. I won't let you do this to me. I'm not in the wrong here. You were cruel last night, Phil. Vicious and brutal. You did horrible things to me.'

He shrugs. 'You never complained.' Then he squints at her. 'You don't look well, Clarice. Are you sickening for something? Let me make you a cup of tea.'

Clarice stares at the carpet, and she takes a deep breath.

'I'd like you to leave, Phil. I want you to get some help. I'm not ending it. I need you to leave now.'

'Leave? I don't understand.'

'Get your stuff and go.'

'I don't want to. You can't chuck me out.'

'This is *my* house, Phil, and I don't feel safe when you're like this. You're scaring me!'

'What's wrong with you? Have you lost your freaking mind?'

'How dare you talk to me like that! Get out, or I'll call the police.'

She sees his fist clench and unclench. She steps back into the hallway and takes her mobile phone from the table.

'I'm sorry you're being like this. It's probably the change. HRT may help you.'

She doesn't answer. Phil curses her under his breath and goes up the stairs. She hears him opening the wardrobes and drawers, arguing with himself. He rattles around in the bathroom and then comes down with the bag he brought with him a few months ago.

'Your key,' she says to him, her voice trembling.

Phil shakes his head. 'Of course. Look, I'm sorry. Work has been difficult. Late nights with clients.' He removes the front door key from his keyring and puts it on the table. 'Will you call me?'

'Yes. When I'm ready, but you need to sort yourself out first.'

'Okay.'

He smiles at her and leaves through the front door. She pushes it closed behind him and slides on the door chain. She can see his shadow through the frosted glass, searching for something—his car keys. His shadow disappears. It's done. Clarice sighs, and tears run down her cheeks. She leans back against the front door, closes her eyes, and lets out a sigh of relief.

The glass shatters behind her. A bloody hand reaches through the door and around her neck. It pulls her head through what's left of the broken glass in the door frame. The glass pierces her cheek and sinks deep into her neck. He leaves her there, impaled, and walks back to the car.

After Ella left, I returned the call to the consultant at Holly Grange in Haslemere. He gave me the news I knew would come someday soon. He suggested it was time to say my good-byes. Carrie's kidneys and liver have stopped functioning. It's as if she gave up after I left her. I had said I would never return, but after talking with Ima, I wonder if that's what has been screwing with my head for the last few days. I've been cursing her, punishing her for the deception and her affair with my uncle. Yet the truth is, I had done the same thing to her long before she did it to me. It was all in the name of The Job, but it was the same. So now I'm back at her bedside after speaking face-to-face with the consultant.

Her room is in semi-darkness, lit only by a side lamp and the soft glow of electronic displays from the medical equipment. Through the glass, I see the nurses talking to each other, giving me reassuring glances. I move the lamp so I can see her more clearly.

Sitting beside her bed, I study her serene face. The rosy, oxygenated glow is now gone. Her skin is sallow, and her breaths are slow and shallow. Carrie is leaving me for good.

'I'm sorry for what I said, Carrie,' I say. 'I'm a hypocrite. Never saw it that way, of course. The Job confused my moral compass, but I was always responsible for my actions. Maybe you knew and didn't tell me. I'm sorry for lots of things. I never took you to see that play you wanted to see—the musical. What was it now? I can't even remember it. The woman with a green face. Anyway. You wanted to see it, but I never took you. I was a rubbish husband, Carrie. You should have married that other guy who tried it on with you that night at the bar. The rugby player. He was better looking than me.'

Shona, the nurse comes in. 'Can I get anything for you, Mr Fortis?'

I shake my head. 'No, thank you, Shona. You've done enough.'

'She's still very beautiful,' she says.

I nod. 'I wish I had done things differently.'

'Lots of people say that, Mr Fortis. But none of us are gods. We make the best decisions we can at the time.'

'True.' A shadow creeps over Carrie's face. She's barely breathing at all. 'It's time for her to go.'

A machine makes an unfamiliar sound, and the nurse taps on the window. A doctor comes in and watches Carrie's heart rate for a moment and then silences the machine's alarms.

The nurse makes me focus on her, and I see something in her eyes.

'We had some fun times,' I say to her.

'Precious memories, Mr Fortis,' she says. 'Hold on to them.'

The doctor moves over to Carrie's head and pulls open an eyelid. He checks her pulse with his fingers and then checks the monitor. Glancing at his watch, he writes a time on his hand and steps away from her.

'She's gone, Mr Fortis,' he says. 'It's all over.'

CHAPTER 36

They are in Marlowe's executive apartment, overlooking Gunwharf Quays. It's a bright October morning, and the light floods into an expansive lounge diner with wide windows and a polished oak floor. Marlowe has turned this space into his private office. There's a double bedroom with a view of the Spinnaker Tower and the shopping centre below. Marlowe keeps quiet about this place so only his most trusted employees know he's here.

Frank Pinto has finished redressing Marlowe's hands. He's removed the shards of glass he can see and used sterile strips to close the wounds. Luckily, he didn't sever an artery. They need proper stitches, but Marlowe won't go to a hospital. Pinto's done a professional job with the bandages, leaving enough room for Marlowe to use his fingers if he needs to.

'It was your temper that did this,' says Pinto.

Marlowe agrees.

'I've got some green in my bag. That might help.'

'No. I need to keep my head clear.'

Pinto knows what Marlowe has done. It's in the news. It

won't be long before the police know he killed her. He had been living with her for months.

They are already at the club, too, and evidence is being gathered from Marlowe's office. They will find traces of blood there. It's almost impossible to get rid of. Pinto knows that himself. Bleach helps to a certain extent, but it's the microscopic droplets—they go everywhere and cover everything. That's why he prefers disposal at sea.

He's watching Marlowe wincing in pain. On the bedside cabinet beside him are painkillers and antibiotics they used for the girls. He's mixing them with brandy and becoming maudlin. He looks pathetic lying on the bed, and Pinto wonders why he has to babysit him. It's only the money that's keeping him here. His loyalty to Marlowe is wearing thin.

'Are you going to tell me your plan?' says Pinto. 'Or are you just going to hide here? They've closed the club, boss. You're wanted. Why haven't we gone yet?'

'You know why, jackass!' Marlowe throws a glass of water at Pinto. 'Will you stop questioning me!' He's slurring his words.

Pinto stands at his full height. The room seems to shrink around him. Marlowe feels under his pillow and finds what he is looking for.

'One of these days, *boss*, you're going to go too far.' Pinto's voice is low and rumbling. 'I could snap you just by looking at you.'

'Don't you dare threaten me!' Marlowe pulls out the gun and aims with both his shaking, bandaged hands.

'Go on then! But you'll have to shoot me in the head. Because it will only take me seconds to get to you.'

'Sit down, oaf! I don't want to fight you. I've already told you the plan. This is for your benefit, too. It was all about getting Max Fortis. That's all we wanted.'

Pinto sits down, and Marlowe lowers the gun.

'We?'

'Yes! Come on, Frank! The club can't work now. Fortis has broken the supply chain. But we're not broken. Once I get Fortis, we can leave here. Where did you say you wanted to go? Spain, was it? A nice villa somewhere with all the girls you could want.'

Pinto nods. 'When? We don't have long. They'll find us, boss. It's a matter of days.'

'I've had news about the girl. She's not with Fortis any longer. She was seen walking with an older woman. I've made a payment to a crew from Hammersmith. Reliable. They're going to bring her to us. Once we have her, we'll have Fortis.'

'And then?'

'And then, Frank, we can go. I've chartered a flight. It's on permanent standby. What do you think? Eh? You and me off to Spain. I may go down to Morocco. You don't need me snapping at your ankles any longer. You've got savings, and I've got a lump sum for you, too. More than you'll ever need. All you have to do is get me there.'

'Spain?'

'Yes, Frank. Come on, man! Think about it. We need to get Fortis first. I need him to pay for what he did. It's simple.'

Pinto smiles. 'Spain. That's all I wanted, and the money to see me comfortable for the rest of my life. Then perhaps I'll find my girls again. Convince them to talk to their old man.'

'You see, Frank. That's my plan! Help me with it.'

Pinto hesitates. 'I don't know. I could go now, but the extra money would be helpful.'

'You still don't trust me? After all this time.'

'You have those photographs. Remember. They're a noose around my neck.'

Marlowe points to a bedside cabinet. 'Take them. There's one more job, and it's over.'

Pinto's waiting for the catch, but Marlowe points again at the drawer. Pinto gets up and peers inside. There's an A4 brown envelope. He opens the envelope and removes the two photographs. Pinto is dragging Mariana's unconscious body in front of the van's headlights. Then he's manhandling her over the wall on the bridge.

'And I thought you took these for your own pleasure,' he says. 'I didn't realise you were going to blackmail me.'

'Take them and destroy them,' says Marlowe. 'There aren't any copies.'

Pinto leaves Marlowe. He takes the photographs into the lounge and runs them through the paper shredder. Then, he returns to Marlowe.

'I will do one last job for you, boss. But don't let me down.'

There's a tap on the door, and Pinto peers through the spyhole—it's Mikita.

When Mikita sees the state of Marlowe's hands, he screws up his face.

'What is it?' says Marlowe.

'There's only a few of us left now, boss,' says Mikita. 'The others have done a runner. There are four of us.'

'That's okay, Mikita,' says Marlowe. 'You will all be rewarded for your loyalty. Tell them all to go back to their families. Then I'll call you for one last job.'

'Boss?'

'Yes, Mikita. Sadly, after that, I will let you all go. Do this last thing for me, and you won't have to work for a long time.'

'I'm sorry, boss. Things were going well for us. I wish we had finished Fortis at the club. Why did you stop us?'

'Think, Mikita! You had everyone watching. It wasn't the right time. I have a way to bring Fortis to his knees. I have found his weakness. You'll see—one last thing to do.'

'Yes, boss.'

'Now go home to your family. Look after your wife. Plan a holiday together. I'll call you.'

Mikita leaves with a glance at Pinto.

'Loyalty, Frank,' says Marlowe. 'That's true loyalty, right there.'

'Yes, boss.' Blind loyalty, thinks Pinto.

CHAPTER 37

Relief. That's what I'm feeling. I've been trying to work it out for a while I'm sitting on a bench next to the boathouse, staring over the water. The bench overlooks the Bosham Deeps and Chichester Marina on the other side. A mud bank is below me, submerged by the high tide. The water is sparkling in the cool sunshine, and I feel fine.

It's been six days since Carrie died, and I think I have it straight in my head now. There are things I regret. Things I've said and done. In the end, though, Carrie not only betrayed me, she betrayed Ima and Leon, too. I won't tell them that. It would break their hearts. No. I'm grateful for our early days, but I choose to let go of the rest.

I hear Ima calling me. She walks across the lawn towards me from the house, clutching her cardigan tightly around her against the chill air. We meet halfway, and a sudden wind tosses her hair over her face.

'Commander Lacey is here,' she says. 'She's in the study with Leon.'

'Thank you, Ima.' I smile at her and rub her shoulder, and we walk in with our arms around each other.

Lacey is looking out of the window as I come in. She's wearing something different now. A blue trouser suit. I've never seen her wear blue before. I sit opposite her, behind my desk. A Post-it note where Ella has drawn doodles of hairy monsters with stick legs is on the computer monitor beside me.

'Your report into Philip Marlowe—Andrew Harman—has caused quite a stir,' says Lacey. 'Harman has indeed risen from the dead, but his nefarious operations don't involve government officials this time, which ends my involvement in the case. What I can tell you is Philip Marlowe was Harman's trusted accountant once upon a time. Harman kept him hidden from all of us. He has used Marlowe's persona to create a new identity for himself.'

'Not the Los Angeles private eye, then,' I say.

'No, he was a real person. Marlowe was a genius with accounts,' says Lacey. 'He's the one who buried Harman's paper trails. I suspect it was Marlowe's charred remains they scraped out of the burnt-out warehouse, and Harman escaped.'

'Then he used Mariana's murder attempt as an opportunity to disappear.'

'There's no evidence to suggest Mariana Garcia attempted to murder her husband. But it seems that Harman believed she did. And he hates you for destroying his business and screwing his wife. Very inconsiderate of you.'

'Do you think?'

'Well, that's that. Major crimes in Hampshire have got the case now.'

I nod.

'You've got a nice place here, Max,' she says. 'I would

happily retire if I had your money. Sorry to hear your new office was destroyed.'

'It's okay. I might move into Old Bosham. It's quieter there. Even less chance of getting clients.'

'Well, don't forget our agreement. I'm happy to help you if needed, and hopefully vice versa. I've nothing for you at the moment. But—'

'Carrie is dead.'

Lacey's eyes widen. 'Oh.' She swallows. 'I'm sorry to hear that. I'd hoped she would rally so we could arrest her.'

'It's okay, but you may want to put that at the end of a file somewhere. Don't be sorry. I have mixed feelings about it.'

'Your wife?'

'Yes.'

'Well, that's your story, Max. Not mine.' Lacey gets up to go and looks around one more time. 'This money doesn't sit comfortably with you.'

'No.'

'Your mother and stepfather seem happy here.'

'It's the only reason I'm keeping it. It's safe here for them.'

'I can understand that. And where's the beautiful Ella? She's rather sexy, don't you think?'

'She's gone home. We finished the case, so…'

'She's very good.'

'She is. I'll hire her again one day soon.'

Lacey nods and smiles. 'I would.' She gives me an unsettling wink.

Leon appears and leads Lacey to the front door. As I watch her go, I'm wondering about Harman. As far as he was concerned, we still had something to settle. I expect he will be arrested soon, and his club will be shut down. It's possible someone will turn it into a friendly family pub. Even so, something's still gnawing at me, making me feel uneasy. Something feels exposed, and I can't think what it is.

I must shrug this feeling off. Ima and Leon have their coats on and are waiting for me in the hallway. They are coming with me to the funeral directors so that I can arrange Carrie's funeral. It feels unreal to be thinking of this. This is one last thing to do before I can move on.

Ella's morning didn't start well, and now it's gone from bad to worse. The telephone and broadband have gone down, and she needs to get online for some extra job prep. The mobile signal is intermittent at her mother's house, and using mobile data is tedious. She has a job interview, courtesy of *Jack the Hack,* at the offices of a local newspaper. While it's something she can do standing on her head, she's left it too late to do her research. She can't let the man down now.

Her mother is out with friends, and Ella has no one to moan to. She half-thought of seeing Shira and asking to use their broadband, but that didn't seem appropriate.

She makes herself a coffee and tries to use her mobile. There's no signal at all now.

'What's wrong with this bloody place?' she says to herself.

A blue van pulls up outside. It triggers memories of the one that followed her and Max two weeks ago, ending up on its side on the A3. Such a lot has happened since then. But now it's silence from Max. He's not returning her calls or messages. He's paid her as promised, and she's used the money to clear some of her debt. It's a huge relief for her.

Two men in yellow reflective jackets and white hard hats step out of the van. Ella is watching them from the front window. They look through and see her. Then they're looking around at the cables running along the telephone poles. They come to the front door, one of them with a clipboard. Ella answers the door cheerfully. Maybe they've come to fix the phone.

'Hello, my love,' the tall one says. 'We're investigating a telephone outage. Have you lost your telephone and broadband?'

'Yes,' she says. 'It was okay first thing, but now it's gone.'

'Is your mobile signal okay?'

'As bad as it usually is.'

'The thing is, we think we've traced the fault to your house. It's taken the entire street down.'

'Our house?' she says.

'Yes, weird, isn't it? It could be something simple, like a short circuit somewhere. Insects can do it, and spiders.' Ella grimaces, and the man nods. 'Can we check the box where your phone's plugged in? It shouldn't take a moment.'

She squints at the lanyards around their necks. It says something about telecoms, but the photo is on the other side. The man smiles at her.

'Does it need both of you?'

'No, my love. Just me. I won't keep you a minute. I'm pretty sure this is where the fault is.' He gives her a cheeky smile.

Ella steps aside while the taller man comes in.

'I'll get the van ready,' says the other man.

'Where's your box?' the engineer asks.

'I don't know. It's not my house.'

He brings out a white spray can and goes on his knees, following the cable from the landline phone.

'Ah,' he says with a smile. 'It's behind the TV.'

'Can you pull it out for me, love?'

'I'm sorry?'

'The TV. Can you pull it out of the way for me? We're not allowed to touch your stuff.'

'I should think not.' Ella pulls at the TV unit. 'This old thing is heavy,' she says.

'Perfect,' says the man. 'Now, say cheese!'

She turns around and sees the spray can pointing at her face. A cloud of white vapour engulfs her, and the man steps back. The gas hits the back of her throat, and her eyes close. She gasps. She can't breathe. She panics and staggers forward towards the man. She tries to open her eyes again, but her peripheral vision goes dark, and her head spins. She's desperate to catch her breath, but soon, all she hears is a long, sharp hiss in her ears, and she feels herself hit the floor.

CHAPTER 38

We're returning after organising the coffin and service for Carrie. The undertakers were professional and as friendly as they could be, but I still hated every moment. It's going to be a simple cremation. She had a brother and a few cousins. We'll invite them and pay for a wake, but I don't want to attend. I'm about to explain to Ima when Gary calls.

'Where are you?' he says.

'Chichester—heading back to my house,' I say. 'Leon's driving.'

'Mate, I've had a call from the Portsmouth Investigations Centre. They went to arrest Philip Marlowe at his home address—some executive apartment in Gun Wharf Quays. He wasn't there, and he's not at the Obsidian Rooms.'

'You know his name's Andrew Harman, don't you?'

'Yes, of course I bloody do!' Gary sighs down the phone. 'Let me finish. We got the intel he was seeing a woman and staying with her.'

'I'm not in the mood for this, Gary.'

He ignores me. 'It turns out she's the same woman who

was murdered in her home last week. It hit the news and everything. Someone dragged her through broken glass, cutting her throat open.'

'They reckon that was Harman?'

'Yes. He was in a relationship with her—poor woman. And there's another thing.'

'Can't this wait?'

'No! The body of a waitress who worked at the Obsidian Rooms has turned up, dumped in a ditch in the woods somewhere. She was the wife of Dennis Palmer, the man you put in hospital from the hotel.'

'Okay, then his wife's death was some kind of punishment for Palmer. We know Harman's a nasty bastard.'

'He's a total nut job. He's in hiding, and there's a huge search on for him.'

'This could have been an email, Gary. I'm not working on this case anymore. I'll be going over to see Grace Garcia this afternoon to give her the news. Now, if you don't mind—'

'He's coming for you and Ella!' Gary blurts out at the end of his breath. 'Intel says he's got money to burn and has stuck a reward on your head. He wants your blood, mate. And hers, too. He's hired a hitman to find her.'

'Ella?'

'Yes. She's still with you, right?'

My blood runs cold. I feel a panic I haven't felt before. I can't let anything happen to her.

'She's at her mother's. She left me last week.'

'Shit! Where does she live?'

I give Gary Ella's address and end the call. Leon is looking at me in the rearview mirror.

'Is everything okay?' he asks.

'No. Take us to Ella's mother's house in Fishbourne. Ella's in danger.'

Cold metal presses against Ella's face. The pain in her shoulders is the first thing that bothers her. Nausea washes over her, and she retches and coughs. Then comes the realisation of what's happening.

She opens her eyes—darkness. A noisy rumble is coming from everywhere, especially beneath her head. Then the floor jolts and moves, and she's sliding over a ribbed metal floor that smells of bleach.

She brings her knees to her chest and tries to sit up, but her arms are stuck behind her with her hands tied. She retches again.

Fear. Real fear. She can barely breathe. It's a panic attack.

'Come on, Ella!' she says to herself.

Her voice echoes above the rumble. She takes deep breaths, and then she screams for help. It's a sound that's lost in the noise.

Now, she can think more clearly. She knows she's inside a van, going somewhere fast. She kicks out against the sides until her feet hurt. She's looking for the doors, but her feet find a cage. She screams for help again, but it's wasted energy.

The rumbling changes in frequency. Then comes the sound of changing gears, and the noise reduces. The van lurches left, and her shoulder smacks against the side. Then she's thrown to the right.

Everything is out of control. She doesn't even have her mobile on her. Who will know where she is? Her mother won't be home until later. Max would know what to do, but he's not here. Not anymore.

Ella thinks about Shira, pictures her in her mind, and slows her breathing. A sudden growl comes from beneath her, and then a vibration shakes everything. The cage rattles, and the van slows, swinging left and right.

Then everything stops. The engine is cut, and two doors open. Ella cries out again as light pours in. The cage rattles and opens. She sees the silhouette of two men standing against a blue sky. The stench of rotten fish and diesel fills the van.

Her eyes adjust to the light, and she sees the telephone repairmen at the doors, smiling at her. Then comes another shape—wide and tall. A bald head and a goatee beard. He's pointing something at her.

'Ella,' says Frank Pinto. 'Wonderful to meet you again.'

He's pointing a pistol at her, and Ella can't swallow. She takes a deep breath to scream, but he's shaking his head.

'If I hear as much as a whimper from you, I won't hesitate to kill you. I don't care what happens to you. You may even come out of this alive if you are a good girl. It's your boyfriend we want, not you.'

'He's *not* my boyfriend.'

Pinto steps up, and his left arm reaches in, grabbing Ella. He drags her towards the rear doors and holds her there. He glances around him, and the two other men cover him from either side. Ella feels the pistol digging into her stomach.

'You made a sound. Now, what did I tell you, bitch! Did you think I was joking? I warned you.'

Ella's car is in the driveway, but no one answers the door, and she's still not answering her mobile.

'Maybe she's walking with her mother,' says Ima.

'Max!' Leon points to a severed telephone cable on the wall.

I bang on the front door again and hear another car arriving. It's Gary, and he joins us outside the house.

'No answer?' he asks.

'Of course, there's no bloody answer! She's not picking up her mobile, either.'

'We'll force our way then. I'll call up for a method of entry team.'

'Don't bother,' I say, looking at Leon.

Leon returns from the Range Rover with a crowbar, and he makes quick work of forcing the door open. I know better than to run in there. There could be anything inside, even tripwires, but there's nothing to see. I can smell a heady vapour I recognise.

'They've got her,' I say, looking at Ima.

She sniffs the air and nods in agreement.

'Here,' Leon says.

A handwritten envelope has been placed on the hall floor. There's a mobile number scrawled on there with the initials *JM. We have Ella.* Gary puts on some protective gloves and checks the envelope. There's nothing in it.

'This is Harman,' I say. 'He's calling himself Jethro Matisse again, and he wants me.'

'Leave it to us, Max,' says Gary. 'We'll find her.'

'Sorry, Gary. I can't.'

I snatch the envelope from him. Ima and Leon run with me back to the Range Rover, and Leon speeds us towards home. I read the number on the envelope and then punch it into my mobile. There's a delay before it's answered.

'Max Fortis, I presume,' the voice says. It's Harman.

'Where is she?' I say.

'You know I'm not interested in the girl. I just want you. She's a feisty thing! She's practically castrated one of my men.'

'That's good to hear.'

'Well, she's under control now, and my boys are getting restless just looking at her. She's a pretty thing. And scrubs up well, from what I remember.'

'Where are you, Harman?'

'Ah, you remember my name! There's no fooling you, Fortis. You were right all along.'

'Stop playing games with me, freak! Where are you?'

'Old Portsmouth. Camber Quay with the moored fishing boats. There's a storage unit with a bright red roof and an old sign on the wall saying fresh fish. Come alone in that pretty red car of yours. If I see the police or even that Range Rover with your friends inside, then she dies. Take your time, Fortis. I'll give you two hours. Any longer than that, then my boys will start playing with your friend here.'

'Let me hear her. I want to know she's alive.'

The phone goes quiet, and then I hear rapid breathing.

'Max!' It sounds like Ella. She's distressed and tired. I can't be sure if it's really her or a recording.

'I need to know it's you, Ella. What's my code name?' I say.

'Achilles. Please, help me.'

'I'm on my way.'

'Achilles?' Harman laughs down the phone. 'Achilles, the great Greek hero.'

'You're so screwed up.'

'I've grabbed you by your heel, Achilles. She's here with me, and I'm about to deal the final blow. Two hours!'

'I'm coming for you, Harman.'

The line goes dead.

CHAPTER 39

I'm driving the red car, doing over a hundred along the A27 towards Portsmouth. I wish I had my Volvo—it would be less conspicuous than this machine. Ima and Leon give me a twenty-minute head start, following on behind in the VW Caddy. We've discussed tactics, like in the old days, and it's a high-risk operation, whatever we do. I've called Lacey and left a message about Harman, asking for another favour.

I already know he has access to guns, and I have nothing other than my hands and feet. My training has taught me to focus, plan, and adapt. Our subconscious is always searching for threats, but most people don't know what to do with those primeval feelings we get when something is wrong. I've trained my mind to always assess information, create options, take action, and never give up. Fears and phobias inhabit our imagination, creating negative scenarios. I deal only with facts. Fear is a misuse of our imagination.

I blast down the M275, then take the route through the city to Old Portsmouth. After crossing several traffic lights and roundabouts, the cathedral passes on my right, and then the heavy stone defences of the Hotwalls. I'm now driving onto gentle cobbles, inset with old tramlines.

Stopping for a moment, ahead of me is Gosport across the harbour. An Isle of Wight ferry glides by, blocking my view. I take a right past a large white structure on my left and into a car park with boats stored in rows on dry land, hemmed in by tall, galvanised fencing.

To my right is the Camber Quay, running along a channel around me. Fishing boats and pleasure craft are moored here, accessed by steep aluminium gangplanks. The air is heavy with the smell of fish and diesel. There's a constant growl of boat engines. Above are the plaintive cries of herring gulls bothering the fishing boats below.

Surrounding the quay are flats and houses—tall, glass-fronted buildings. A little further to the left is a row of tall storage units in corrugated steel, with rolling doors and slanting roofs. They are rusty blue and grey, except one has a red roof. I park the car and slow my breathing. I check my phone and see Ima and Leon's GPS location inching towards me. They must be stuck in heavy traffic. Something's happened on the motorway.

It's been over an hour and a half since I spoke to Harman, and I guess he must be getting tetchy by now. I can't wait any longer for Ima and Leon, so it's time I put Harman out of his misery.

I approach the building, noting the fire escapes and the boarded windows. There's an old sign on the front of the building. *Fresh fish sold here every Friday.*

The building is abandoned. The rolling doors have a heavy padlock and a rusty chain, but a smaller entrance is to the right. The padlock to this door lies on the floor. That must be the way in. I snap a photo with my phone and send it to Ima.

I push the door, and it opens without resistance. Coming in from the light, the inside appears in darkness. I don't step in straight away. I'd be going in blind.

'Don't be shy,' says a voice from inside. It's not Harman. The voice is coarser. It must be Frank Pinto.

'I'm here,' I say. Remaining outside. 'Now, hand over Ella. I'm not walking into the darkness.'

'Come and see her for yourself,' Pinto says. 'I'm not bringing her outside.'

I take one step inside and wait for my eyes to adjust. It's then I see Pinto. Standing next to him is Mikita, the man from the nightclub. The building is an empty shell with rubble, netting, and other detritus across the floor. A musty, sour smell hangs in the air—the distinct stench of dead rodents.

Tall steel girders support the roof and walls like skeletal legs. People are standing in the darker shadows beside the furthest of these girders.

'Bring her over here,' I say. 'You've got me, so let her go.'

Pinto glances behind him, and the shadows move. Three men appear, and Ella is in between two of them, held like a rag doll. Her hands are tied behind her, and her shirt is torn and grubby. I hope, for their sake, they didn't touch her.

I call out to her. 'Ella?'

She lifts her head. 'They have guns, Max. They're going to kill you.'

I walk towards them. It's a distraction, a movement, information for them to assess for danger.

'Release her, and I'm all yours.'

They push Ella towards me, but the door slams behind me.

'You're all ours anyway,' says a voice echoing against the steel walls.

I keep pacing. 'Harman,' I say. 'What a joke you turned out to be.'

'The joke's on you, Fortis,' he says. He's in near darkness —just a shadow. The only light coming in is through the fibreglass skylights.

I can make out five men in here, and Harman makes six. They're only here because he's paying them well. Harman's desperate now. The police are searching for him, and he will have to run to get away. But first, he wants to deal with me. That would make him feel like he's won something for all his efforts.

It's time to assess.

First, threats. There are six targets and an unknown number of weapons. Ella is bound by her hands and vulnerable. Harman covers the main exit. Pinto and Mikita are blocking my way to Ella, and three other men are close to her. Those are not good odds. Harman is clever but not good in a fight, so I'm guessing he will keep his distance from me. At least one of the men with Ella must have a gun. Would Harman trust anyone else with a weapon? Pinto, maybe. I reckon that's it.

Next, environment. It's dark and cluttered where I'm standing, making it difficult to move around freely. Possible cover from gunfire, but not guaranteed. There's one exit near Harman and another on the side—a fire door. The building is a steel shell. A gun going off in here will sound like a thunderclap, alerting everyone around us. Firing their weapons is going to be a last resort.

Last, capabilities. I'm a skilled fighter and fit. Harman isn't. Pinto can fight, but he's not agile. The others are unknown but unlikely to be skilled.

'Achilles, how pathetic,' says Harman.

'It wasn't my idea,' I say. 'Better than Philip Marlowe, anyway. Using a dead man's name.'

'Hmm. Marlowe was Shakespeare's contemporary. But he was a Christopher, not a Philip. Some say he was the real bard.'

'You've lost it, Harman.' The Real Bard, Mariana's stalker.

'I wouldn't want to be you now, Fortis. I'm going to kill you, but not until I've made you suffer like you've made me suffer.'

I turn to the side. 'You didn't suffer enough, Harman. And what about the suffering of those innocent girls? Do you enjoy that?'

'Do you know how I found out you bedded my wife?'

'Were you watching? That's something you like to do, I seem to remember.'

'I found one of your shirt buttons in our bed. Mariana had ripped off your shirt. That was something she liked to do—rip the shirts off her lover's backs.'

Now I realise the button I found inside Mariana's desk was most likely mine. Spencer hadn't been sleeping with her after all. Something else I got completely wrong.

'Let Ella go,' I say. 'Then you can do what you like with me.'

'No. You will watch her die first. Then you will suffer.' Harman addresses his goons. 'Follow the plan. Take them away to the usual place. Then get back here quickly. I need to take a trip.'

A gun is pressed against my neck. Pinto grabs my hands and uses a cable tie to bind them behind my back. Then he leads me to the side door with Ella in front of me. Pinto takes the phone from my pocket and destroys it with his boot.

'Where are you taking us?' I say.

'You'll see. We can't very well kill you in here,' says Harman. I can see his hands are bandaged now that he's stepped into the light. 'Your DNA will spread everywhere.'

Pinto pushes me forward, closer to Ella, and the barrel of the pistol digs harder into the back of my neck. He grabs my hair and yanks my head back. Pointing a spray can into my face, he pulls the trigger, and I'm suffocating.

CHAPTER 40

Leon jumps the red light amid an angry cascade of car horns and heavy braking. The van swings and lurches across the roundabout, turning right, and he forces a blue Hyundai into the bus lane and slips in front of it.

'Just like the old days,' he says to Shira with a wide grin.

Shira's eyes are fixed ahead, her expression like stone. Nothing but solid concentration, calculating outcomes, devising strategies.

'Can't you go any faster?' she says.

'Not without killing someone.'

'Then kill someone. Max and Ella need us.'

Leon slips down a gear and floors the accelerator. The van responds, cutting up a taxi. More noise and abuse come from behind, followed by the crunch and scrape of metal as two cars collide. He pushes through another set of red lights and dodges a motorbike. A bus slams on its brakes, and Victoria Park rushes past. He spots a gap in the traffic and pushes his way over a junction. Then, a silver Audi pulls diagonally in front of them, stopping hard. The abusive taxi driver is right against their bumper. He's out of his car, followed by the man in the Audi. Both are tall and threatening. The tattooed Audi driver hoists his jogging shorts up to his vest top.

The Audi driver thumps on Leon's window, who smiles and waves.

'We don't have time for this,' says Shira.

Leon pushes the door open on the Audi driver, forcing him backwards.

'You got a death wish?' says Audi-man, head forward like a fighting cock.

The taxi driver has backed off. He can see where this is going.

'Not at all,' says Leon. 'We have an emergency. So get out of the way.'

'You hit my car.'

'That was your careless driving. Not mine. Now move! I'm in a hurry.'

The inevitable haymaker flies towards Leon, but he catches the fist, bends it upwards, and wrenches his arm away. Audi-man creases at the waist, and Leon grabs the man's shorts and pulls them to his ankles. It's only a second before he plants his face on the road with his purple boxers on show to the world.

Leon returns to the van and mounts the pavement, squeezing past the Audi and dropping back onto the road.

He glances at Shira. 'Which way?'

'Straight over.'

Shira holds onto her seat as they take a hard left and right, passing the university. They're doing sixty past the library and over another roundabout. The cathedral flashes past on their right, and they're heading towards the Hotwalls.

'Follow the road right,' says Shira. 'It's not far now.'

'All good, and no one died.'

Leon slows the van over some cobbles and takes a right into a car park. The Ferrari sticks out like a sore thumb.

'There.' Shira points to the grey corrugated unit with the red roof, the same as in Max's photograph.

Leon stays away from the Ferrari and parks facing the building.

'What now?' he says. 'I assume he's in there.'

'We assess. Come on. Get out slowly and walk with me.'

Leon follows his wife towards the east side of the quay, standing beside a small crane holding its rusty jib over the water.

'The building has a fire exit on the right,' says Leon. 'That roller door is locked. No vehicles in or out.'

'Hold my hand,' says Shira. 'Look like you love me.'

'Hey, I *do* love you!'

Leon and Shira walk hand-in-hand towards the west side, passing around the back of the building. They're circling the row of units and walking beside the fishing boats and pleasure craft on their moorings.

A side door of the red-roofed building opens, and a man in dark clothes hurries down the fire escape, heading their way. But he ignores them—some middle-aged couple out for a walk. He looks rough and unshaven, with greasy black hair. He peers over the side of the quay and then checks his watch. After a few moments, he scampers off again, back into the building through the fire escape, slamming the door behind him.

'What was he looking for?' says Leon. 'A boat?'

'Maybe. I have a hunch. We need to wait. I need to think.'

They return to the van, and Shira stares at the building and the fire exit. They count five more trips by men in dark clothing onto the quayside, looking for something. It's been forty minutes since they've arrived, and still nothing.

'I think we should go in,' says Leon.

'No. We should wait. They're nervous. See how they check their watches and make phone calls. No one answers. Something's gone wrong for them.'

'But where are Max and Ella? They could be hurt.'

'No. Not Max. And if they've hurt Ella, he'd be carrying out body parts by now.'

'So, we wait.'

'Yes, we wait.'

I feel sick. My eyes are blurry, and the sky is above me—white clouds on cold blue. I can sense the world moving, swaying beneath me, and a deep, growling sound rumbles through my body. I'm lying on something cold and wet. My lips taste salty. Diesel fumes fill the air, and sea spray is soaking me. Two men in black are standing above me, looking out onto the horizon. We are on a boat with a noisy engine pushing us further out into the waters of the Solent.

I turn my head and see a mop of red hair next to me. Bright green eyes are staring at me, willing me to move. I lock eyes on hers and smile.

'I'm sorry,' she says. Tears have made her eyes red. Her face is white with fear.

'Don't be,' I say. 'You did great.'

'I hope my mum will be okay,' she says. 'She'll be lost without me.'

'Ella, listen to me. It's not over until it's over. Trust me.'

She frowns at me and is wondering what I mean.

The shorter man on the boat's controls clicks the throttle lever into neutral, and our forward motion stops. He drags Ella to her knees. The other man has a Glock 17 in his hand. Seems to be the weapon of choice for these people. They look around them, and I sit up. There's open water everywhere. Portsmouth and Hayling Island are on one horizon, the Isle of Wight on the other. I hear waves lapping against the hull and the slow-running engine. They haul Ella to the side of the boat. Her legs kick out, but they have a firm grip on her hands bound behind her. She shrieks and curses them, and the one with the pistol digs the barrel into the back of her head. Then she falls silent.

'Make a wish,' he says to her.

'It seems such a waste,' says the other one.

'What? You want a piece of her before we sink her?'

'No. We don't have time. Let's do it.' He pulls back the barrel an inch.

'Let me go, please,' says Ella. 'I have someone at home who needs me.'

The tall man laughs. 'Do I look like a social worker? How shall we do this? Do I count to three or count down from three?'

'Down from ten,' says the other man. 'Make it last.'

'Sure. Ten... nine...' He's jabbing the gun into her neck with every count. 'Eight... five... three...'

But it isn't over until it's over. They never bound our feet. What kind of fools wouldn't bind our feet? Dead ones. I've already shuffled along the deck, and my feet have reached the throttle lever. There's a blue switch underneath that locks it in neutral. I push it up with the end of my foot.

'Two...' He pulls the gun back. 'One...'

I kick the throttle. The engine revs, and the boat lurches

forward. They all fall backwards in a heap. Ella lands on top of both men. The gun is to the left of her head, and the arm holding it is trapped beneath her. She lifts her head and rams it backwards into the man's face. She does it over and over. He drops the gun and shouts for his friend to pick it up. He's desperate to use his trapped hand to stop her. But his friend is busy pulling himself free, and when he stretches for something to grab, he sees me standing over him, legs apart to keep my footing. My foot lands hard on his stomach, then a kick in his side, and lastly against the side of his neck. I press it down hard, grinding and stamping until he is no more. The man beneath Ella can't see with all the blood in his eyes. I kick the gun into the sea and use my feet to roll Ella away, where she swivels on her bottom and drops onto her feet into the cabin. The man left behind is in a bad way. His nose is broken. He tries to get up, spitting out blood, but the chopping of the boat through the waves makes it hard.

'Big mistake, little man,' I say. 'How did you get so full of this dark, hateful shit? Killing innocent people like it's a game? The world doesn't need people like you. You're beyond repair.'

He curses me, and I kick his face. He screams, and I silence him with a stamp on his head—twice. I make it back into the cabin and lean against the wheel. The boat turns hard, dropping the two men's bodies into the sea.

Ella can't speak, so I leave her alone. I use my elbows to push the throttle back to neutral. Now, to get this cable tie off. I drop onto the deck, sit on my hands, and lean tight forward. I move my hands to the front of me from under my feet and use my teeth to pull the cable tie as tight as it goes. With my hands above my head, I jerk them down hard to my sides. The tie snaps, and I'm free.

Digging around the boat, I find some heavy pliers, and I free Ella with them.

'You're safe now, Ella. It's over.'

She hugs me tight, and I stroke her hair. The boat rocks us together, and we hold each other until Ella can speak again.

'I thought that was it, Max.'

'Take some deep breaths. You're safe now. I've got you.'

'I'm so sorry.'

I kiss the top of her head. I don't know why, but it's the right thing to do. I can see the lump on the back of her head. That's got to hurt.

'There should be enough fuel in this thing to get us back,' I say.

'They were evil.'

'Did they hurt you?'

'No,' she says. 'But one of them thought it was funny to grope me. The one with the broken face.'

'They'll wash up in a few days, bloated and unrecognisable. You won, Ella. You won.'

'I did.'

CHAPTER 41

I run the boat aground by the Hotwalls, jamming it onto the granite rocks below the water.

'I'm guessing Harman wants his boat back to make a getaway,' I say.

'Screw what he wants!' says Ella. Using the pliers, she severs the fuel line.

We get our feet wet climbing onto the beach and pass through an archway in the wall. It's only a few minutes back to where I parked the red car. Ima and Leon have arrived and are inside the white van. They are shocked to see us.

'What happened to you?' Ima says to Ella. She gives Ella her seat while she checks her over. 'You have a cut and a lump on the back of your head.'

'That was me rearranging someone's face.'

'Good girl. Did they hurt you in any other way?'

'No. I'm okay.'

'Thank God you are safe.' Ima and Ella hug each other. 'You're shaking.'

'I think it's relief. I thought I was going to die.' Ella sobs, and Ima holds her tight.

'Have you seen anyone leave?' I ask Leon.

'No,' he says. 'Someone keeps going out to the quayside, looking for something.'

'They're waiting for the boat to return. Harman's in there. I think he wanted it for his escape.'

'What boat?'

I tell Leon about our adventure in the Solent.

'They think we're dead,' I say. 'This will be a bit of a shock for them.'

'You're going back in there!' says Ella. 'Are you crazy?'

'Oh yes. I'm going to give Lacey's clean-up team something to do. They don't have you anymore, Ella, and I have the element of surprise.'

'And now you also have me,' says Ima, tying back her hair.

'Ima?' I say. 'Are you sure?'

'Of course, I'm sure. They hurt our Ella, so now I'm going to hurt them.' She says something to Leon in Hebrew.

He nods and kisses her hand. 'Come back to me safe.'

'Let's go,' I say.

'The side door,' says Ima.

'I'll update The Controller,' says Leon.

We walk around to the side door and listen. People are talking inside, but we can't hear what they are saying. I turn to look at Ima. You wouldn't believe she was in her sixties. She's strong, noble, and fierce. One of the elite.

'Let's get in there,' she says. 'You go left, and I'll go right. It's dark in there, yes?'

I nod. 'There's crap all over the floor, so be careful.'

'I'll be fine. I'll leave Harman to you. I promise.'

I count to three, and I kick the side door open. We run in, splitting left and right into the shadows.

'Who's that!' shouts Harman. 'Frank, who is it? Is the boat back?'

'Someone's here,' says Pinto gravely.

We're in the shadows, and I can't see Ima. A man with a gun moves forward. He's reluctant to shoot—it will bring trouble running towards them.

I step out, distracting them, while Ima moves behind.

'Surprise!' I say. 'I bet you didn't expect to see me again.'

'Fortis!' shouts Harman. 'How…'

'We'd had enough of playing on your boat. Now I've come back to finish you.'

'The girl must be with him.'

'No,' I say. 'But I brought my secret weapon with me—my ima.'

'What are you talking about?' says Harman. 'Frank, what is he talking about?'

'I don't know, boss.'

'He said he's brought his ima,' she says, emerging from the darkness. 'His mother.'

They all spin around, looking bemused. There are four of them left, including Harman. The man with the gun moves forward, aiming at her, enjoying the suspense. Then she strikes. Her action is faster than his reaction. She twists on the spot, spinning, and both feet leave the ground. Her legs shoot forward and wrap around his throat. She sweeps him off his feet, breaking his neck before he hits the floor. Three are left.

'Holy shit!' says Pinto. He moves forward and turns to Mikita. 'Come on!'

They both run at her.

I've seen this scenario countless times, and I've stood in awe every time. Ever since I was a boy, my mother would allow me to watch the demonstrations at army bases throughout the world, to the applause of majors and dignitaries. And now I stand in awe once again. The years have barely touched her, and I have learned so much from her.

Mikita produces a switchblade with a bone handle. He arrives first and runs straight at her, thrusting the blade. He's too far away—most of it was for show. He lunges forward again, but he's overreached. She catches his wrist after a block and puts her fingers on top of his hand. She snaps it upwards, and now the knife points back towards him. She steps in and makes him implant the blade into his own neck. He falls and bleeds out onto the floor.

'God, Mikita!' shouts Pinto. 'He had a family! He had a daughter.'

'I have a family, too,' she says. 'And he was the one with the knife. Not me. So what about you, big man?'

'You're a monster.'

I move round to stand in front of him.

'Monster?' I say to his face. 'What about those kids you enslaved, raped, murdered? Who's the monster, Pinto? I'm looking right at it!'

He grunts at me and faces Ima. She readies herself. He steps back, looking at Mikita, lying in a pool of blood, and the other man with a broken neck, the gun at his feet. He's trying to work it out. Can he get to it before she can stop him?

'You'll never make it,' I say. 'Accept defeat. Both of you.'

Pinto lunges towards Ima, trying to grab her. It's probably what he knows best—close combat. But Ima sidesteps him and smiles.

'Try again?' she says.

Pinto roars. 'You bitch!'

He turns to the side with a heavy swing of his fist, but Ima dodges, using his momentum to push him away. Now he's furious. He goes in with his fists swinging. They are heavy blows that would crush most men, but Ima swipes them away. She's had enough. She rotates, raising her knee high. Her leg extends, sweeping from the right, and her foot strikes hard against Pinto's temple. He staggers to the left, dazed, and his hands come down. Then a front kick to his sternum. It's a blow that would stop the hearts of most men. Pinto falls onto his back. He's struggling for breath. Ima stands back. She doesn't finish him.

'Try again?' she says. She's not even out of breath.

Pinto waits on the floor, catching his breath. 'This isn't going to happen. We're not heading for Spain anytime soon, are we, boss.' He rolls onto his side and stands bent over. He laughs, defeated, and looks up at Ima. 'I can't handle her. I'm beaten.'

'She's a woman!' says Harman. 'What do I pay you for?'

'You don't pay me enough,' says Pinto. 'I told you not to let me down, Harman. She's all yours. You take her.'

'Are you done?' My mother asks him the same way she asks me when I'm defeated.

Pinto lowers his head and nods. 'I'm done.'

'What are you doing!' says Harman. 'Frank! I've spent too long and sacrificed everything to get where I am. I will not let you win, Fortis. Not again.'

Ima takes Pinto hard to the floor, resting him on his side so his giant bulk can breathe. She can show compassion when she needs to. She's leaving Harman to me.

I walk over to him and look him up and down.

'What shall I do with you, Harman?' I say. 'All I can think about is that poor girl who came to my hotel room. The misery you caused her, her sister, and countless others. Those women you controlled and personally murdered. The others you killed by your orders.'

'You don't know half of it,' he says, smirking at me.

'You're not helping yourself, Harman. I know how to make your death slow and painful. It's what you deserve. I can walk away, and no one will know. Only me and my mother. She's done the same in the past.'

He's edging towards the gun on the floor. 'You've already caused me to suffer,' he says. 'You even took my wife. Now let me go. There's a plane waiting for me, and I'll be out of your life forever. I have money. I will pay you.'

'That's mighty generous of you. But I don't need it. I already have money in the bank that I don't need. Dirty money, most of it. Contaminated with the lust for power and wealth like you. It's all mine, and I never asked for it. Why would I want your filthy pennies to add to it?'

He dives for the gun, but I'm already there. I kick the gun away and stamp on his bandaged hand, breaking several phalanges in his fingers. He'll never play the piano again. Then I punch his ear, dazing him. Looking at him there, I see a pathetic piece of scum whimpering, rolled into a ball and clutching his hand, begging for mercy. He's arguing with himself, cursing, crying. It would be easy to put him out of his misery—one swift kick to his head. But I don't.

'There's a better way to make you suffer, Harman. You're going to stand trial and face your victims, those young people you tortured, and their families. The courts will find your money and every asset you own and claw it back from you. Then you'll make new, special buddies in prison who'll make you pay every day for what you've done to those kids. You're going to rot in hell, Harman. And hell starts right now.'

The door opens, pouring in light from outside. It's Leon. 'Commander Lacey and the police are here.'

Lacey pushes past him and makes her way inside. She laughs at the mess we've made, at Pinto lying on the floor and Harman sobbing at my feet.

'Clean up on aisle one,' she says. 'Reasonable force, I assume.'

'Yes,' says Ima. 'Knives, guns, and so on.'

'And you're his mother. Shit!' Lacey whistles. 'I hope I look as good as you when I'm your age, Shira.'

'And this one isn't dead,' says Ima, looking at Pinto.

'No. I'm very much alive,' he replies. 'Just uncomfortable.'

'How did you get here so soon?' I ask Lacey.

'I got a call from DC Bates before I heard your message. He told me Harman had abducted Ella, so I guessed you'd be making a mess of someone somewhere. Let's get the living ones outside, and I'll send my Home Office approved cleaners in. Then the local bobbies can take over. Mr Pinto, Mr Harman. Come with me.'

Ima walks behind Pinto, watching his every move. I drag Harman with me through the door, and I can see him in the full light of day. He's a pale, scrawny worm with broken glasses and blood-soaked hands in dripping bandages. He's nothing. He's a mouse making scary shadows of monsters on the wall. He's not the man I remember at all. This Harman is broken. It was his money that gave him power. It bought him muscle and the reputation of Jethro Matisse. He was that controlling bully everyone feared, but in himself, he was nothing but a gutless, toothless lion. All roar and no bite.

'There are two more somewhere in the Solent,' I say to Lacey.

'Leon told me. I've sent the Marine Support Unit to fish them out if they can find them.'

We watch Harman and Pinto being arrested and leave Lacey to order the clean-up. Ima and I arrive at the white Caddy van. Ella has more colour in her cheeks now. She is relieved to see Harman and Pinto placed in the backs of the police vans. Ima and Leon leave us to talk. I watch them walk away, hand-in-hand, almost as if nothing has happened.

'You didn't tell me about your wife,' says Ella. 'I'm so sorry, Max.'

'Did Leon tell you? There's no need to be. She was on the same level as my uncle. Literally sometimes.'

'Oh.'

'So, changing the subject,' I say. 'We both have statements to write up for the police. Why don't you come back to ours to get yourself cleaned up? You don't want your mother to see you like this.'

Ella nods. 'Only if we can go in your car.'

I pat down my jeans. The red car's key fob is still tucked in there. 'Sure.'

'You were right,' she says. 'It isn't over until it's over. Is that job still going? I missed my interview today.'

'We'll have to see.' I smile at her. 'I'll have to interview you first.'

'Piss off! The job's mine, or I'll tell your mother.'

'Fair enough.'

CHAPTER 42

The sunlight this October morning follows us on the way to Emsworth. My beloved blue Volvo V70 is back on the road. Dave, the mechanic, has done a fine job with her, and she's like new again. She's not lost any of her comfort, and the replacement engine is a dream with a power upgrade. Ella is disappointed the red car wasn't taking another outing.

As we leave Bosham, she takes an incoming call on my mobile for me.

'Max Fortis,' she says. 'Ah, Gary!' She listens to him, nodding even though he can't see her. She turns to me. 'Gary says he wants to talk to you about a job offer. He says he's handed in his notice.'

'Ask him what job offer that was.' I'm trying to keep a straight face.

'He's saying very rude things about you, Max. Shall I hang up?'

'Tell him we don't talk to rude people.' Ella laughs when she hears his reply. 'And tell him I'll call him later. We can discuss if this is something he really wants to do.'

Ella ends the call and sighs, enjoying the smooth ride in the Volvo to Emsworth.

We park outside the house where Grace Garcia is staying, and she opens the door to us. The difference is remarkable. The bruising has almost gone, and her confidence is returning.

Her friend leaves us to talk in the front room, and we sit facing each other, hunched forward. The atmosphere is tense, and Grace looks between Ella and me, waiting for one of us to speak. My lips are dry, and I glance at Ella. She knows what I'm about to say. I take a deep breath and start by telling Grace about the Thai girl I met in the hotel—Janie. I tell her what I know about her story and what Harman and his men did to her and the others. Janie is safe now. She's given evidence, and her mother has flown out to be with her while she recovers—as much as she will ever recover. I wanted Grace to know what her father did to those kids. So she knows this case was about more than her mother's murder. Sadly, most of it has gone over her head.

'Andrew Harman has been remanded,' I say. 'It's still early days, but he's admitted to ordering your mother's murder and killing another woman in her home. His bodyguard, Frank Pinto, is telling all, hoping for a more lenient sentence. But that won't happen.'

'That's something, at least,' says Grace. 'I had no idea about my father's past. My mother kept it all from me.'

I very much doubt that.

'Strange that,' I say. 'He was very protective over you. He ordered Spencer's killing after he beat you up.'

She blushes. She's not going to answer that one.

'But one thing is puzzling me,' she says. 'Why did she look for you that night, Mr Fortis?'

'This is going to be hard to answer. There are things I can't tell you, but that won't make this any easier. I knew your mother when she was still married to your father. I was a police officer back then, investigating him for people trafficking, sexual exploitation, and influencing important government ministers.'

'Okay, she knew you already. But why did she go to you that night and not the police?'

Grace doesn't seem at all surprised by her father's nefarious activities. She says she didn't know anything about his past, but I've just dropped a bombshell about him, and she hasn't batted an eyelid about it. Maybe she knows more than she's letting on. Perhaps she's always known, and the thought of that pisses me off big time. But I'm sure she knows nothing about what I'm about to tell her, and I won't go in gently.

'Your mother and I had a physical relationship. It was a short one, but enough. Your father found out.'

Grace's eyes go wide. 'You were having an affair!'

'Yes. As I said, I was investigating your father and had to do it as an undercover operative. I was successful. Your father went into hiding after I brought down his business. With his accountant's help, he successfully moved a load of money offshore. And I mean, a *load* of money. Your mother found him and tried to kill him when he planned to escape. She thought she had locked him in his office when she set fire to it. But she didn't realise it was his accountant in there, not your father. She was responsible for the accountant's death—a man called Philip Marlowe. Andrew Harman faked his own death and slipped away somewhere. When he was ready, he set up business again, but he was out for revenge. He planned to kill your mother, but first, he used her to lead him to me. But your mother's friend, Daniel Cole, warned her that Harman was still alive. She must have asked him to find out where your father was. He told her about his alter ego, Jethro Matisse. But Daniel Cole ended up dead, too—killed by Frank Pinto.'

'But what about Spencer?'

'I'm sorry to say I got something wrong about Spencer. As awful as he was to you, he never slept with your mother. That was only me. That button I found was mine. I honestly didn't realise.'

Grace clenches her jaw. I'm expecting something to come flying my way any moment. But she sits still and dignified. Grace studies her hands.

I glance at Ella. 'Harman paid Spencer to find out more about your mother's movements and what she was writing. Nothing more. He never slept with her. Spencer had proven himself weak to Harman and had threatened to talk. And after he attacked you, Harman ordered his death.'

The room feels suddenly cold. Grace's friend pops her head around the door to check on her and glances at Ella and me.

'I accused Spencer of cheating on me with my mother,' says Grace, rubbing her hands together. 'You made me look a fool.'

'I'm sorry,' I say and shrug. 'But he lied to you about his motives. He was passing information about your mother to your father. This is going to hurt.' This isn't going to make things any better, but she has to know. 'Your father paid Spencer to form a relationship with you. He had no real feelings for you. He was one of your father's men.'

'Well, congratulations. You can pat yourself on the back, Mr Fortis.' She's talking through gritted teeth. 'You must be very proud of yourself for being so clever. Why didn't you tell me about your relationship with my mother?'

'I was a police officer, Grace, and it was an undercover operation. I didn't think it would help. I'm sorry.'

'And that's why you took so much interest in this case?'

'Yes.'

'So, in truth, what I thought Spencer had done to me was no different from what you had done to my mother.'

'If you put it that way, you're right.'

Grace takes a deep breath. 'Thank you for your honesty.' She stands and stares out of the window. 'While I feel sorry for those girls, I can't apologise for my father's actions, as he had nothing to do with me. I'm grateful I know the truth about my mother and that she never betrayed me, despite your best efforts to convince me otherwise. You did warn me you might uncover things that could be unpleasant.'

'Yes, I did.'

'For me, the most unpleasant thing in all of this is you.' She glares at me with cold eyes. 'Send me your bill. After that, I never want to hear from you again.'

'There's no bill,' I say. 'Give the money to a sexual exploitation charity. They need all the support they can get. Just send me the receipt.'

Grace nods and turns away.

Ella and I walk back to the Volvo and gaze over the water. Grace's final words to me are still ringing in my ears, so we don't speak for a while but watch the swans preen themselves in the soft autumn light.

Relief washes over me as this case closes, but so many have been hurt in Harman's wake, it's hardly a satisfying ending. Will it ever be over for those kids they found locked up like animals in the factory?

'Grace was so ungrateful,' says Ella. 'We almost got ourselves killed.'

'It was harsh,' I say, 'but it went better than I thought it would.'

'With all those secrets you have,' says Ella, 'you must be like those swans, hiding all that frantic activity under the waterline to keep you afloat. It must be hard work.'

'It's exhausting sometimes.'

'What's next, boss?'

I look at her and smile.

'Lost pets, nuisance neighbours.'

'No thanks,' she says.

'Lacey forwarded me an email—a father whose son went missing. I think that will be next. He wants to meet me.'

'And me.'

'And you?'

'Give the nuisance neighbours to Gary when he starts.'

I laugh. 'He'd love that.'

Ella pokes me in the arm.

'If we're going to work together in the future, I need you to be honest with me.'

'I will.'

'And we have to promise something to each other.'

'What's that?' I say.

'You won't fall for me, and I won't fall for you. Deal?'

I look into those gorgeous green eyes and smile. 'Deal.'

And we shake on it.

ACKNOWLEDGMENTS

I'd like to thank Val Evans once again for her love, encouragement, and support, even when she had major projects of her own going on.

Again, my heartfelt thanks go to my family and friends for your continued love and support, read-throughs, and suggestions. This includes my fantastic beta-readers: Bob Lock, Beth Leeworthy-Evans, and Caitlin Gale. Your insightful feedback is invaluable.

Any mistakes that are present after publishing are entirely my own.

TO THE READER

I'm truly grateful for your support as a reader, and it would mean a lot to me if you could share your thoughts by leaving a review on Amazon. Your feedback is invaluable, helping both me and fellow readers. Thank you for being part of my writing journey.

MODERN-DAY SLAVERY AND SEXUAL EXPLOITATION

While these are topics explored as fiction in this novel, it's important to remember that they are all too real for countless individuals worldwide.

The following resources offer information, support, and ways to get involved in the fight against modern-day slavery and sexual exploitation.

Information is correct at the time of publication.

Unseen UK - unseenuk.org
Helpline: 08000 121 700. The UK Modern Slavery & Exploitation Helpline operates 24/7, 365 days a year. It is free to use, available in more than 200 languages and confidential. Helpline Advisers are there for support and advice, not only for victims of modern slavery, but for the public, businesses and statutory agencies like the police, NHS and local government.

The Salvation Army - salvationarmy.org.uk/modern-slavery
Helpline: 0800 808 3733
From website: 'The Salvation Army provides specialist
support to protect and care for all adult survivors of modern
slavery in England and Wales through a government contract
which was first awarded in 2011.'

Yada - yadauk.org
From website: 'Working to prevent sexual exploitation
throughout coastal West Sussex. Yada delivers frontline
projects aimed at raising awareness and preventing the sexual
exploitation of self-identifying women. We work across Adur,
Worthing, Arun and Chichester local authority districts.'

ABOUT THE AUTHOR

Matthew Evans lives in Chichester, West Sussex, UK. He is married and has three children and two grandchildren. He served as a police officer for 18 years. He's a folk musician and the proud owner of 'Betty', his 1962 Morris Minor.

Email: matt@matthewjevans.co.uk
Website: www.matthewjevans.co.uk

Visit my website to subscribe to my newsletter, where you can read my latest updates, find out about new releases, and get exclusive inside information on my creative processes.

ALSO BY MATTHEW J. EVANS

The DI Angelis Supernatural Crime Thriller Series

Chasing Shadows

Hide Her Away

Take You Home

The Chichester Crime Mysteries Series

The Dead Beneath Us

Our darkest places are never far away.

When a brutal murder strikes a prestigious private school, DCI Dinescu finds himself entangled in a complex investigation, including the mysterious disappearance of a schoolgirl in the 1980s. How are these two cases connected? Confronting his deepest fears, Dinescu must uncover the dark secrets of the past to bring justice and closure to the present.

This is the first police procedural crime novel in the Chichester Crime Mysteries series.

Printed in Great Britain
by Amazon